THE ULTIMATE

WAVE

written and illustrated by

TERRY DENTON

ALLEN&UNWIN

FOR MAX

First published in 2001

Storymaze: The Ultimate Wave was first published in 1999 as a hardback picture book, by Silverfish, an imprint of Duffy & Snellgrove.
This paperback edition has been completely revised and reillustrated.

Allen & Unwin
83 Alexander Street
Crows Nest NSW 2065
Australia
Phone: (61 2) 8425 0100
Fax: (61 2) 9906 2218
Email: info@allenandunwin.com
Web: www.allenandunwin.com

National Library of Australia
Cataloguing-in-Publication entry:

Denton, Terry, 1950– .
  Storymaze: the ultimate wave.

  New ed.
  ISBN 1 86508 378 X.

  I. Children's stories. I. Denton, Terry, 1950– Terry
  Denton's storymaze: the ultimate wave. II. Title. (Series: Storymaze).

A823.3

Cover and text design by Terry Denton and Sandra Nobes
Set in Helvetica by Sandra Nobes
Printed in Australia by McPherson's Printing Group, Maryborough, Victoria

10 9 8 7 6 5 4 3 2 1

YES, HELLO!

I'm the Narrator.

You can call me…**The Narrator.**

My job is to tell you this story.

I'm not the only Narrator in the universe. In fact everyone on my planet is given a Narrator at birth. We exist to tell you what is going on.

'*You are sitting on a couch. It is Tuesday. You are reading this Storymaze book – the bit where the Narrator talks about his job. He is telling you how he is a Narrator telling you that you are sitting on a couch, reading this book…*'

Narrators can be very annoying.

Imagine a classroom full of kids on my planet. Each kid has a Narrator jabbering on about everything their kid is doing. The teacher is up the back of the classroom screaming, and next to her is her Narrator calmly explaining that her teacher is screaming because her room is full of people talking, and all their Narrators are talking about what they are talking about. It's worse on planet Norsebum12, a planet in a parallel universe, where everyone has two very loud Narrators. One is always three seconds behind the other – so they drive you as mad as a dolphin in a toaster. It's like Friday night tea with my family.

Come to think of it, nothing's like Friday night tea with my family. I'd prefer to be a dolphin in a toaster.

BUT ENOUGH ABOUT ME! I HAVE A STORY TO TELL.

It concerns some humans from a planet called Ithaca. You know Ithaca. It's that planet in a parallel universe that is identical to yours and full of humans just like you, except that each one has an animal head instead of a human head. To balance things up, all the animals have human heads. Seems perfectly normal to them.

Like most Ithacans, our heroes love surfing. And Ithaca is a surfer's paradise.

Nico and Claudia are gun surfers. Mikey would love to be, but he has two left feet and can't even manage to stand up in the bath. I know how he feels.

So, let me set the scene for you in my best Narrator's voice.

Nico, Claudia and Mikey set out for a brilliant day's surfing. The sky is a brilliant green, all three suns are a brilliant pink, the sea is a brilliant chartreuse – whatever that is. There's only one small problem…

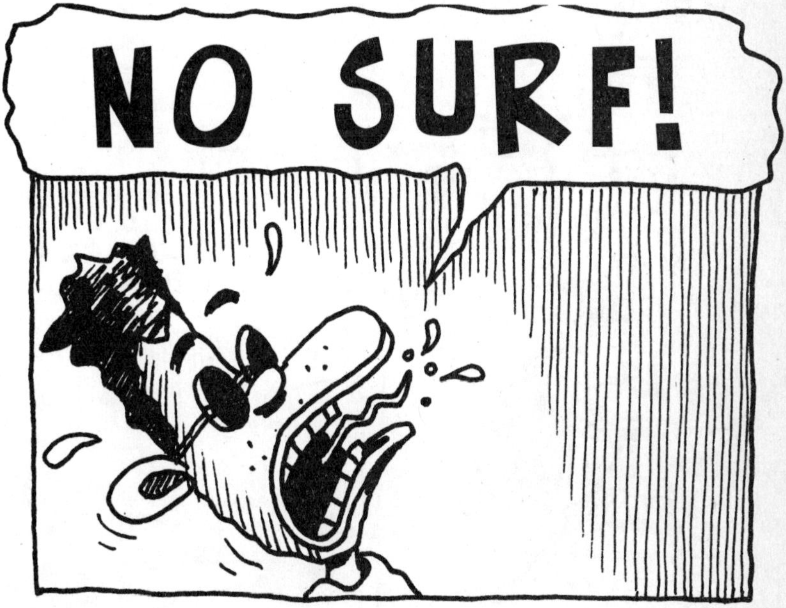
NO SURF!

'Didn't I tell you two blockheads we should go to Bonecrunchers Beach?' yells Claudia.

'Ah, so that was you talking,' says Nico. 'I did hear a noise but I thought it was the cat caught in the clothes-dryer again.'

'Idiot!'

By the way, that noise you can hear in the background is the desperate sound of Mikey trying to stay upright on his board. He finds it so much harder when there are no waves.

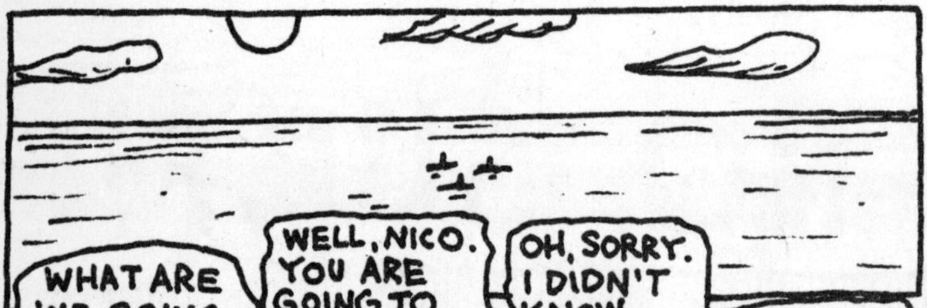
WHAT ARE WE GOING TO DO NOW, BABE?
WELL, NICO. YOU ARE GOING TO GET YOUR ARM OFF MY SHOULDER.
OH, SORRY. I DIDN'T KNOW IT WAS THERE. IT MUST HAVE A MIND OF ITS OWN.
WELL, IT'S LUCKIER THAN YOU, THEN.

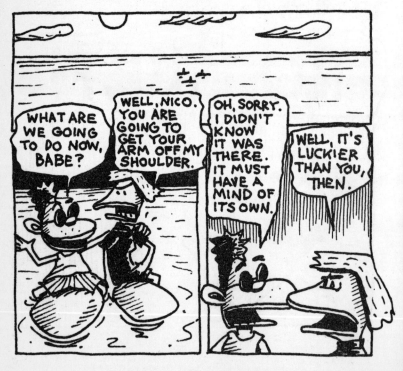

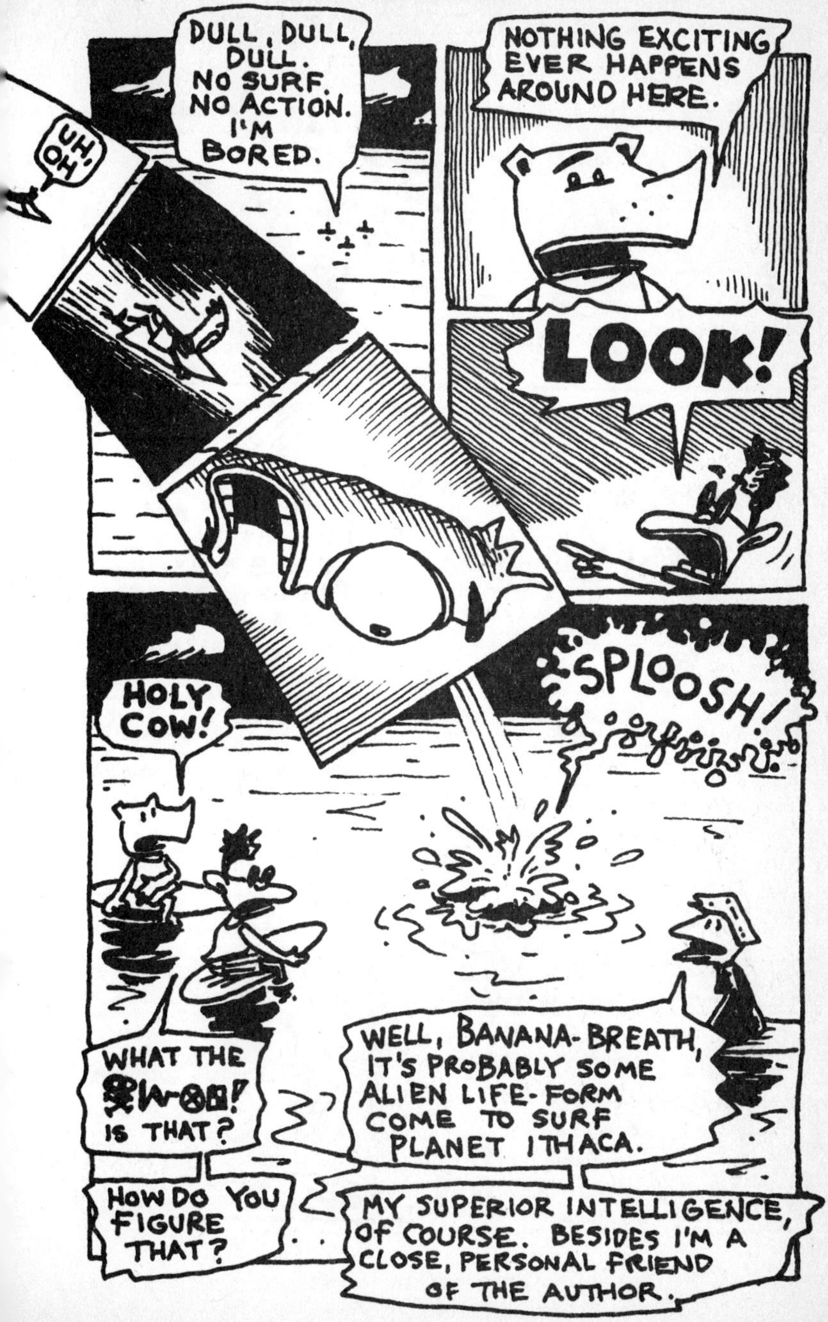
DULL, DULL, DULL. NO SURF. NO ACTION. I'M BORED.
UH, OH
NOTHING EXCITING EVER HAPPENS AROUND HERE.
LOOK!
HOLY COW!
SPLOOSH!
WHAT THE IS THAT?
WELL, BANANA-BREATH, IT'S PROBABLY SOME ALIEN LIFE-FORM COME TO SURF PLANET ITHACA.
HOW DO YOU FIGURE THAT?
MY SUPERIOR INTELLIGENCE, OF COURSE. BESIDES I'M A CLOSE, PERSONAL FRIEND OF THE AUTHOR.

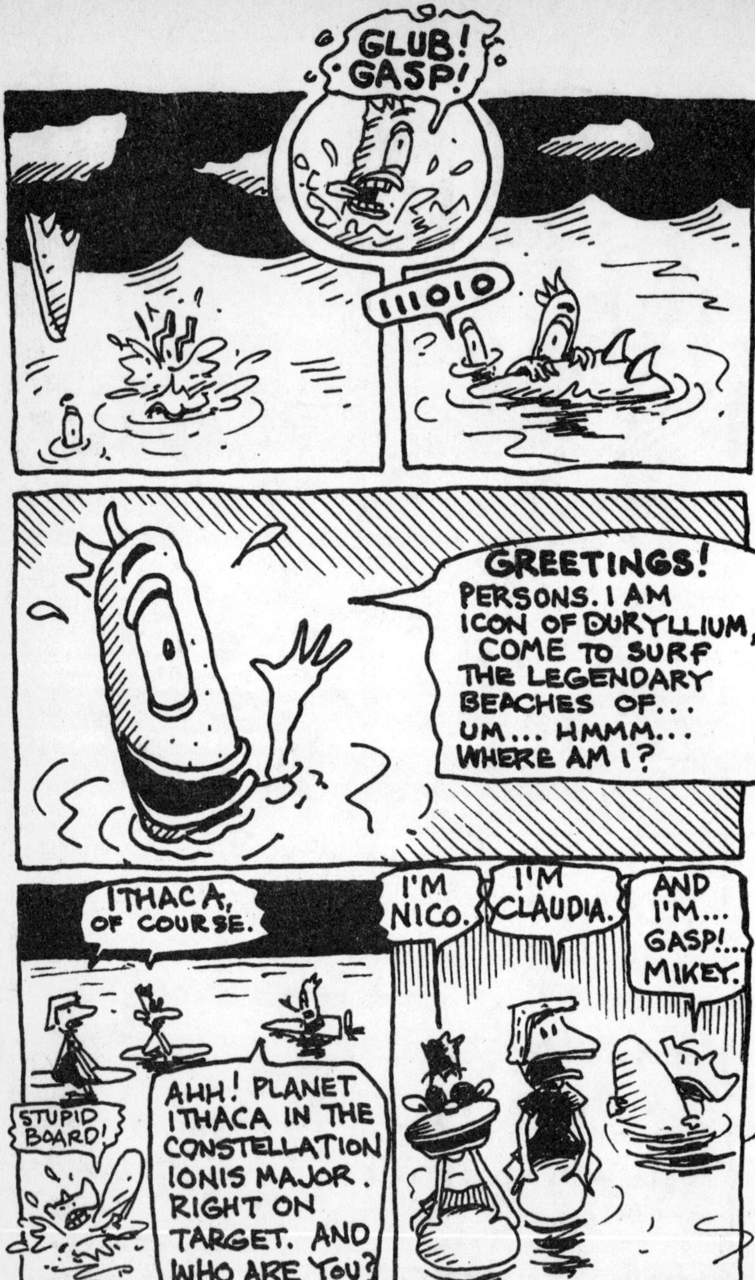
GLUB! GASP!
111010
GREETINGS! PERSONS. I AM ICON OF DURYLLIUM, COME TO SURF THE LEGENDARY BEACHES OF... UM... HMMM... WHERE AM I?
ITHACA, OF COURSE.
STUPID BOARD!
AHH! PLANET ITHACA IN THE CONSTELLATION IONIS MAJOR. RIGHT ON TARGET. AND WHO ARE YOU?
I'M NICO.
I'M CLAUDIA.
AND I'M... GASP!... MIKEY.

A cosmic disturbance, caused by Icon's sudden plunge through the Ithacan atmosphere, has stirred up some truly awesome surf. Blue with envy, the Ithacans watch Icon strut his stuff. I've seen better, but they haven't.

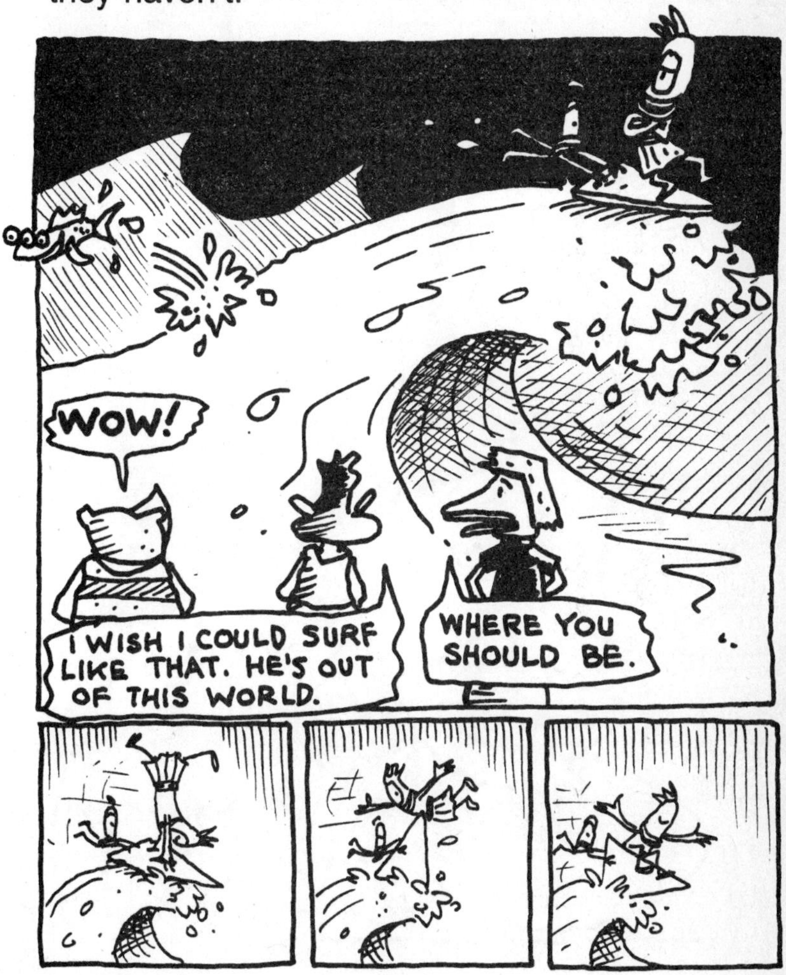

WOW!
I WISH I COULD SURF LIKE THAT. HE'S OUT OF THIS WORLD.
WHERE YOU SHOULD BE.

Without going on too much, what you need to know is that they all surf together for the rest of the summer. Icon teaches Nico and Claudia a few of his best moves. Especially the Layback Snap in Pike Position with a Double Goose. Mikey learns nothing.

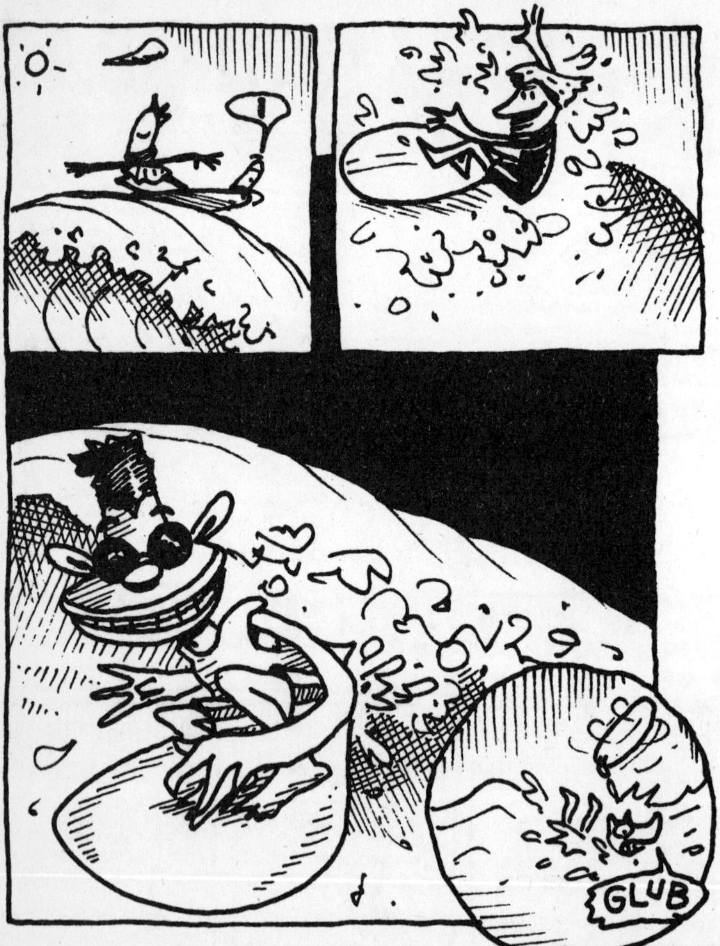
GLUB

2

Are you a bit confused about Icon, this pencil-headed mutant from another dimension? Well, I was. Narrators are very suspicious by nature. So I looked him up in the *NCGUB* (*The Narrators Complete Guide to the Universe and Beyond*).

Icon comes from Duryllium. Have you heard of it? I hadn't, until one day I was fiddling around in my auntie's wardrobe. I slid the door closed. Suddenly I felt a bit of a head-rush – it could have been the stench of my uncle's socks (pheeewww!!!) – but when I opened the door again, I was on this strange planet. Well, that's what I thought it was. Later, a wise old Narrator tried to tell me that it was just my own planet 26,457 years later. But I think he was wrong. The people were different. The landscape was different. It even smelt different. And there was this huge billboard that said:

WELCOME TO DURYLLIUM

So that's where Icon comes from. Duryllium. He says he is in Ithaca to surf, and that sounds fair enough. But there's more to it, of course. He doesn't want to tell the whole story. And I know why.

Let me explain.

I was in Duryllium a few years ago, not long after the disappearance of the old King of Duryllium. I was there to cover the story for *The News behind the News behind the News*. The rumours said the King had fallen into the palace's giant waste-food grinder and was eaten by his own chooks. Some say he was pushed. (And I think I know by whom.) But no trace of him was ever found.

The old King had twin sons. The younger son, by 13 minutes, was called Vidor. Within a few days he had taken control of Duryllium and started calling himself King Vidor. I guess he thought he was the best man for the job. He didn't bother to tell his older, by 13 minutes, twin brother, who was away surfing at the time. (He was *always* away surfing.) In fact, Vidor sent the Black Raiders out to track down his brother. He probably wanted to capture and imprison him or have him accidentally fall into a waste-food grinder.

Or more likely he just wanted to scare him off so he'd never return.

That older twin brother is Icon. He should really be King. Instead, he's spent the last few years keeping just one planet ahead of Vidor's Black Raiders.

But does he want to tell his new Ithacan friends all about this? I don't think so. He just wants to surf. That's all he's ever wanted to do, travelling the universe looking for new and awesome beaches.

That's OK for him. But the rest of us have to work. I wish I'd been born a Royal. Playing golf seven days a week, beautiful women hanging off my arms, shooting small defenceless creatures. But I wasn't, so on with the Narration.

3

Let's shift this story along a bit, or we're all going to die of old age before we get to the end.

They sleep. They wake. They surf. They get hungry. They go to a pizza shop.

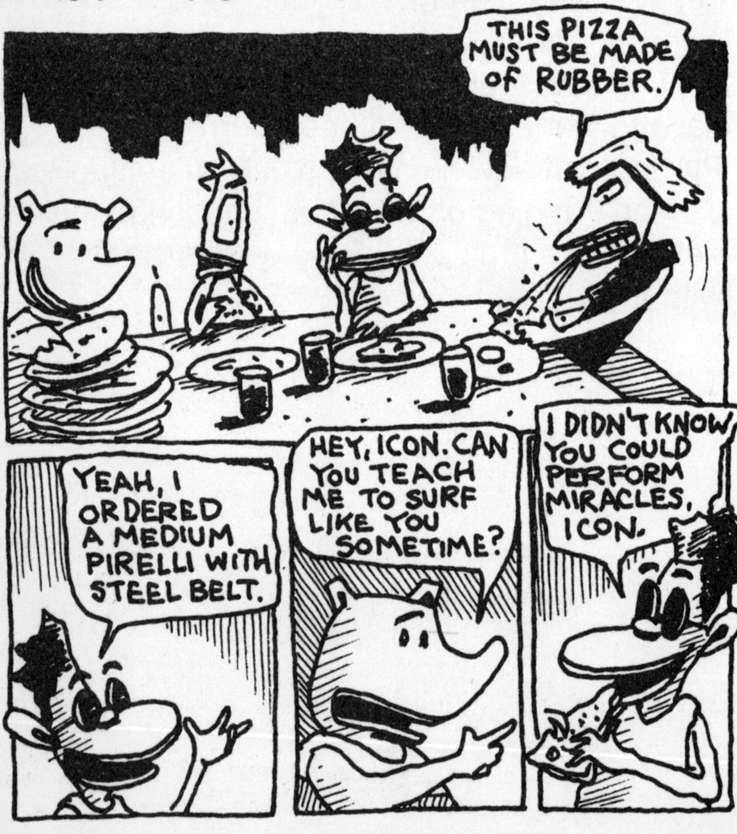
THIS PIZZA MUST BE MADE OF RUBBER.
YEAH, I ORDERED A MEDIUM PIRELLI WITH STEEL BELT.
HEY, ICON. CAN YOU TEACH ME TO SURF LIKE YOU SOMETIME?
I DIDN'T KNOW YOU COULD PERFORM MIRACLES, ICON.

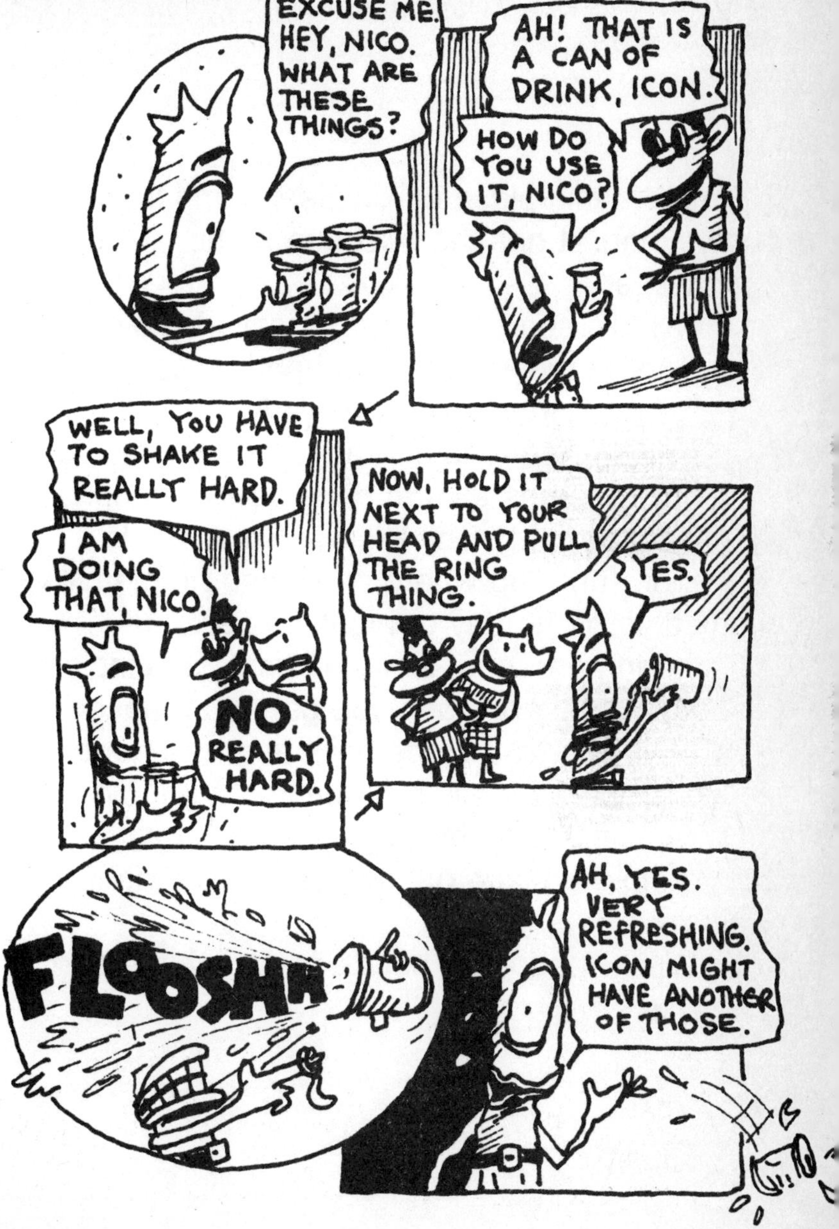
EXCUSE ME. HEY, NICO. WHAT ARE THESE THINGS?
AH! THAT IS A CAN OF DRINK, ICON.
HOW DO YOU USE IT, NICO?
WELL, YOU HAVE TO SHAKE IT REALLY HARD.
I AM DOING THAT, NICO.
NO. REALLY HARD.
NOW, HOLD IT NEXT TO YOUR HEAD AND PULL THE RING THING.
YES.
FLOOSHH
AH, YES. VERY REFRESHING. ICON MIGHT HAVE ANOTHER OF THOSE.

4

'There is this place called Eeeno, my friends,' says Icon. 'It has the best surf in the Universe.'

'What's so good about it?' says Mikey.

'Maybe the waves have handles so you can't fall off them, Mikey,' says Nico.

In fact, Eeeno is a strange and mysterious planet. It seems to float quite freely through space and time. A bit like my Great Uncle Gregor. Turns up where and when he pleases, any time of the day or night. Sits around blathering on about stuff you know nothing about. And then, when you get up to make him a snack, you come back and he's gone. Door's open and all that remains is his old Cuban cigar still smoking in the ashtray, smelling the place out and setting off the fire alarms.

Well, Eeeno is a bit like that, plus the surf is bliss.

'It is the waves, old friends,' says Icon. 'They are big and even and constant all day long. And if you were ever to fall off the waves, the rocks would be as soft as a baby's bottom. So you bounce. And the sand is like velvet between your toes. And the water! It's as smooth as milk, so there is NO chafing.'

'I like the sound of that,' says Nico.

'So, when can we go and try out this Planet Eeeno?' says Claudia.

'Hmmm,' says Icon. 'Sometime, Claudia. Sometime soon.'

5

Icon is lying in a dark world. He can hear his father talking to him.

Which doesn't make much sense, seeing as he was just in a pizza parlour on Ithaca, chatting on about Eeeno. But sometimes a fragment of reality just appears from nowhere, calling itself Chapter 5. You are not sure where it comes from. Or where it is headed. Or where it fits into the whole picture. It just turns up and you have to deal with it. Like Uncle Gregor again!

It's like you are sitting in a cinema, watching a movie. And the projection booth just blows up. Boom! The place fills with bits of film. Little scraps from all over the movie flutter down past your eyes. You catch one, and if it's not a bit of the projectionist, you look at it. This is one of those fragments.

So Icon sees his father, standing in front of him, talking to him.

'Someday, my boy, all of this will be yours. You will be King of Duryllium. A great King.'

'But where will you be, father?' asks Icon.

'Me? I will be long gone. And the people will need a great King to rule over them. And you will be the one.'

Young Vidor is in the room next door with his friend Crundor. He can just hear what his father is saying.

'But why not me?' he thinks to himself. 'I would make a great King, too. I should be King!'

Icon, in the room with his father, sees his brother watching...and hears him saying, 'I should be King.'

And now Icon looks around. The vision is gone. He is back in the Underworld. There is no warm bedroom. His father is gone. So has Vidor. Icon is alone again, in the cold Underworld.

6

Now, I hate to do this to you, but we are almost back where we were before that little interruption. Except that Icon and the Ithacans have used the M.I.T. and have landed on Eeeno. Which is almost where they wanted to be.

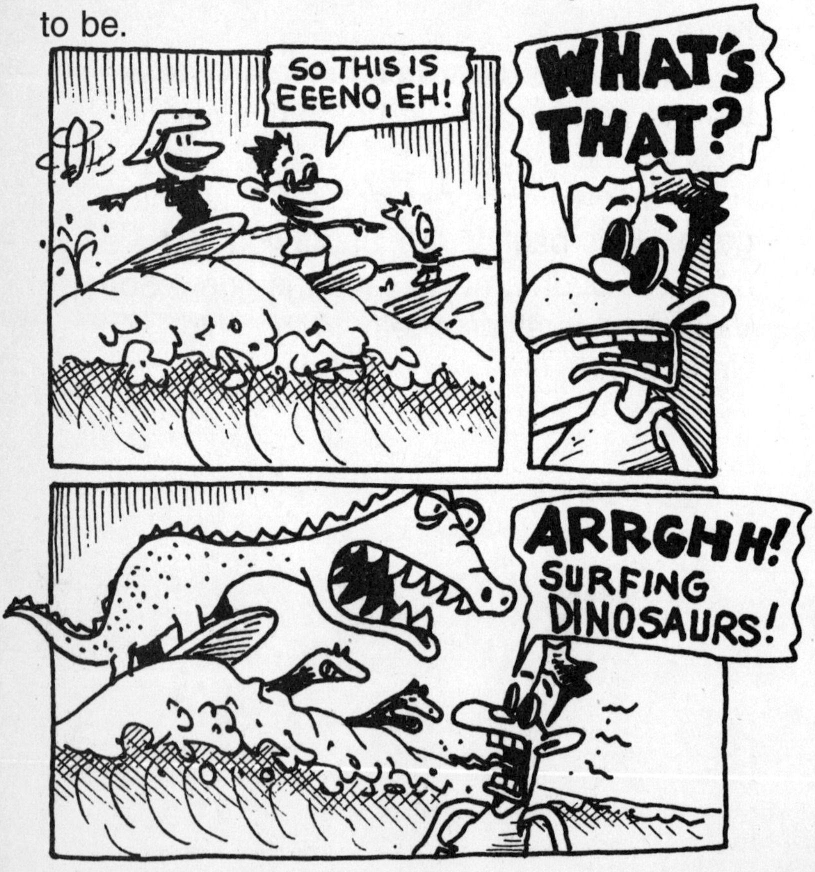

SO THIS IS EEENO, EH!
WHAT'S THAT?
ARRGHH! SURFING DINOSAURS!

I wouldn't trust them to shoot an apple off my head. Their aim is pathetic. Instead of landing on Eeeno in the present, they miss and arrive during the Proto-Durassic Era, a time when the planet was famous for its surfing dinosaurs. Which is fine if they are not surfing right next to you, trying to snack on your head as they pass by.

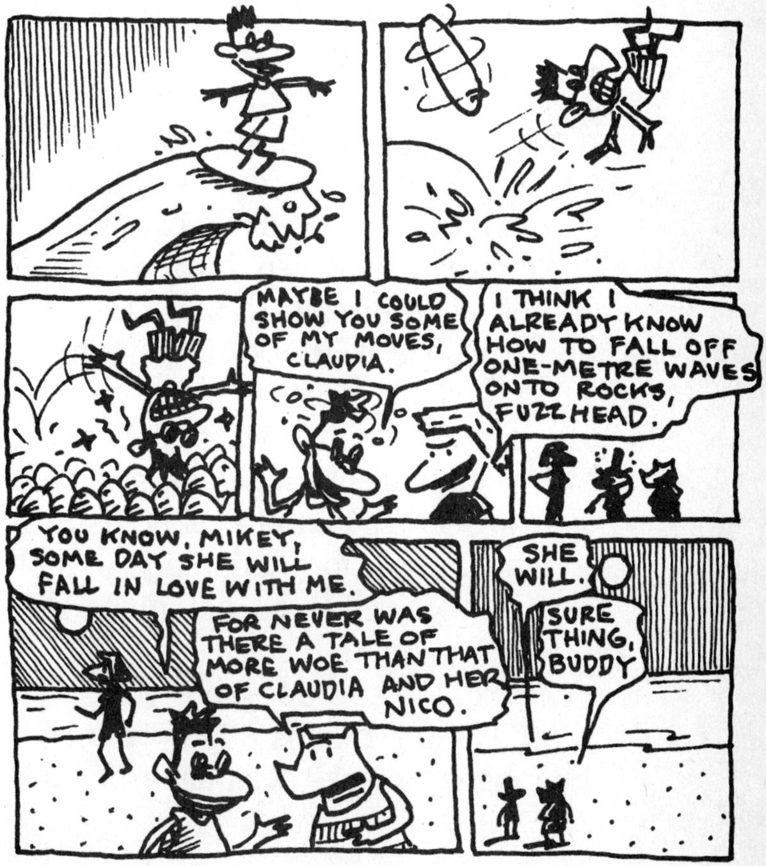
MAYBE I COULD SHOW YOU SOME OF MY MOVES, CLAUDIA.
I THINK I ALREADY KNOW HOW TO FALL OFF ONE-METRE WAVES ONTO ROCKS, FUZZHEAD.
YOU KNOW, MIKEY, SOME DAY SHE WILL FALL IN LOVE WITH ME.
FOR NEVER WAS THERE A TALE OF MORE WOE THAN THAT OF CLAUDIA AND HER NICO.
SHE WILL.
SURE THING, BUDDY

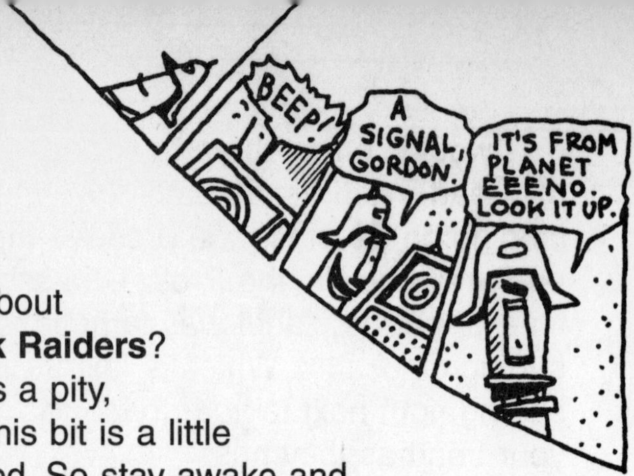
BEEP!
A SIGNAL, GORDON.
IT'S FROM PLANET EEENO. LOOK IT UP.

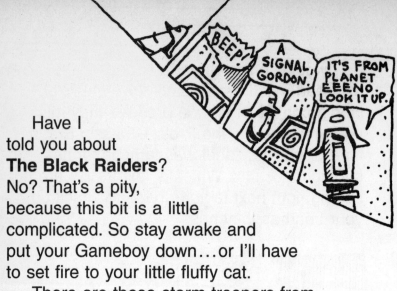

Have I told you about **The Black Raiders**? No? That's a pity, because this bit is a little complicated. So stay awake and put your Gameboy down...or I'll have to set fire to your little fluffy cat.

There are these storm troopers from Duryllium called **Black Raiders**. Their job is to do whatever the King orders. If he wants them to blow up Planet Earth and all its contents, they do it. No questions asked. If he wants a pizza from the corner store in 5000 B.C. Egypt, these guys get it. That's not as hard as it might seem if you have an M.I.T..

You see, everyone on Duryllium has an M.I.T. – a small genetically engineered biomorph. Why? So they can travel across space and time. People form an image in their mind of where they want to go, command the M.I.T. and **PLIK!** they are there.

The tricky bit is to end up where you wanted to go. The universe is a big place, and you only have to make a small error of

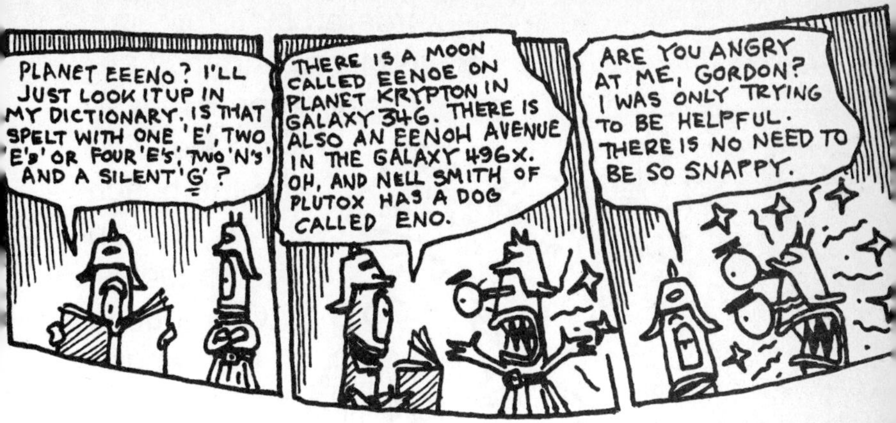
PLANET EEENO? I'LL JUST LOOK IT UP IN MY DICTIONARY. IS THAT SPELT WITH ONE 'E', TWO E's' OR FOUR 'E's; TWO 'N's' AND A SILENT 'G'?
THERE IS A MOON CALLED EENOE ON PLANET KRYPTON IN GALAXY 346. THERE IS ALSO AN EENOH AVENUE IN THE GALAXY 496X. OH, AND NELL SMITH OF PLUTOX HAS A DOG CALLED ENO.
ARE YOU ANGRY AT ME, GORDON? I WAS ONLY TRYING TO BE HELPFUL. THERE IS NO NEED TO BE SO SNAPPY.

one tenth of one per cent and you end up in deep space. Or somewhere weird, like in the fridge. The fridge of a gang of bikies. A gang of very short-tempered, grey-haired auntie bikies. Who are holding an afternoon tea party. And you've just squashed their cinnamon tea-cake. And you have your feet in their pav. You are history.

The Black Raiders, on the other hand, are very good at using their M.I.T.s. But they are even better at tracking other people's M.I.T.s. Every time someone uses an M.I.T., it leaves a tiny time shadow. The Raiders have a plane-load of nifty equipment that can track down these shadows.

AND THAT IS WHAT THEY ARE DOING AT THIS VERY MOMENT!!!

They have been ordered by King Vidor to find Icon, and they are closing in on him fast. He is sleeping on the beach with his Ithacan buddies. Oblivious to the danger.

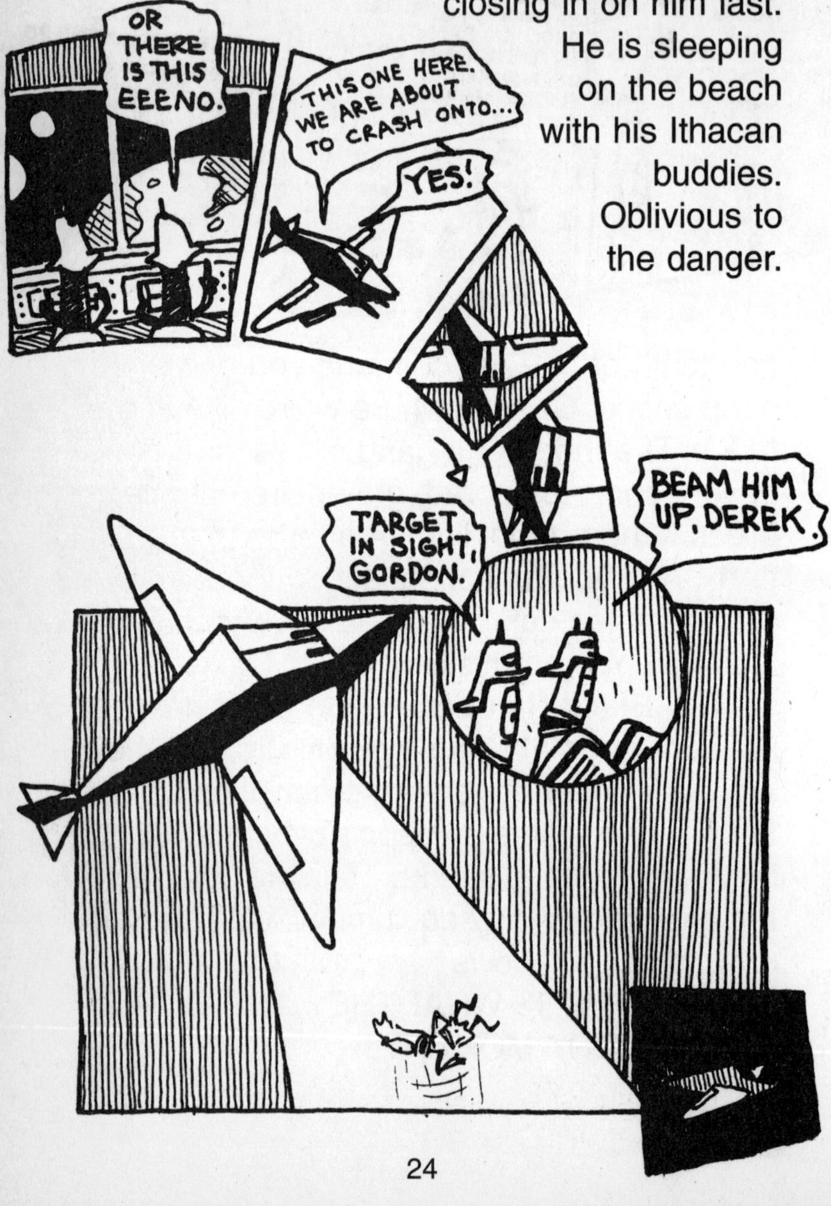
OR THERE IS THIS EEENO.
THIS ONE HERE. WE ARE ABOUT TO CRASH ONTO...
YES!
TARGET IN SIGHT, GORDON.
BEAM HIM UP, DEREK.

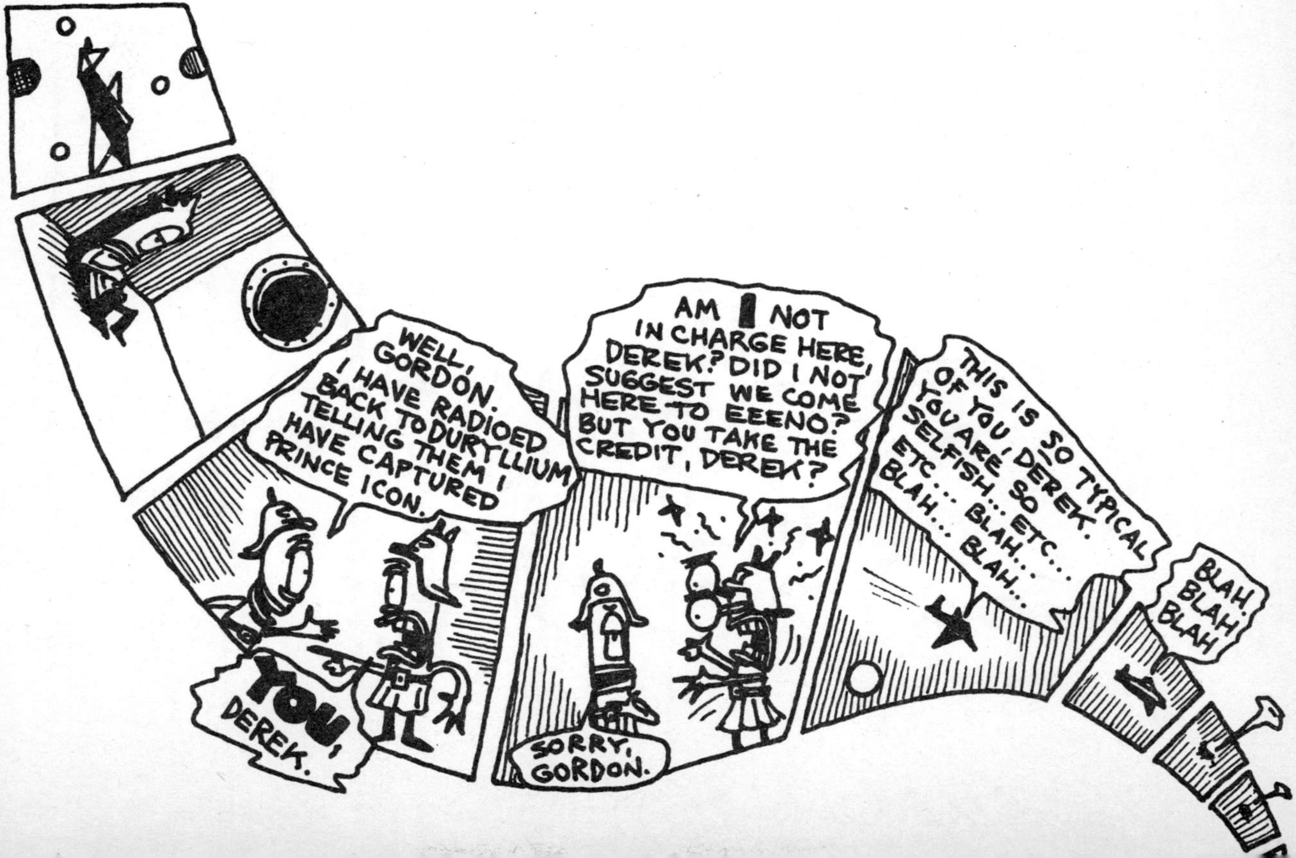
WELL, GORDON. I HAVE RADIOED BACK TO DURTLLIUM TELLING THEM I HAVE CAPTURED PRINCE ICON.
YOU, DEREK.
AM I NOT IN CHARGE HERE, DEREK? DID I NOT SUGGEST WE COME HERE TO EEENO? BUT YOU TAKE THE CREDIT, DEREK?
SORRY, GORDON.
THIS IS SO TYPICAL OF YOU, DEREK. YOU ARE SO SELFISH... ETC... ETC.... BLAH... BLAH... BLAH...
BLAH. BLAH BLAH

8

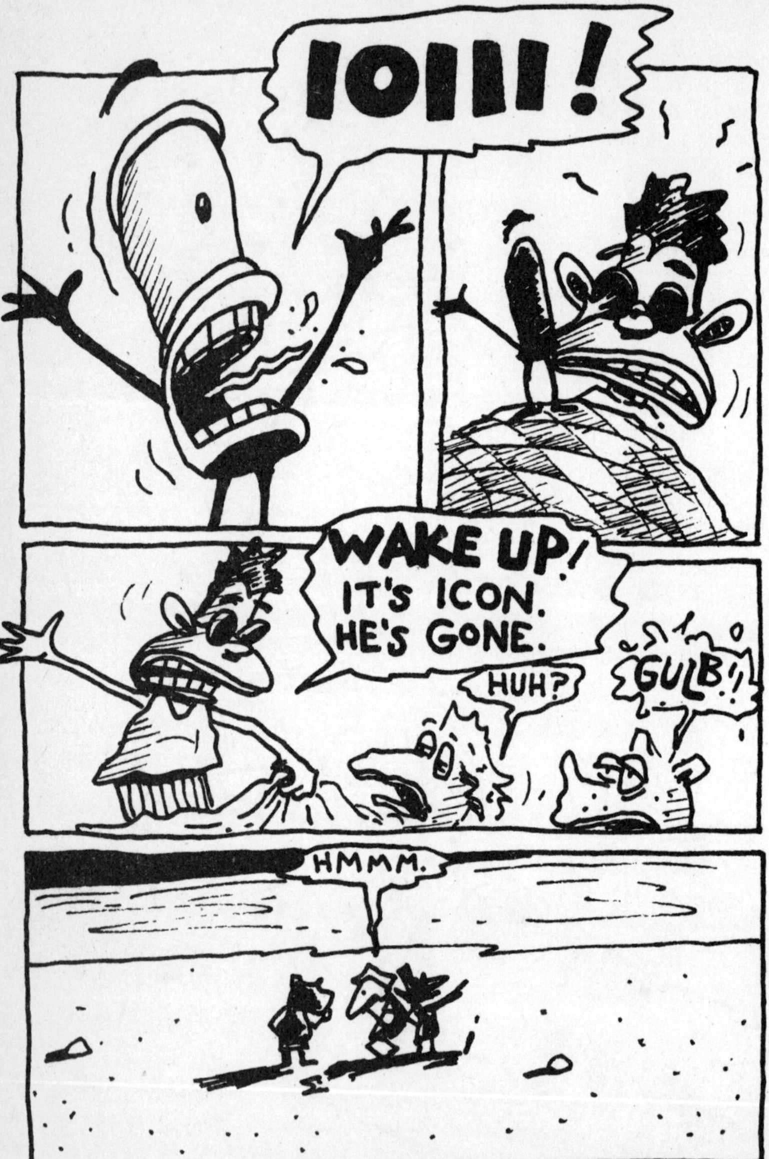
IOIII!
WAKE UP! IT'S ICON. HE'S GONE.
HUH?
GULB!
HMMM.

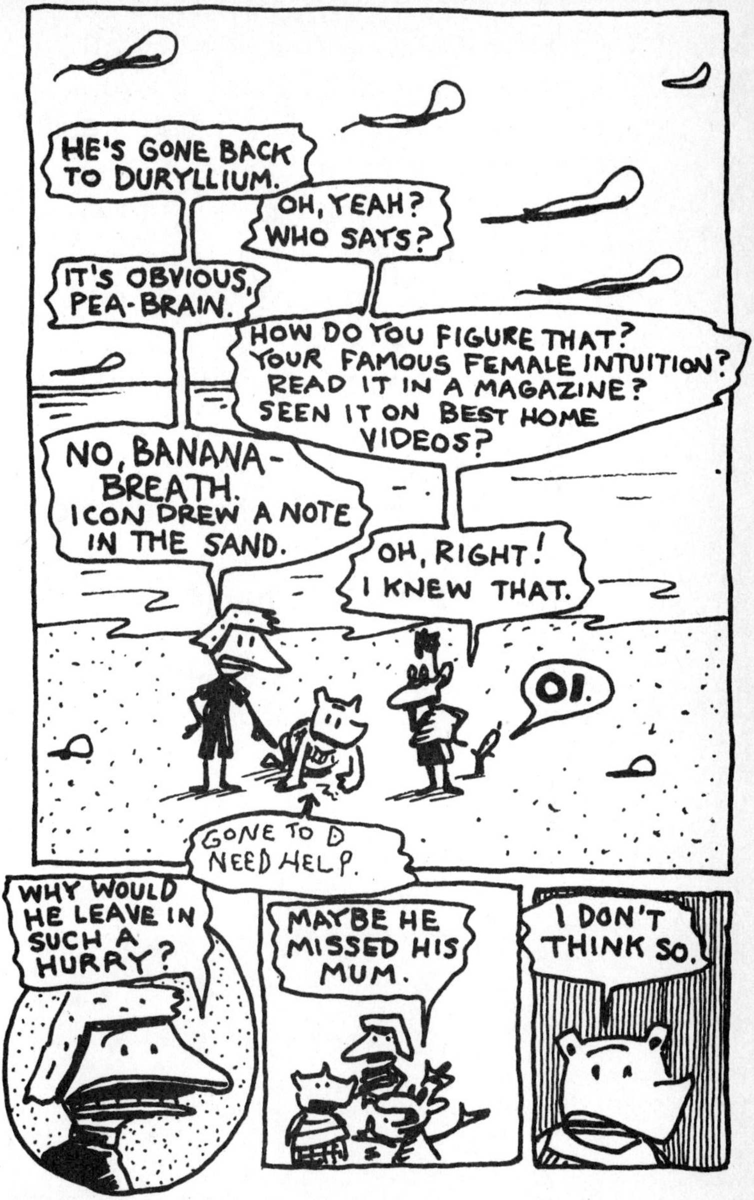

HE'S GONE BACK TO DURYLLIUM.
OH, YEAH? WHO SAYS?
IT'S OBVIOUS, PEA-BRAIN.
HOW DO YOU FIGURE THAT? YOUR FAMOUS FEMALE INTUITION? READ IT IN A MAGAZINE? SEEN IT ON BEST HOME VIDEOS?
NO, BANANA-BREATH. ICON DREW A NOTE IN THE SAND.
OH, RIGHT! I KNEW THAT.
OI.
GONE TO D
NEED HELP.
WHY WOULD HE LEAVE IN SUCH A HURRY?
MAYBE HE MISSED HIS MUM.
I DON'T THINK SO.

Nico, Claudia and Mikey don't know what to do. So they sit around for a couple of hours wondering if they should be thinking about doing something instead of just sitting around. Then Mikey decides it's time to act.

'I don't know about you blokes, but I reckon Icon's in trouble.'

'Yeah, maybe. But we don't know for sure,' says Claudia.

'I just think we should drop in on Duryllium on our way home, to see if he's OK,' says Mikey.

'Good idea,' says Nico. 'But how do we get there?'

'We could use the M.I.T., you blockhead,' says Claudia.

'Oh yeah!' thinks Nico. 'I knew that.'

9

Nico, Claudia and Mikey are holding on to the M.I.T., trying to remember how to use it. If they can't remember, they may be doomed to spend the rest of their lives on Planet Eeeno. Which would be OK, but for the head-chomping, surfing dinosuars.

Lucky break. They find Icon's address on the back of his surfboard: 351 Ocean Boulevarde, Duryllium, 3101. They take hold of M.I.T. and…

PLIK! They are gone.

Unfortunately they are not used to keeping just one thought in their minds for very long. Try it. It's very hard to do. You start thinking about one thing – say it's Duryllium – and for a while that's all you think about. Then you start thinking: Am I thinking about Duryllium? Then you think: By the way, did I pack a hanky? Are my undies clean? Why do fish have only two eyes, not three? And next thing you know, you've sent yourself somewhere really weird. Which is what our heroes do.

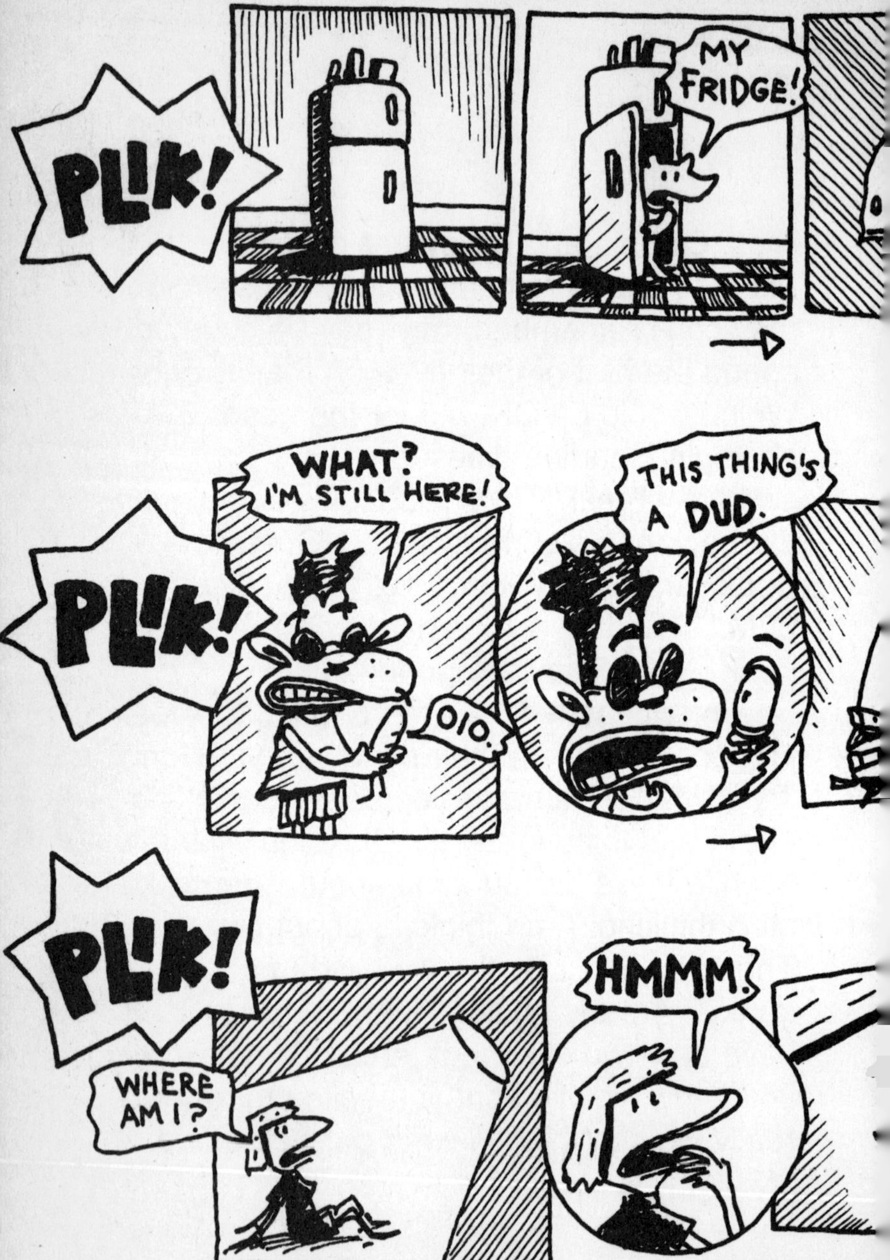
PLIK!
MY FRIDGE!
PLIK!
WHAT? I'M STILL HERE!
010.
THIS THING'S A DUD.
PLIK!
WHERE AM I?
HMMM.

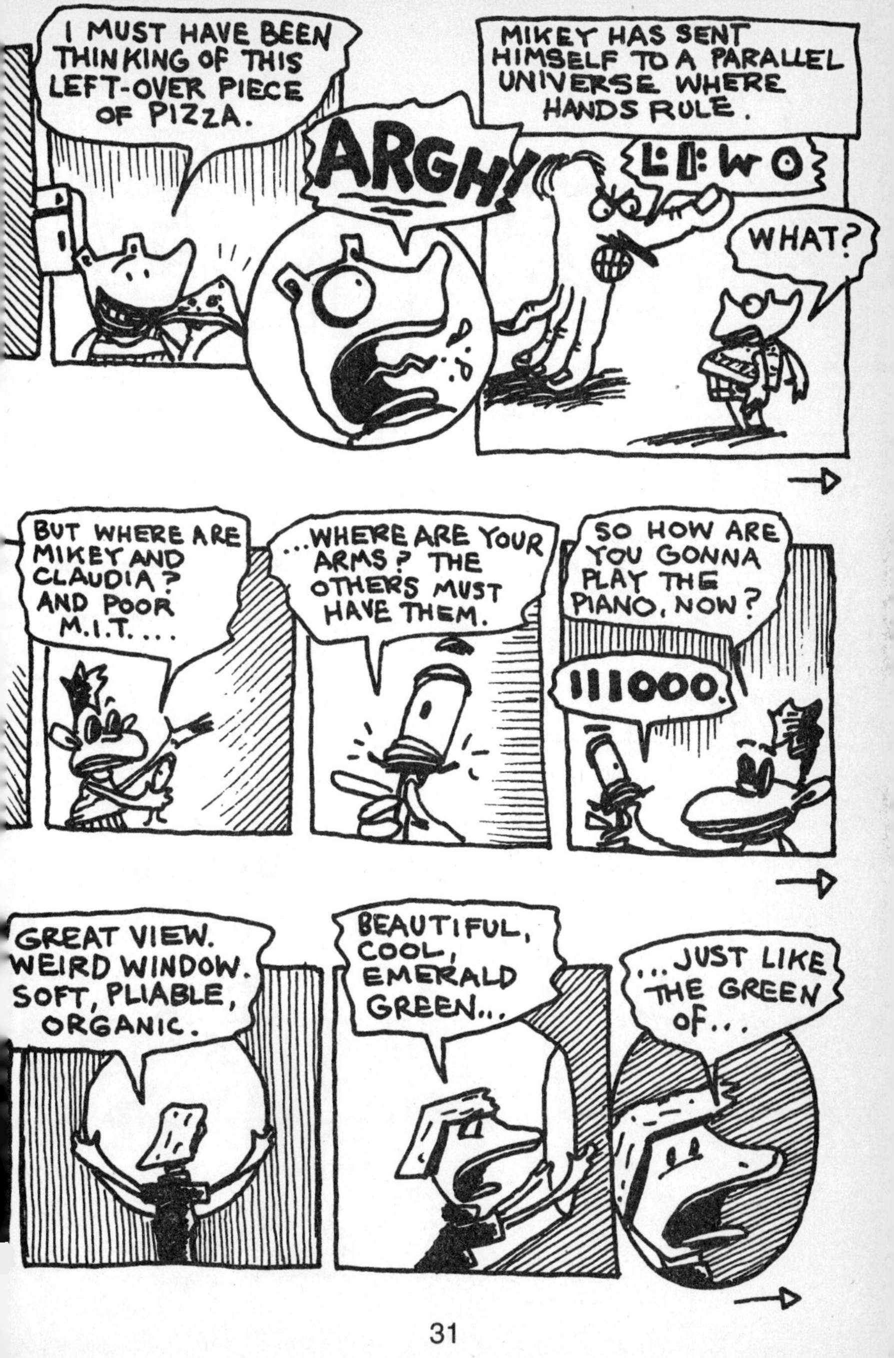

I MUST HAVE BEEN THINKING OF THIS LEFT-OVER PIECE OF PIZZA.
ARGH!
MIKEY HAS SENT HIMSELF TO A PARALLEL UNIVERSE WHERE HANDS RULE.
WHAT?
BUT WHERE ARE MIKEY AND CLAUDIA? AND POOR M.I.T. ...
...WHERE ARE YOUR ARMS? THE OTHERS MUST HAVE THEM.
SO HOW ARE YOU GONNA PLAY THE PIANO, NOW?
111000.
GREAT VIEW. WEIRD WINDOW. SOFT, PLIABLE, ORGANIC.
BEAUTIFUL, COOL, EMERALD GREEN...
...JUST LIKE THE GREEN OF...

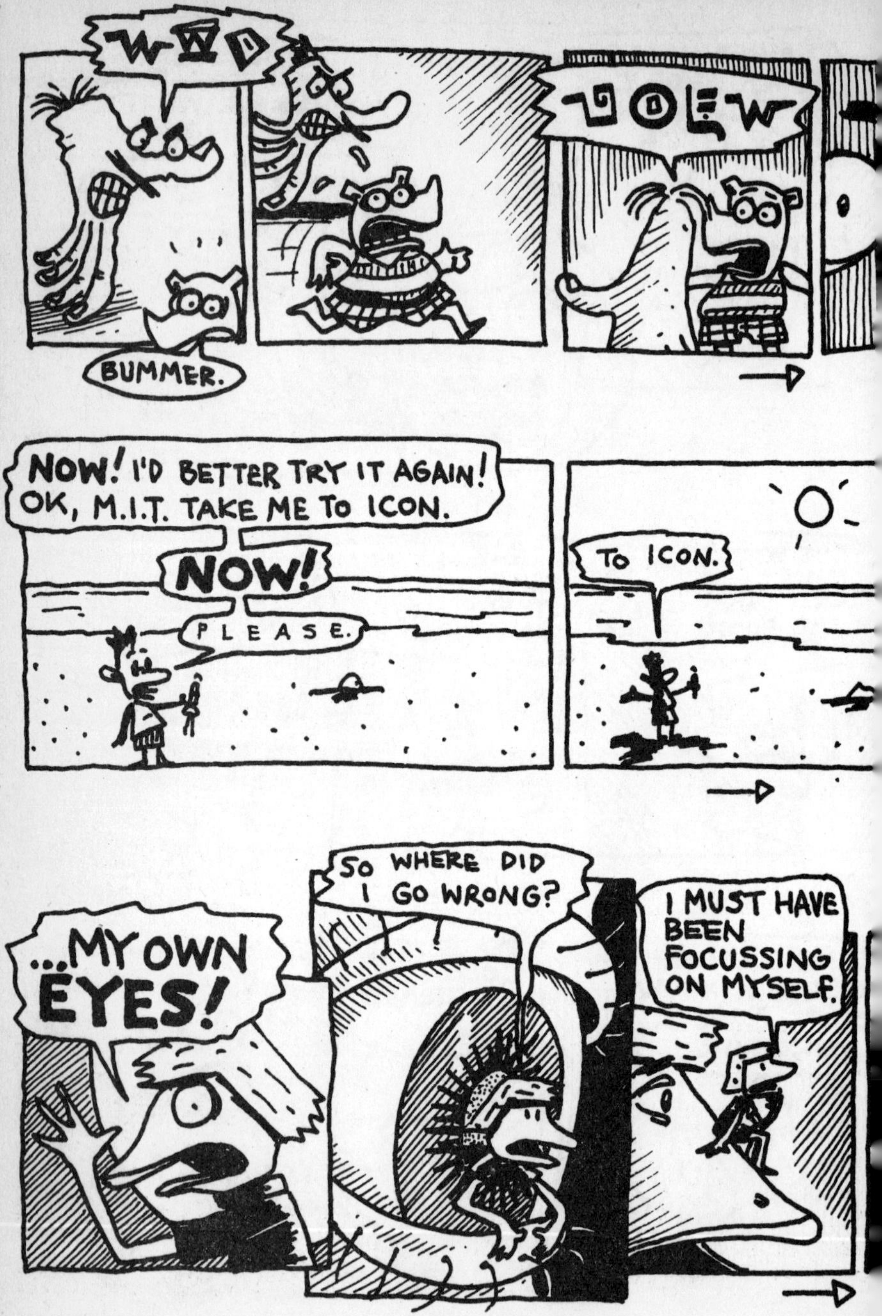
BUMMER.
NOW! I'D BETTER TRY IT AGAIN! OK, M.I.T. TAKE ME TO ICON.
NOW!
PLEASE.
TO ICON.
...MY OWN EYES!
SO WHERE DID I GO WRONG?
I MUST HAVE BEEN FOCUSSING ON MYSELF.

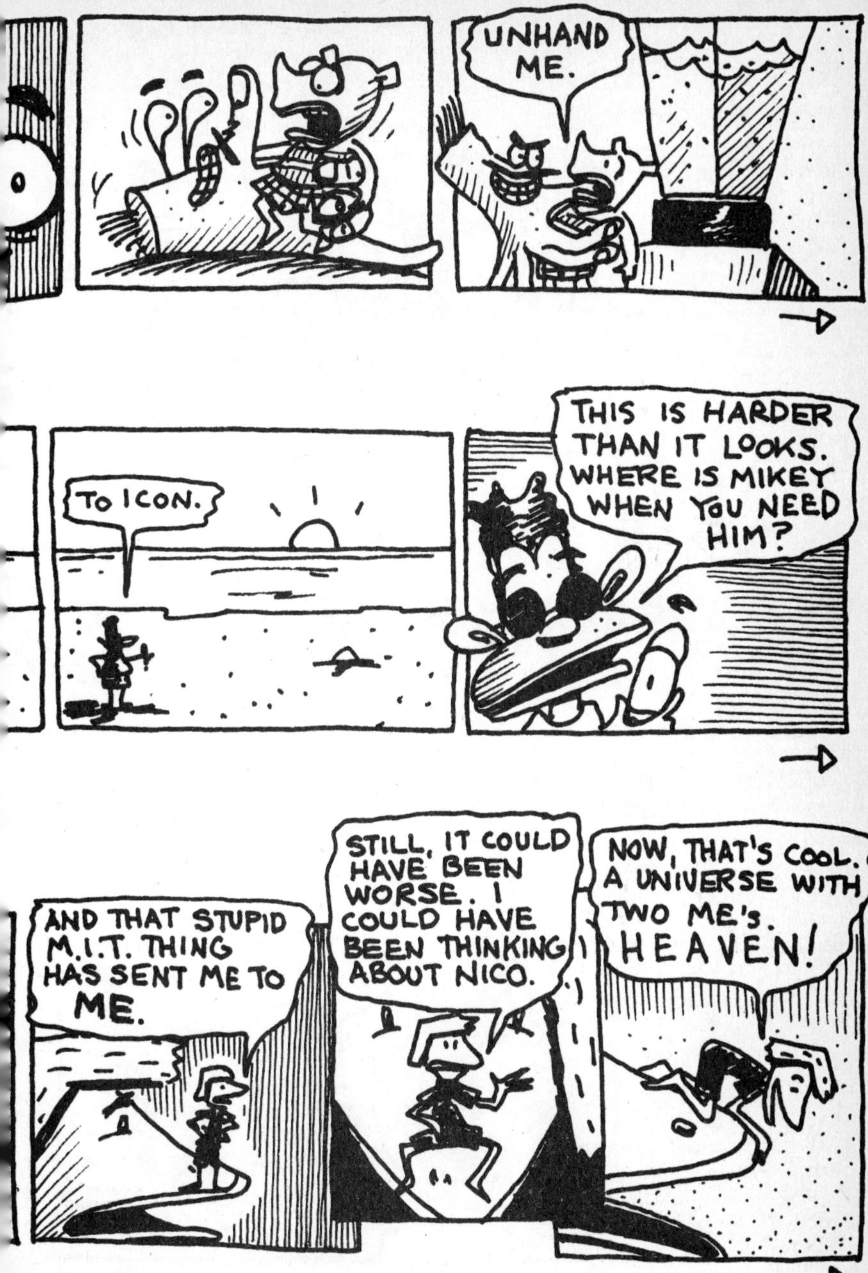
UNHAND ME.
To ICON.
THIS IS HARDER THAN IT LOOKS. WHERE IS MIKEY WHEN YOU NEED HIM?
AND THAT STUPID M.I.T. THING HAS SENT ME TO ME.
STILL, IT COULD HAVE BEEN WORSE. I COULD HAVE BEEN THINKING ABOUT NICO.
NOW, THAT'S COOL. A UNIVERSE WITH TWO ME's. HEAVEN!

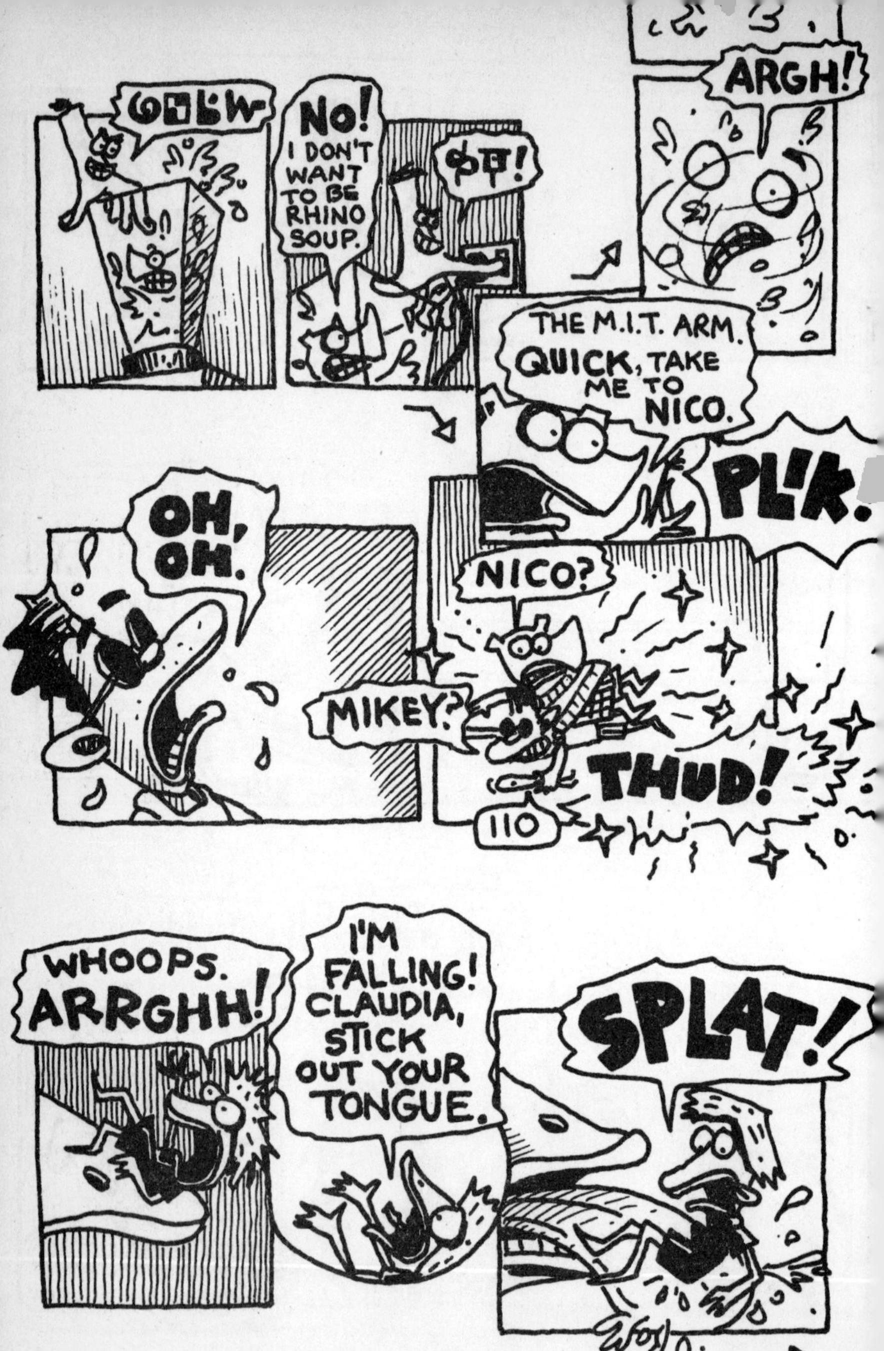
NO! I DON'T WANT TO BE RHINO SOUP.
ARGH!
THE M.I.T. ARM. QUICK, TAKE ME TO NICO.
PLIK.
OH, OH.
NICO?
MIKEY?
THUD!
110
WHOOPS. ARRGHH!
I'M FALLING! CLAUDIA, STICK OUT YOUR TONGUE.
SPLAT!

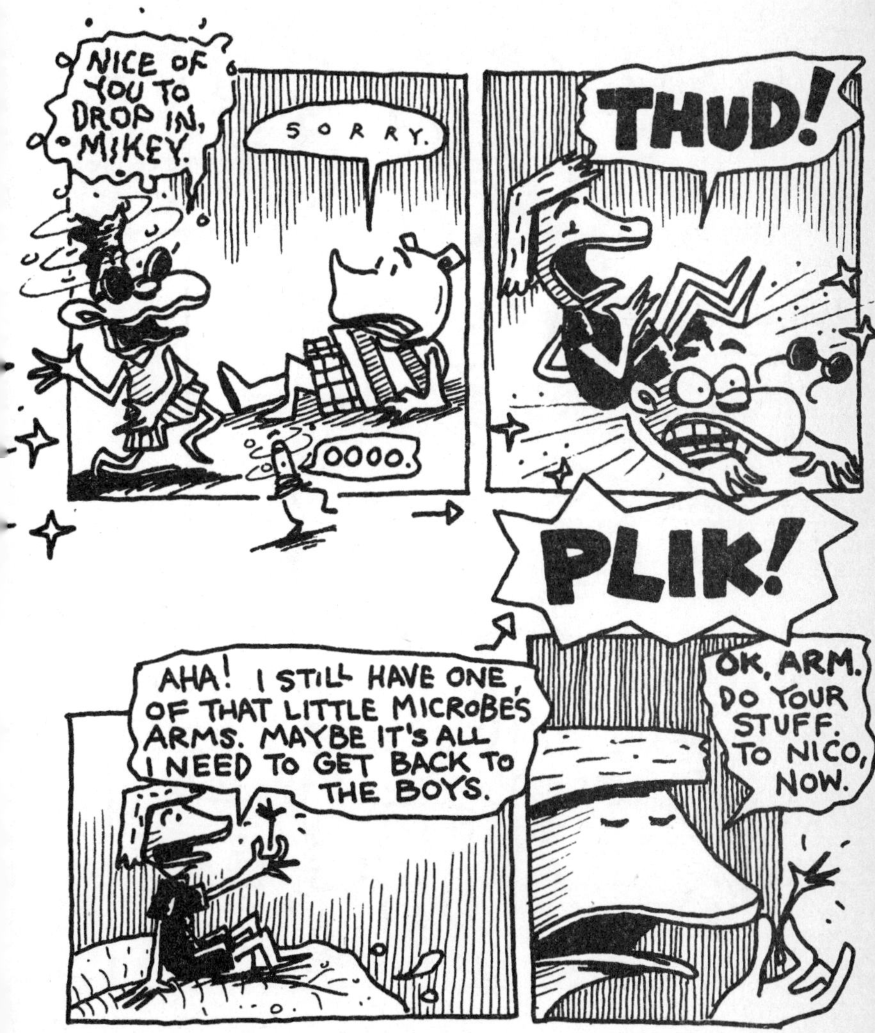
NICE OF YOU TO DROP IN, MIKEY.
SORRY.
OOOO.
THUD!
PLIK!
AHA! I STILL HAVE ONE OF THAT LITTLE MICROBE'S ARMS. MAYBE IT'S ALL I NEED TO GET BACK TO THE BOYS.
OK, ARM. DO YOUR STUFF. TO NICO, NOW.

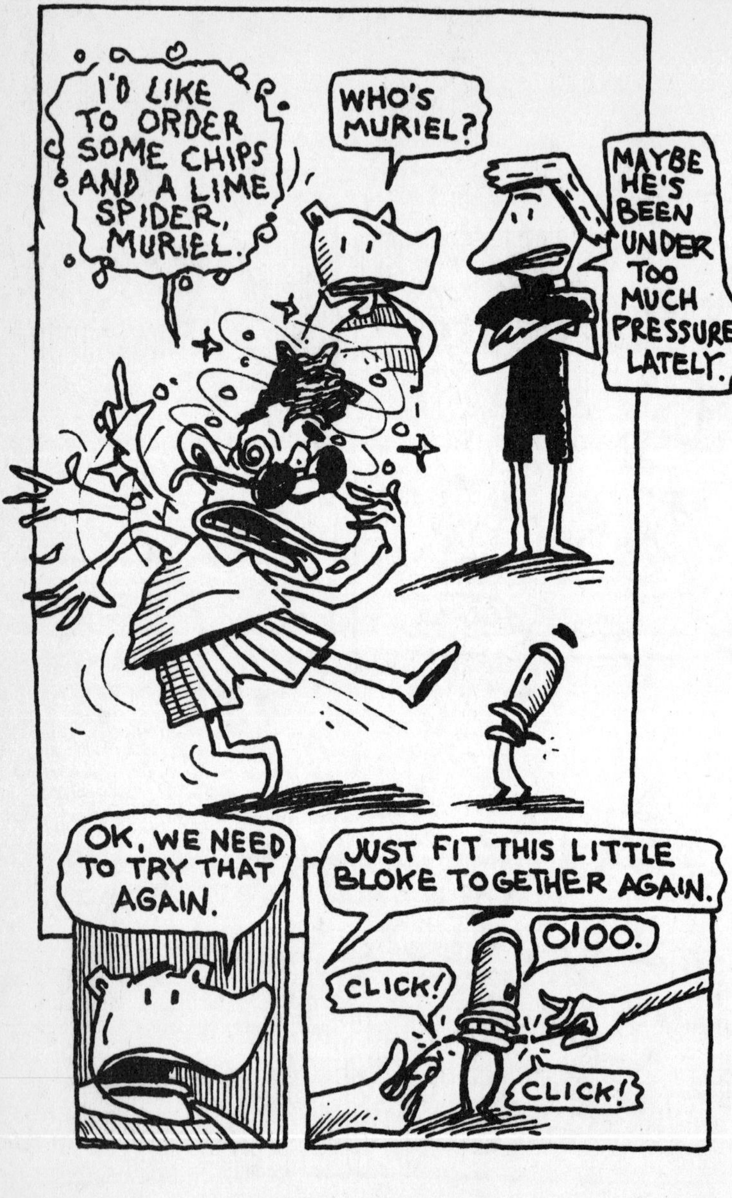
I'D LIKE TO ORDER SOME CHIPS AND A LIME SPIDER, MURIEL.
WHO'S MURIEL?
MAYBE HE'S BEEN UNDER TOO MUCH PRESSURE LATELY.
OK, WE NEED TO TRY THAT AGAIN.
JUST FIT THIS LITTLE BLOKE TOGETHER AGAIN.
OIOO.
CLICK!
CLICK!

10

Nico, Claudia and Mikey stand on the same beach on Eeeno and try the M.I.T. thing one more time. Their heads fill with helium, they expand like large balloons, then someone unties the ends and they fly, *ffffllllllppppppphhhh*, all around the room. Well, that's what it feels like.

Then...

PLIK!

The Ithacans turn to see a pack of vicious, howling bonecrunchers rushing towards them. They run down a corridor of stone walls too high to climb over. At the end of the corridor are two paths. One right. One left. Somehow they agree and take the right path. The bonecrunchers follow. Our heroes realise that they are being chased through a maze. Every time they pass an opening, more bonecrunchers pour out and join the chase.

They go left, the pack goes left. They go right, still the pack follows.

'We're going to be dinner!' screams Nico.

A few more turns and the bonecrunchers are gaining on them. Finally they pick badly. A dead end. The bonecrunchers are growling and licking their foul blood-stained lips. Moving closer. Deciding which one to eat first. Personally, I'd eat Mikey. Tender and meaty.

'The M.I.T.! You idiots. Use the M.I.T.!' cries Claudia.

They take hold of it. They form an image.

PLIK!

They are sitting on their favourite beach, on Ithaca. It is sunset. All is calm.

NO MAZE!!
NO BONECRUNCHERS!!

'You stupid mouldy microbe,' yells Claudia, trying to choke the M.I.T.. 'Why did you take us there?'

'10101,' says M.I.T..

Sometime later, when they have all calmed down, they decide to try again. They take hold of the M.I.T.. They form an image of Duryllium, again. They close their eyes. They concentrate really hard. Which is difficult for Ithacans. Very easy for us Narrators, of course, because we are a higher form of being. But that's another story.

'To Duryllium,' says Nico.

'And on the double,' says Mikey.

11

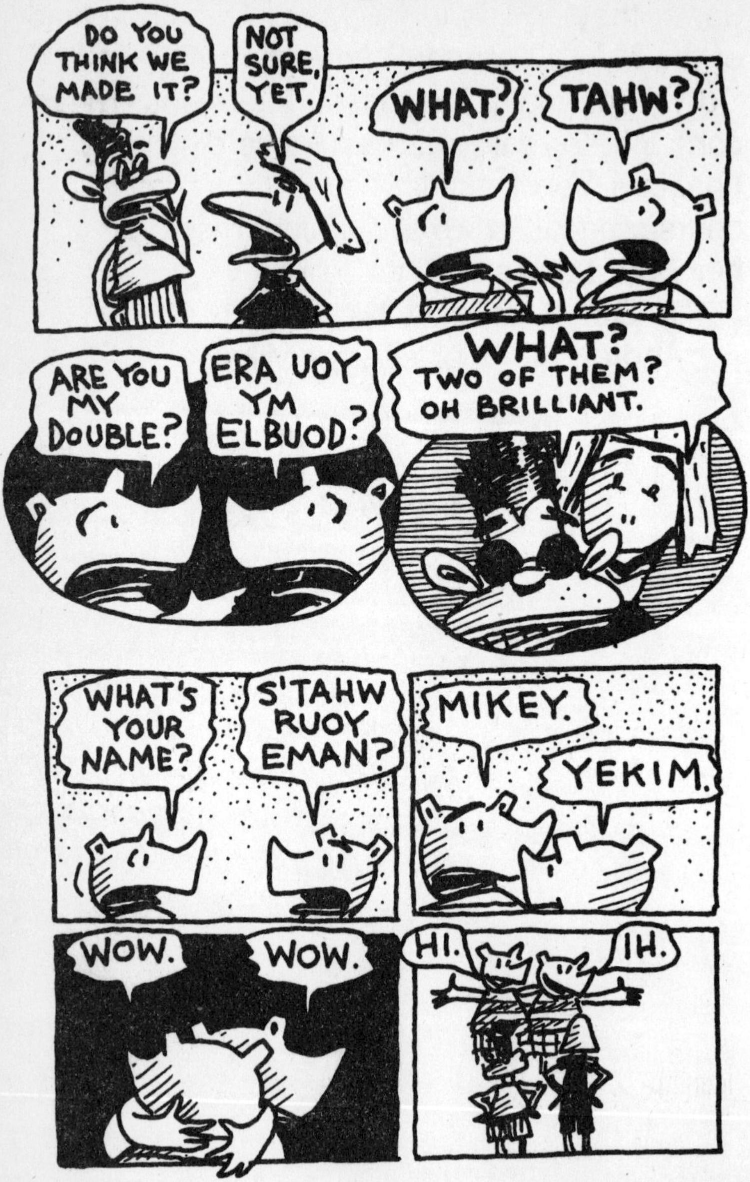
DO YOU THINK WE MADE IT?
NOT SURE, YET.
WHAT?
TAHW?
ARE YOU MY DOUBLE?
ERA UOY YM ELBUOD?
WHAT? TWO OF THEM? OH BRILLIANT.
WHAT'S YOUR NAME?
S'TAHW RUOY EMAN?
MIKEY.
YEKIM.
WOW.
WOW.
HI.
IH.

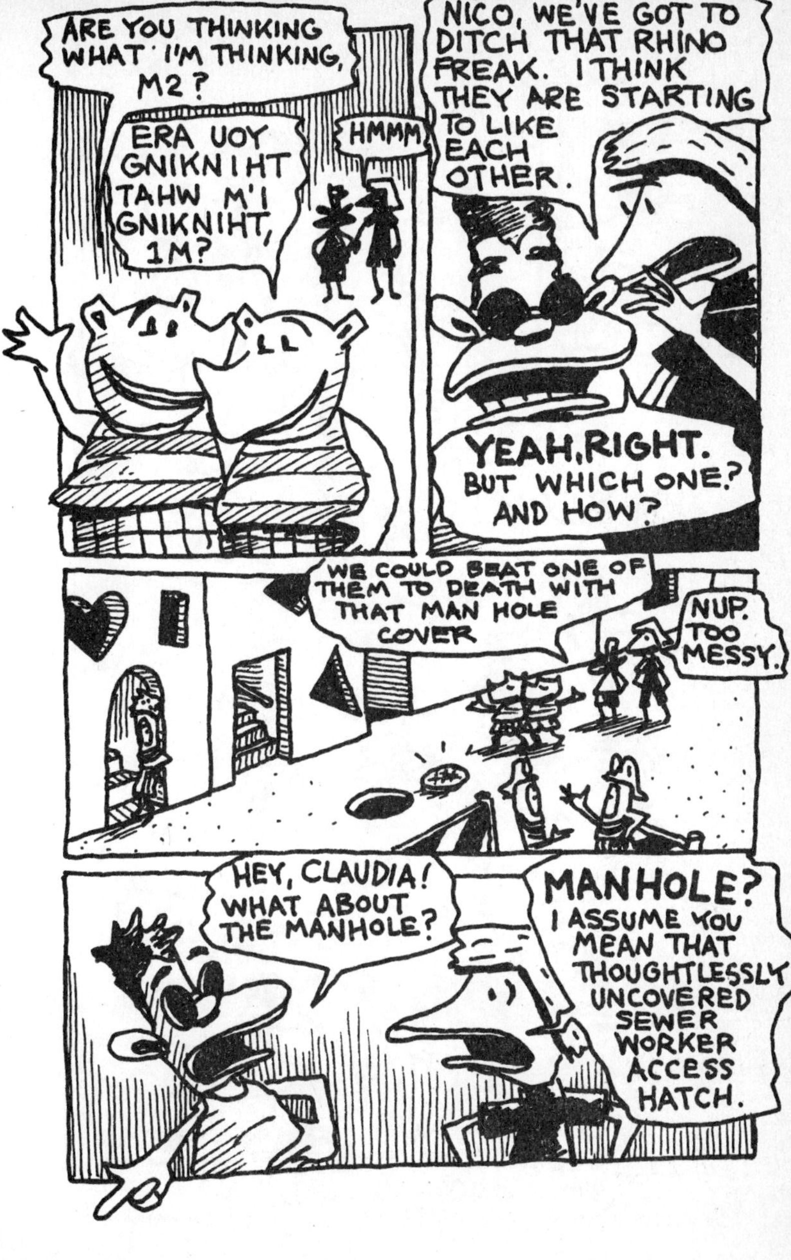
ARE YOU THINKING WHAT I'M THINKING, M2?
ERA UOY GNIKNIHT TAHW M'I GNIKNIHT, 1M?
HMMM
NICO, WE'VE GOT TO DITCH THAT RHINO FREAK. I THINK THEY ARE STARTING TO LIKE EACH OTHER.
YEAH, RIGHT. BUT WHICH ONE? AND HOW?
WE COULD BEAT ONE OF THEM TO DEATH WITH THAT MAN HOLE COVER
NUP. TOO MESSY.
HEY, CLAUDIA! WHAT ABOUT THE MANHOLE?
MANHOLE? I ASSUME YOU MEAN THAT THOUGHTLESSLY UNCOVERED SEWER WORKER ACCESS HATCH.

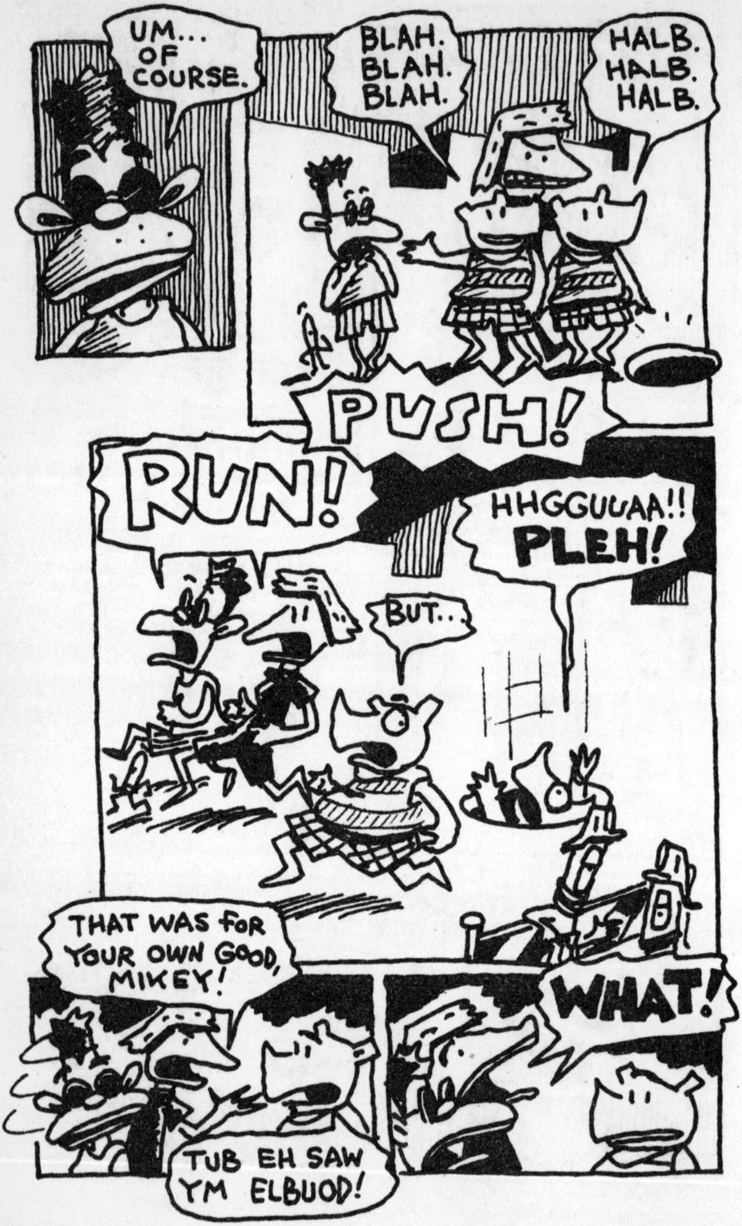
UM... OF COURSE.
BLAH. BLAH. BLAH.
HALB. HALB. HALB.
PUSH!
RUN!
HHGGUUAA!! PLEH!
BUT...
THAT WAS FOR YOUR OWN GOOD, MIKEY!
TUB EH SAW YM ELBUOD!
WHAT!

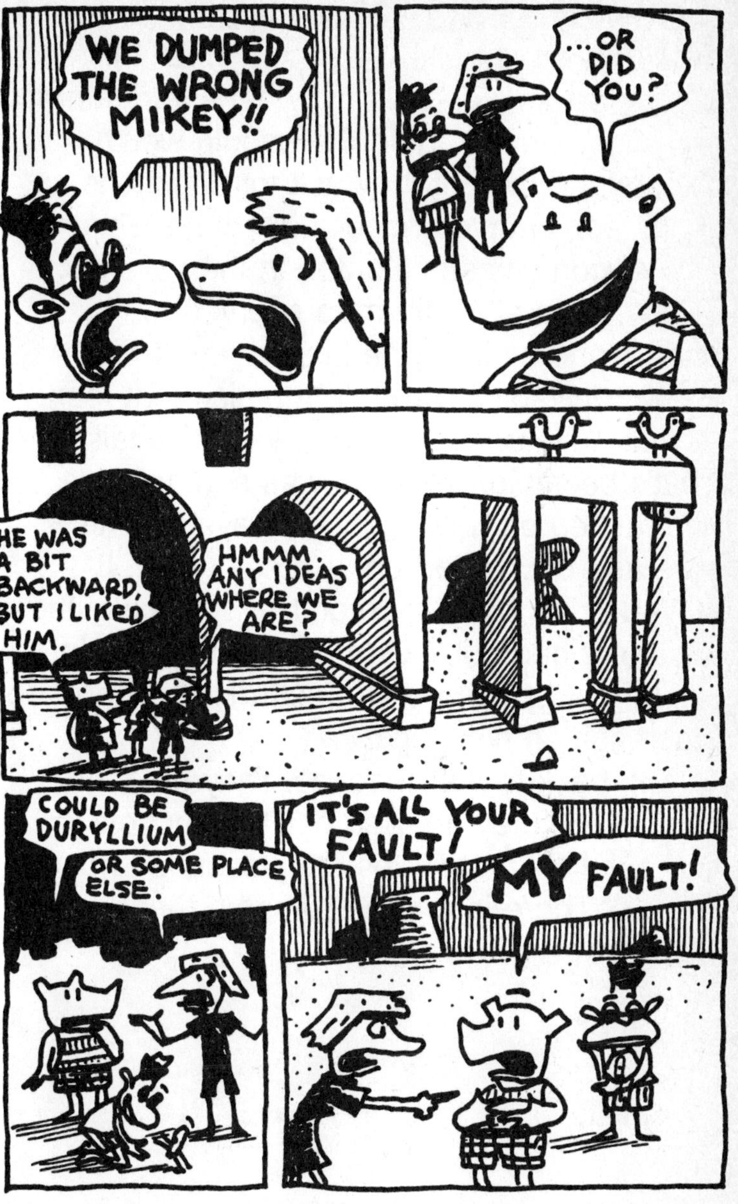
WE DUMPED THE WRONG MIKEY!!
...OR DID YOU?
HE WAS A BIT BACKWARD, BUT I LIKED HIM.
HMMM. ANY IDEAS WHERE WE ARE?
COULD BE DURYLLIUM
OR SOME PLACE ELSE.
IT'S ALL YOUR FAULT!
MY FAULT!

Of course they have no idea where they are. They have never been to Duryllium before, so they don't know what it is meant to look like. They imagine the people won't understand them if they ask for directions.

In fact, people on Duryllium have a pair of nifty silicon chips implanted in their skulls. These chips allow them to speak and understand most of the languages of the known universes. You might notice that Icon makes quite a few mistakes when he talks. That's because, when he was surfing once, he crashed off a really huge wave and his ears and brain filled up with salt water. It stayed in his head for months. Eventually the water drained out, but by then it was too late. His language skills were faulty. He had got too much salt on his chips.

But back to the Ithacans. They have no idea where they are and don't know how to find out. Fortunately they turn around and look up. There is a large billboard that says:

WELCOME TO DURYLLIUM

12

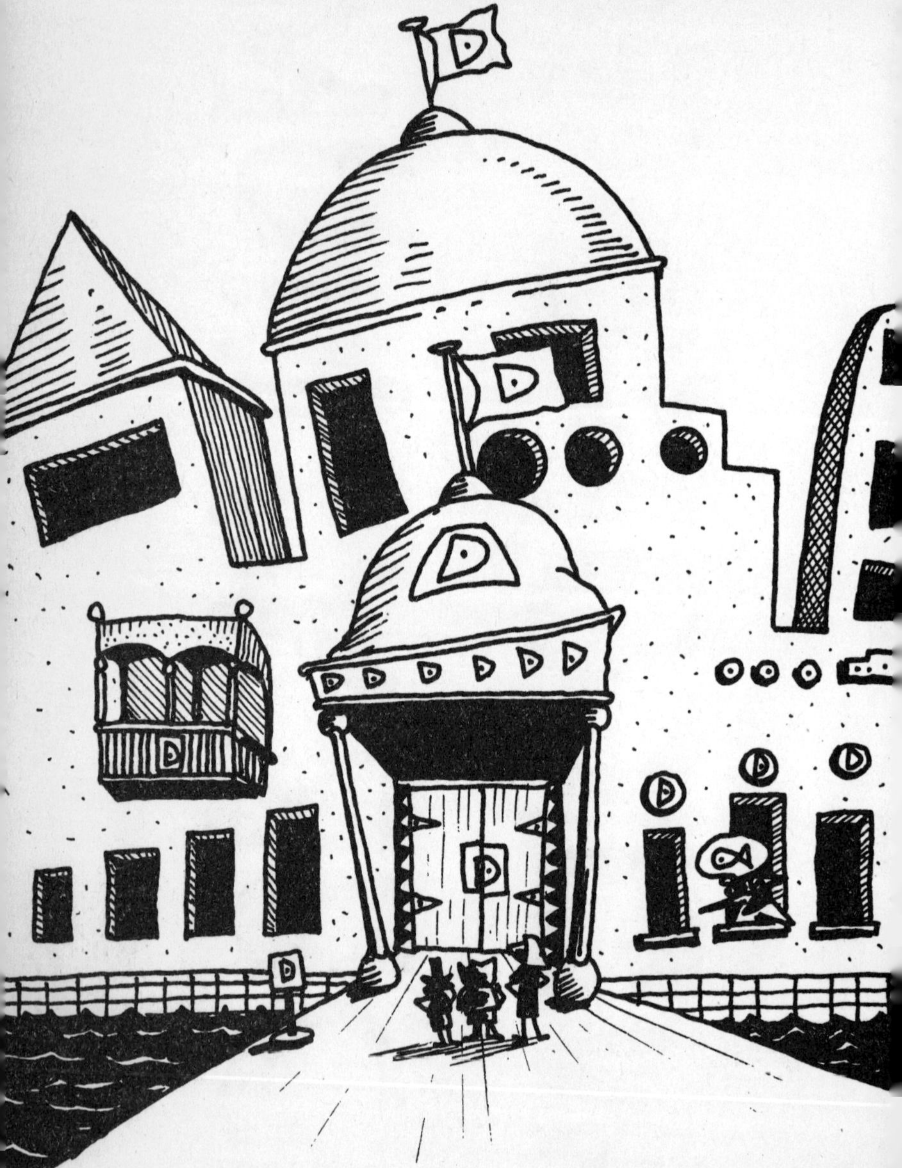

Nico, Claudia and Mikey are not sure if they are in the right place. Before them is a large palace, not the scungy little house they were expecting. They argue for a while, until Claudia becomes impatient.

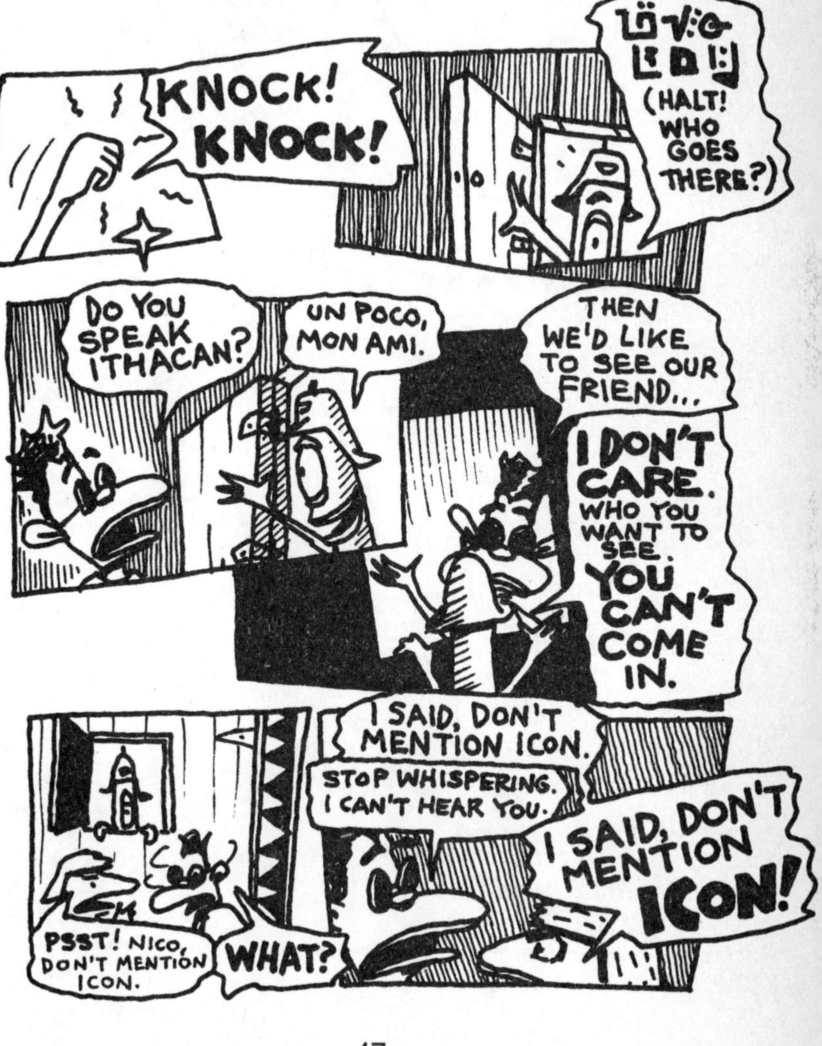
KNOCK! KNOCK!
(HALT! WHO GOES THERE?)
DO YOU SPEAK ITHACAN?
UN POCO, MON AMI.
THEN WE'D LIKE TO SEE OUR FRIEND...
I DON'T CARE. WHO YOU WANT TO SEE. YOU CAN'T COME IN.
PSST! NICO, DON'T MENTION ICON.
WHAT?
I SAID, DON'T MENTION ICON.
STOP WHISPERING. I CAN'T HEAR YOU.
I SAID, DON'T MENTION ICON!

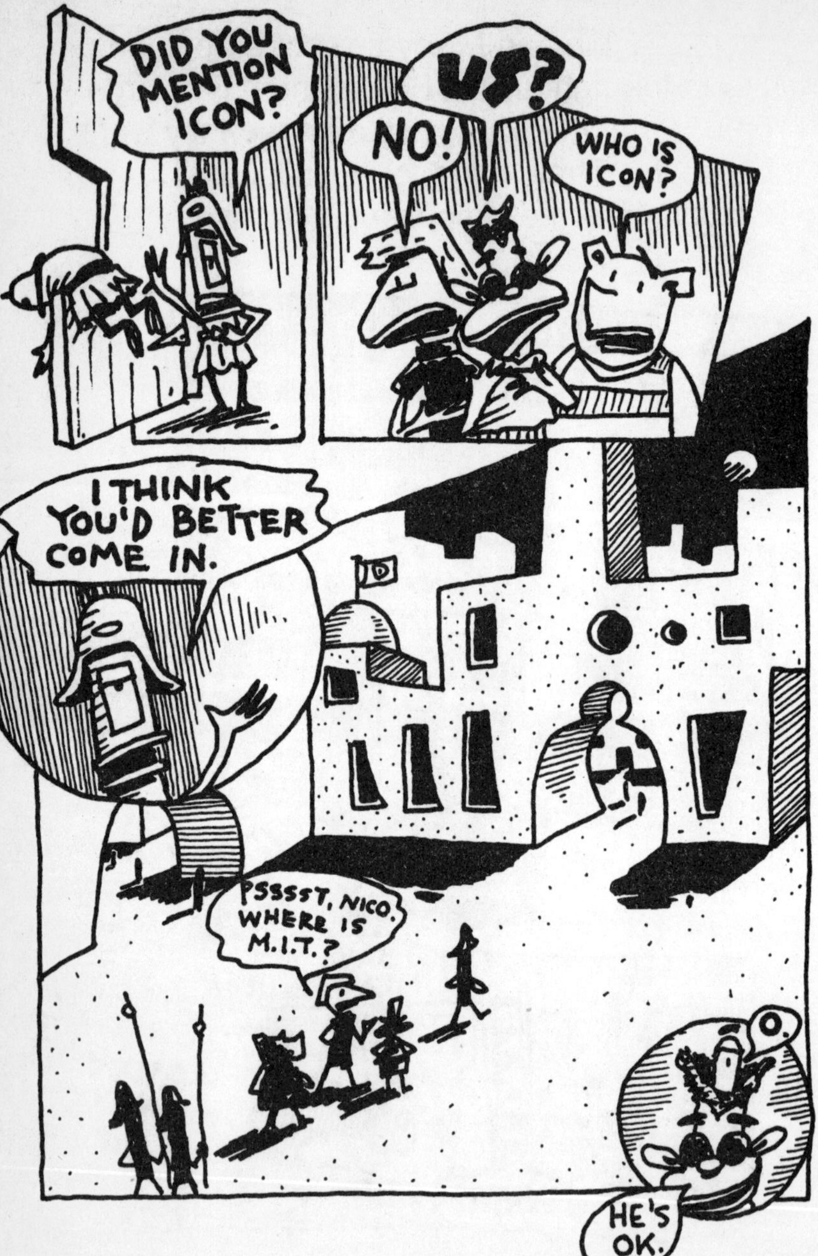
DID YOU MENTION ICON?
US?
NO!
WHO IS ICON?
I THINK YOU'D BETTER COME IN.
PSSSST, NICO, WHERE IS M.I.T.?
HE'S OK.

The tall military officer is Captain Crundor, the highest-ranking military officer in the land. And he's not very high. These days he is King Vidor's right-hand man and a very nasty piece of work. When he was a child he was Vidor's best friend. They would spend their days doing rotten things like sticking dead mice in Icon's muesli, pulling the wings off flying fish or setting fire to important public buildings. And other things too murderous to mention.

Nothing has changed.

13

There is NO Chapter 13. There is no Chapter 13 because to have a Chapter 13 would be considered unlucky…unless you are lucky enough not to believe in luck. In which case you are probably wondering why there is no Chapter 13.

Well, there just isn't one. OK? Narrators can't make everyone happy.

We don't believe in bad luck. We believe that it's bad luck to believe in bad luck. We believe that we make our own luck. If we really want something badly enough, then we can make it happen. Go for it. Just do it. And if things don't work out? Well, then we just find someone else to blame. Usually someone smaller and less powerful than us.

14

'So dark. So cold.'

Icon looks about. He can't see anything. (It's dark, remember!) But now a vision is forming.

'Vidor? Crundor?' he says.

He can hear them laughing some way off.

It is dark. (Did I tell you that?) Icon's hands are tied. He can smell old socks. That's because he is lying in a wardrobe. He has been playing a game of 'kidnap the slightly older twin brother' with Vidor and his friend Crundor. And, as usual, they promised not to pick on Icon. But, of course, they did. And they took his pocket money and have run off to spend it. And Icon is left behind, locked up in the wardrobe.

Rigo, the butler, finds him and releases him.

'Why do you always trust them, Icon?' Rigo asks.

'I won't next time, Rigo. Never again.'

But he will. Vidor and Crundor will trick him again and tie him up, or worse, because Icon wants to believe that they are telling him the truth. And they know he wants to believe them.

It is dark. The vision vanishes. The voices, too. Icon is again alone in the Underworld. And another fragment of the Universe passes by.

15

Nico, Claudia and Mikey are being led by Captain Crundor down a long corridor. He is taking them to meet King Vidor.

'That was your fault, Nico,' whispers Claudia.

'Me?'

'Yes, you!'

'But what's wrong with talking about Icon anyway?'

'I'm not sure, banana-breath,' she says. 'Just don't, OK.'

They enter a big room. On the floor is a long green carpet that looks like it is made of live grass. On either side of the carpet is a shallow pool with long-legged water rats gracefully picking their way through the water lillies. The path leads up to a platform with steps and on top of the platform sits some bloke on a throne. They figure that's probably King Vidor. Smart people, Ithacans. Crundor starts to speak.

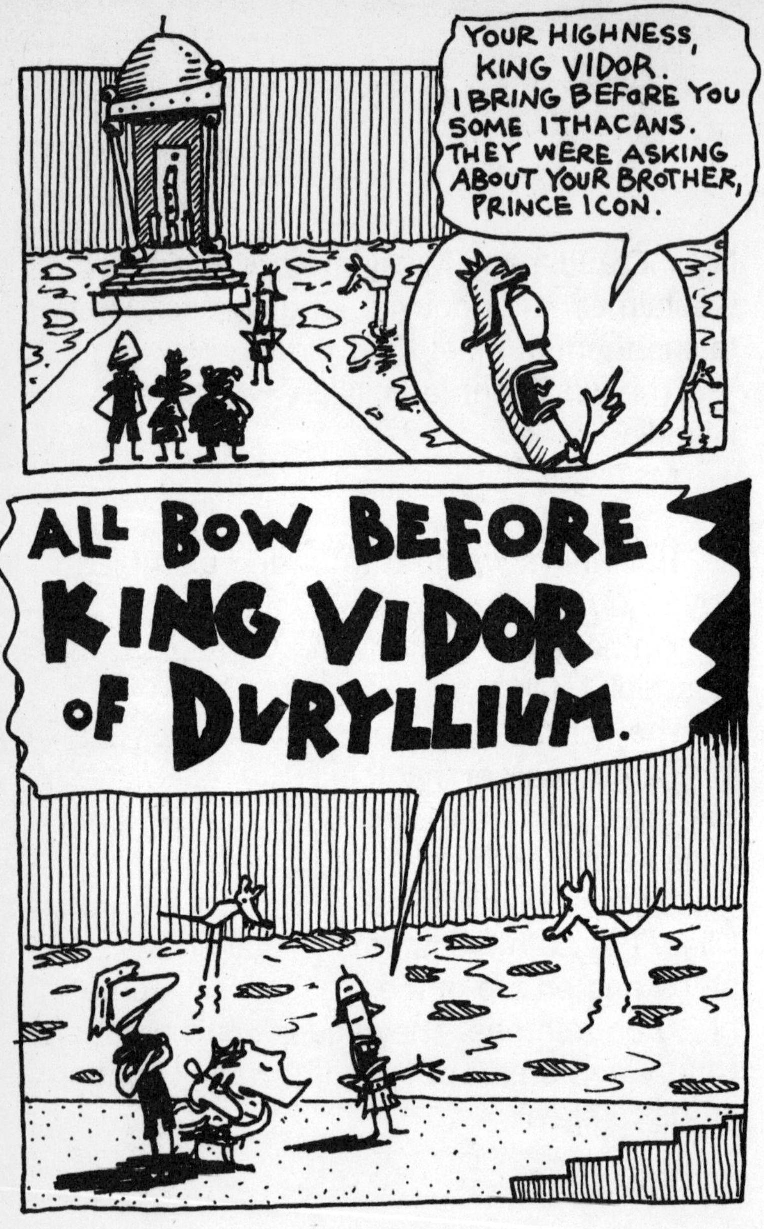
YOUR HIGHNESS, KING VIDOR. I BRING BEFORE YOU SOME ITHACANS. THEY WERE ASKING ABOUT YOUR BROTHER, PRINCE ICON.
ALL BOW BEFORE KING VIDOR OF DURYLLIUM.

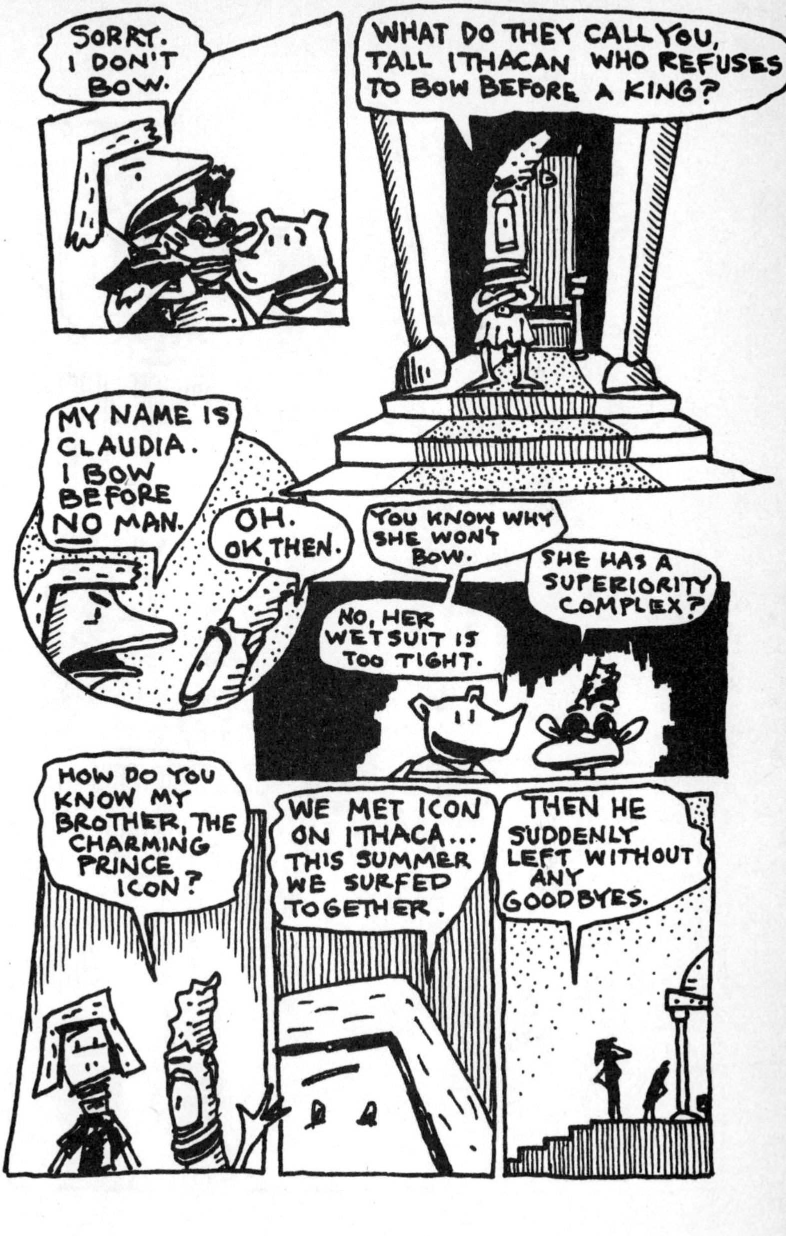
SORRY. I DON'T BOW.
WHAT DO THEY CALL YOU, TALL ITHACAN WHO REFUSES TO BOW BEFORE A KING?
MY NAME IS CLAUDIA. I BOW BEFORE NO MAN.
OH. OK, THEN.
YOU KNOW WHY SHE WON'T BOW.
SHE HAS A SUPERIORITY COMPLEX?
NO, HER WETSUIT IS TOO TIGHT.
HOW DO YOU KNOW MY BROTHER, THE CHARMING PRINCE ICON?
WE MET ICON ON ITHACA... THIS SUMMER WE SURFED TOGETHER.
THEN HE SUDDENLY LEFT WITHOUT ANY GOODBYES.

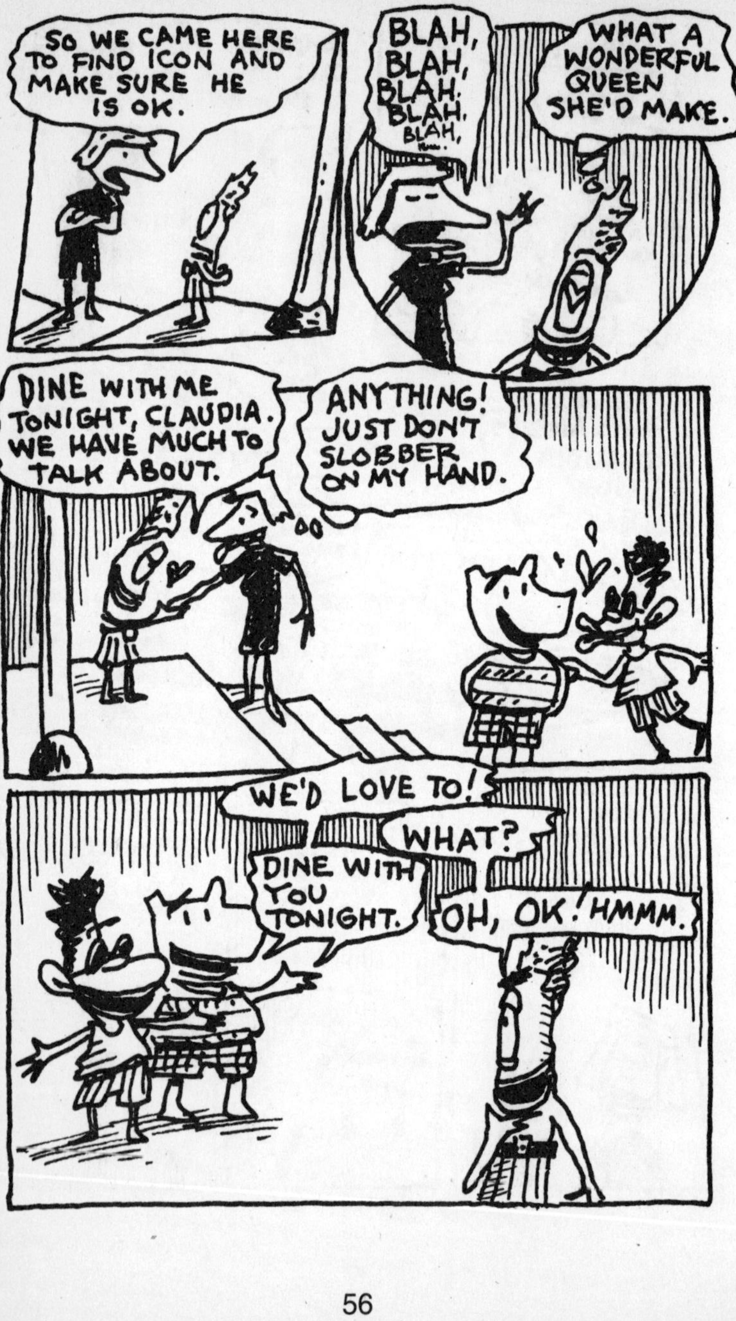
SO WE CAME HERE TO FIND ICON AND MAKE SURE HE IS OK.
BLAH, BLAH, BLAH. BLAH. BLAH,
WHAT A WONDERFUL QUEEN SHE'D MAKE.
DINE WITH ME TONIGHT, CLAUDIA. WE HAVE MUCH TO TALK ABOUT.
ANYTHING! JUST DON'T SLOBBER ON MY HAND.
WE'D LOVE TO!
WHAT?
DINE WITH YOU TONIGHT.
OH, OK! HMMM.

16

Have you ever dined on a strange planet on the other side of the universe, far from home? It's an experience. The meal always looks superb. There's a beautiful table laid out with beautiful cutlery and even more beautiful food. Candlesticks, with weird looking candles. It is usually the cutlery that gives you a clue as to what you are about to eat. Not just knives, forks and spoons, or something simple like chopsticks. But a whole array of tools – drills, pokers, prodders, grippers, plungers, pullers, tweezers, crushers – everything but an X-ray machine.

So Claudia sits at one end of a long table and Vidor at the other. Before them are dishes filled with delicious looking things to eat. If Claudia only knew…

There is a nice dish of prawny looking things – Giant Silver Cockroaches, which feed off the dust and rubbish found in dark, musty corners of old buildings…but they do taste delicious. Equally delicious are the green things that taste like avocado, but are really giant earthworms gutted, skinned and barbecued in a sauce of sewerage algae.

Things that look like small roast pigs are really metal-eating moles from the mountains of Duryllium. The chickens are not chickens, they are roast fleas picked off the backs of Giant Three-tusked Mammoths that roam the plains of Duryllium. If you don't know what you are eating, they are fine. My favourite is the pleche de grommit – a delicate-tasting, small-winged, rodent-like creature that spends its life cleaning up anything that lodges between the toes of the Huge Hairy-nosed Bog Boar of the Duryllium Swamps.

But Claudia knows nothing about this.

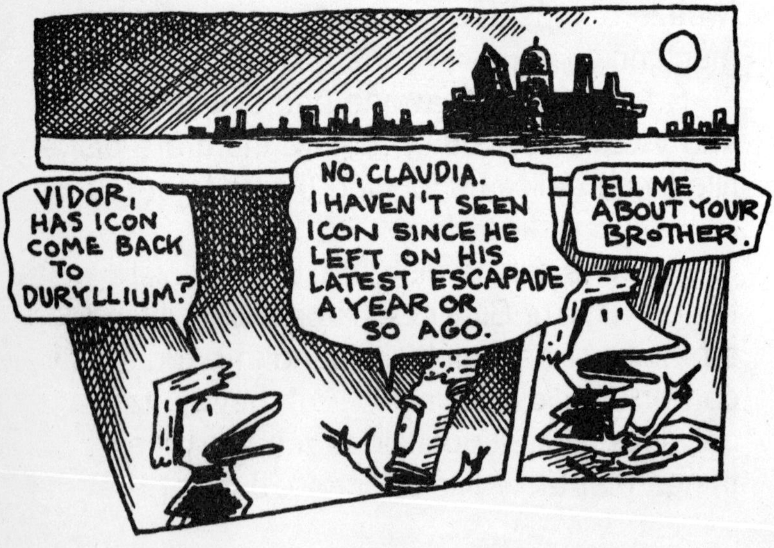
VIDOR, HAS ICON COME BACK TO DURYLLIUM?
NO, CLAUDIA. I HAVEN'T SEEN ICON SINCE HE LEFT ON HIS LATEST ESCAPADE A YEAR OR SO AGO.
TELL ME ABOUT YOUR BROTHER.

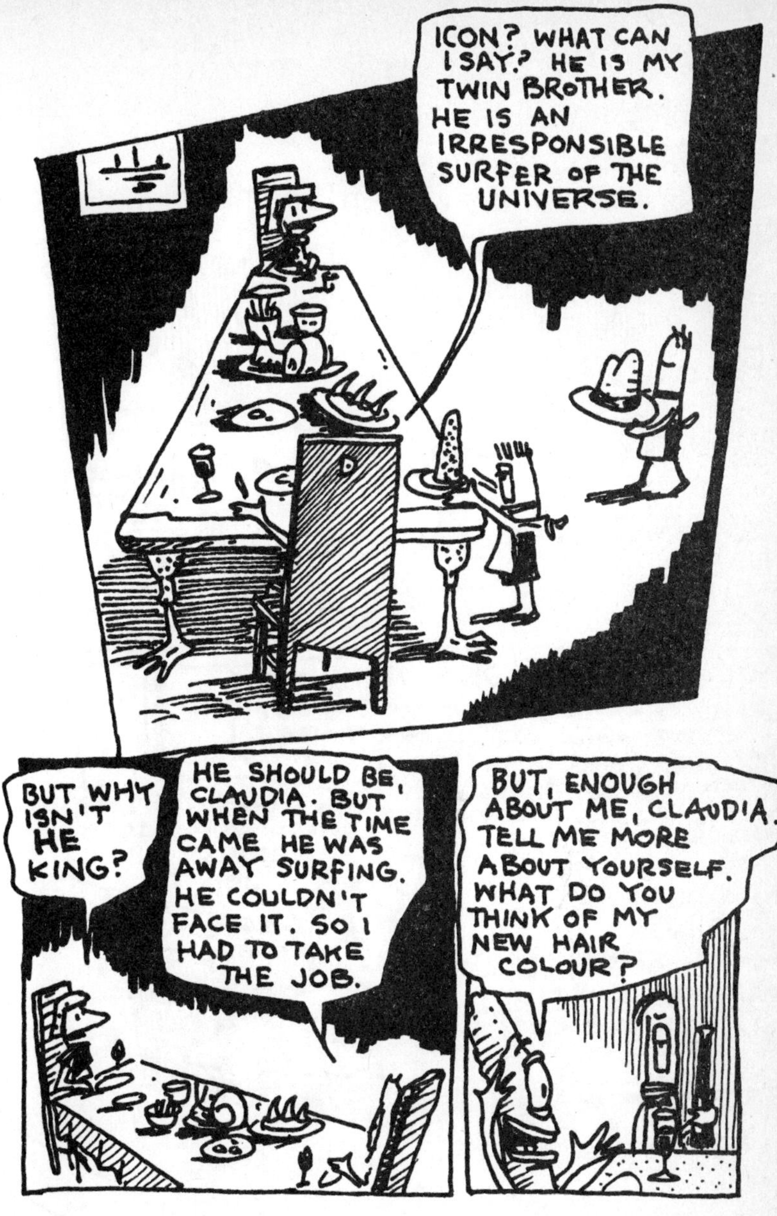
ICON? WHAT CAN I SAY? HE IS MY TWIN BROTHER. HE IS AN IRRESPONSIBLE SURFER OF THE UNIVERSE.
BUT WHY ISN'T HE KING?
HE SHOULD BE, CLAUDIA. BUT WHEN THE TIME CAME HE WAS AWAY SURFING. HE COULDN'T FACE IT. SO I HAD TO TAKE THE JOB.
BUT, ENOUGH ABOUT ME, CLAUDIA. TELL ME MORE ABOUT YOURSELF. WHAT DO YOU THINK OF MY NEW HAIR COLOUR?

17

Meanwhile, in the kitchen, another dinner party is taking place.

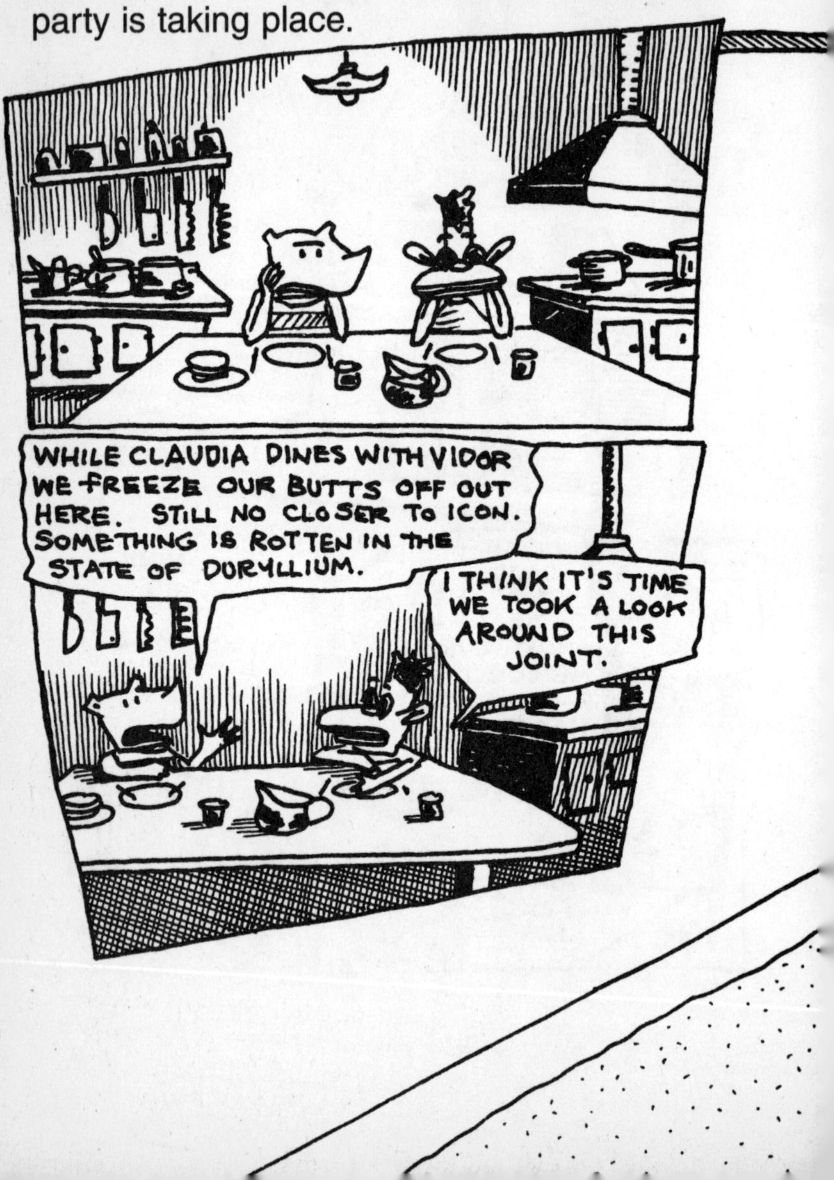
WHILE CLAUDIA DINES WITH VIDOR WE FREEZE OUR BUTTS OFF OUT HERE. STILL NO CLOSER TO ICON. SOMETHING IS ROTTEN IN THE STATE OF DURYLLIUM.
I THINK IT'S TIME WE TOOK A LOOK AROUND THIS JOINT.

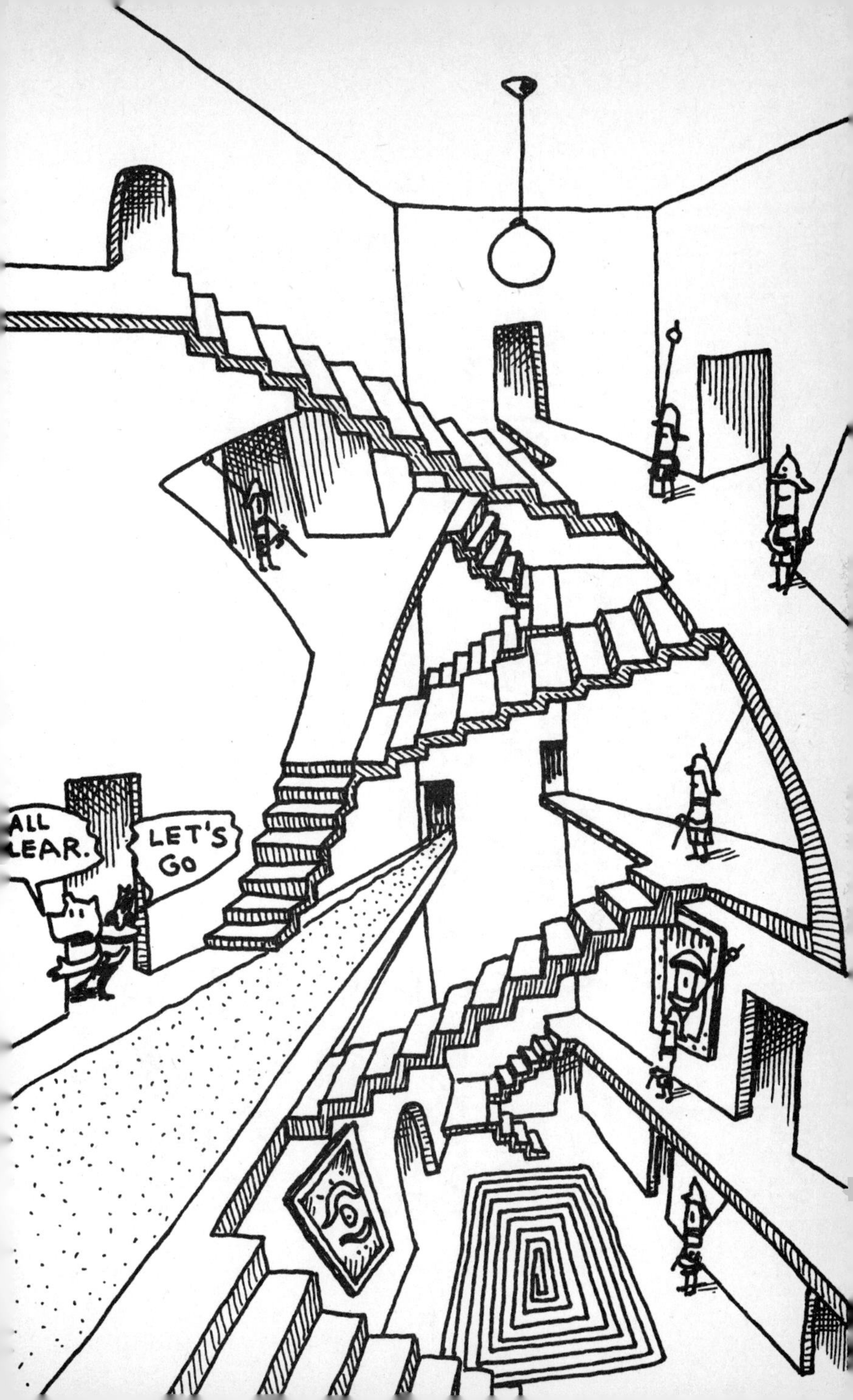
ALL LEAR.
LET'S GO

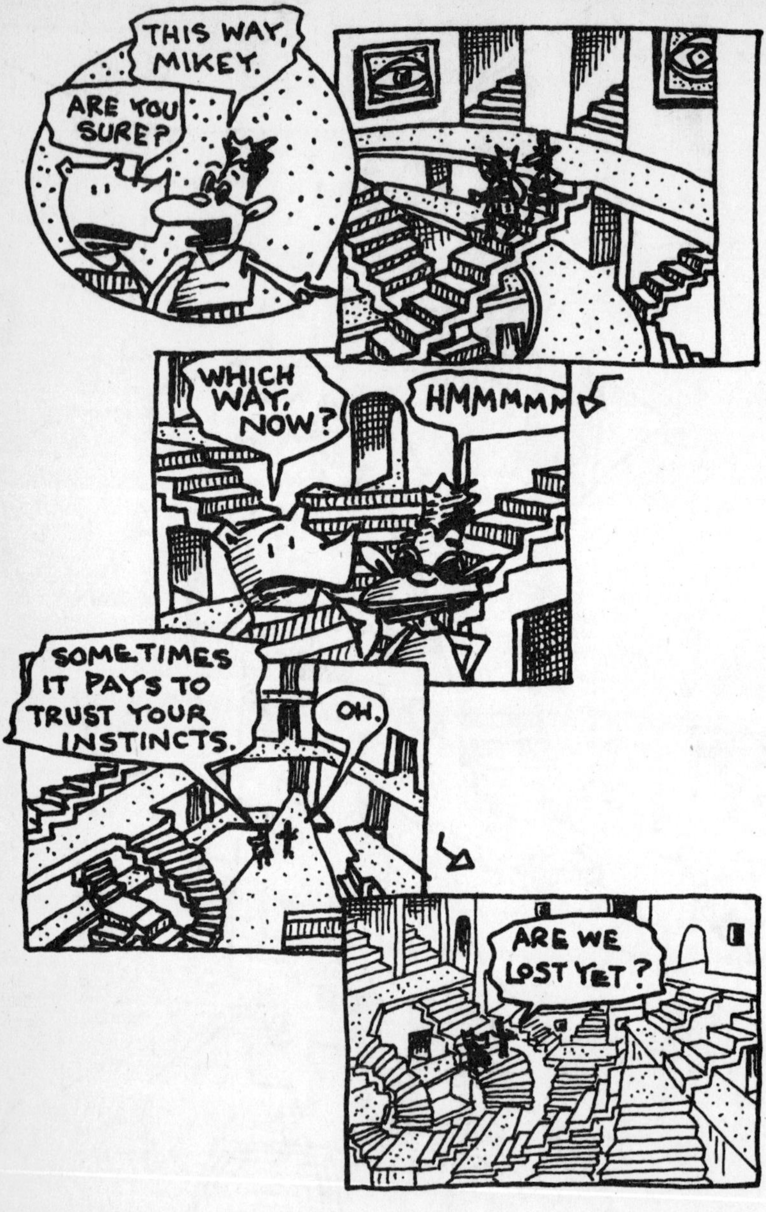
THIS WAY, MIKEY.
ARE YOU SURE?
WHICH WAY, NOW?
HMMMMM
SOMETIMES IT PAYS TO TRUST YOUR INSTINCTS.
OH.
ARE WE LOST YET?

So Nico and Mikey are lost somewhere in the bowels of Vidor's palace.

'This is another fine mess you have got me into, Nico,' says Mikey.

'Well, it's not my fault.'

'**100111**,' yells M.I.T., who has been sleeping in Nico's hair.

'M.I.T.!' they yell. 'You can get us out of here.'

Nico and Mikey take hold of the M.I.T.. They build an image of their destination in their minds. But it was never going to work…

PLIK!

18

They just wanted to get back to the kitchen.
But they missed. And it was a big miss.

'M.I.T., you idiot!!! What do you think
you...'

Nico stops.

Blood. Gore. Stench. Smoke. Mud. And
they are up to their knees in it. The mud, that
is. And noise. Screaming, shooting, exploding,
dying. This is a battlefield.

'**101110**!' screams M.I.T..

In front of them, as the smoke clears, they
can see a gigantic dark shape. Relentlessly, it
is moving forward, spitting fire and metal,
obliterating all in its path. They move back, but
only a short way. Behind them is a stone wall.
Too high to climb over. Too long to get around.
The War Machine keeps coming. Nico reaches
down to pick up a stone to defend himself.

Fool!

I don't know what use a stone is going to
be against a State of the Art Duryllium War
Machine. Nor does Nico, really. But it usually

works with dogs back home on Ithaca. It is in
Nico's hard-wiring to throw stones at things
that are attacking him. To Nico, this War
Machine is just a big, snarling dog.

'Take off your undies, Mikey.'

'WHAT? MY UNDIES?

We're about to be pulverized by a bloody
great fire-spitting War Machine and you want
to inspect my undies? Have you gone – '

'Take off your undies. They're big. Very
big. They'll make a perfect slingshot,' says
Nico.

'But that'll never work.'

'Got any better ideas?'

So Mikey hands over his undies and Nico
drops the stone in.

'Phhheeeww. I'm glad I'm not the stone,'
he says as he swings the slingshot around
his head. He flings the stone at a red, heart-
shaped door on the underside of the
towering machine.

The stone hits its target, but not the one
Nico was aiming for. What Nico doesn't know
is that he has picked up a very special stone.
A very powerful weapon. An ancient

legendary carved stone eye that has been lost for generations. That stone eye flies straight to the true heart and weak spot of the War Machine, which explodes and disintegrates into a big pile of twisted, smoking wreckage.

'How did you do that?' asks Mikey, very confused.

'Lucky shot?' says Nico, equally confused.

'Let's get out of here,' says Mikey.

They take hold of the M.I.T., concentrate hard, and…

PLIK!

They are gone.

19

What has just happened? Well, we Narrators know a great deal about these mysterious things. These tricks of space and time. Of course we know a great deal about a lot of things. But that's not what you want to know.

What we have seen is a glimpse into a possible future. The future of Duryllium under the rule of King Vidor – a King Vidor manipulated, as usual, by the very devious Captain Crundor. A King Vidor who has no idea of the misery he is creating for the people of Duryllium. A king who sits in his tower and dyes his hair new and more interesting colours while his people starve. And when the people revolt, Crundor sends out the War Machines to crush them.

Of course, Nico and Mikey know nothing about all this. They are in the dark, and not just about the War Machines and the stone eye and Mikey's undies.

They are really in the dark. And cold. In a small space. It is not the kitchen of the palace they were aiming for. There is a smell of floor polish and disinfectant.

But there is a door. Nico pushes it open.

'Aha. Good shot, team,' says Nico. 'We're in the broom cupboard, just off the kitchen. Almost perfect.'

He steps out of the cupboard. In his hand is something white. Big and white.

'Could I have those back?' says Mikey.

'AAAARRRGGGHHH!!! YOUR UNDIES!!'

While Nico runs to the sink to wash his hands, Mikey slips his undies back on.

'Do you think it was my undies that gave that stone such power?' Mikey asks.

'I don't want to think about that. Ever!' says Nico.

20

'Excuse me, sirs.'

'What?'

Nico and Mikey turn around. The voice is coming from a small, smooth looking Durylliumite. He is standing in front of the freezer, looking at them. Except that his eyes are closed, and he isn't really looking at them. They have no idea where he came from, or who he is.

This is Rigo, Icon's manservant. He is blind. Which is a great advantage if you are a manservant. People think that because you are blind, you must also be deaf, dumb and stupid. Which, of course, is not true. But, for Rigo, this has been very useful. He has become Icon's spy in the palace. He sees nothing, but hears everything.

'You must be the Ithacans. The friends of Icon.'

'Yes, we are. But who are you?' says Mikey.

'And where is Icon?' says Nico.

'I have no time to explain, sirs. But you are in great danger here.'

Rigo moves to the freezer and starts fiddling. It swings aside and opens onto a secret passage. (Try it on your fridge at home.)

'Follow me, young sirs.'

'Where are you taking us?' says Mikey.

'You are in danger here. Vidor and Crundor know you have come to find Icon.'

He leads them down some stairs and along another dark passageway, talking all the way. Which confuses the guards on the other side of the walls. They keep hearing voices in the walls and think they are going mad.

'Wow! I love secret passageways,' says Nico.

'You must warn the girl, young sirs. She may fool King Vidor, but not Crundor. He will work out you are here to rescue Icon.'

'But we didn't come here to rescue Icon,' says Mikey.

'We didn't even know he needed rescuing,' says Nico.

'Well, young sirs, that may be true. But Vidor and Crundor don't know that.'

They pass through a door set into a bookcase and out into a dimly lit hallway.

'The dining room is through those curtains, sirs.'

'So where is Icon?' says Mikey.

'I don't know, sirs. I believe they have captured him. And they will have sent him far away, to another galaxy, perhaps. To a time lock. Maybe even the Underworld.'

'To the UNDERWORLD? What's that?'

'No time to explain, sirs. I must go or I will be missed. But you must escape from here tonight. You must rescue Icon. Take him away somewhere safe, somewhere they cannot find him.'

'But...'

Rigo turns and slips back behind the bookcase. Now they are together, alone in the hallway.

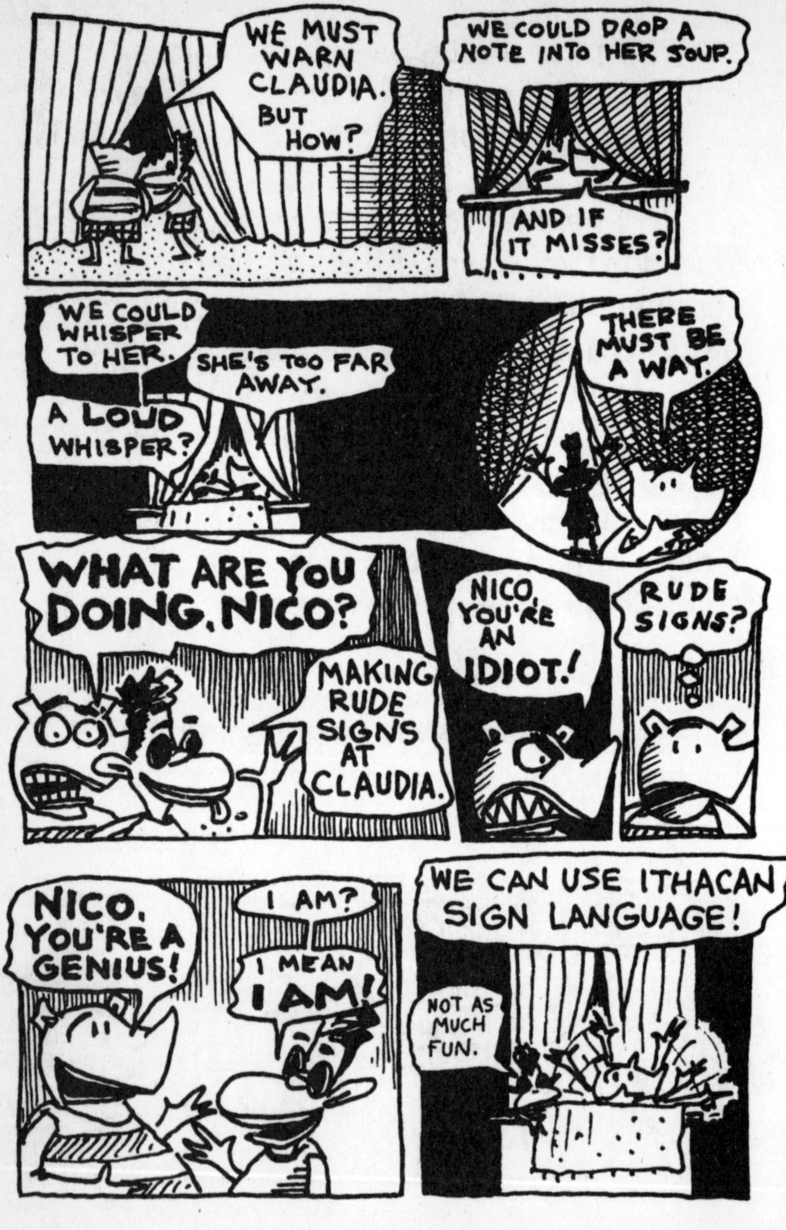
WE MUST WARN CLAUDIA. BUT HOW?
WE COULD DROP A NOTE INTO HER SOUP.
AND IF IT MISSES?
WE COULD WHISPER TO HER.
SHE'S TOO FAR AWAY.
A LOUD WHISPER?
THERE MUST BE A WAY.
WHAT ARE YOU DOING, NICO?
MAKING RUDE SIGNS AT CLAUDIA.
NICO, YOU'RE AN IDIOT!
RUDE SIGNS?
NICO, YOU'RE A GENIUS!
I AM?
I MEAN I AM!
WE CAN USE ITHACAN SIGN LANGUAGE!
NOT AS MUCH FUN.

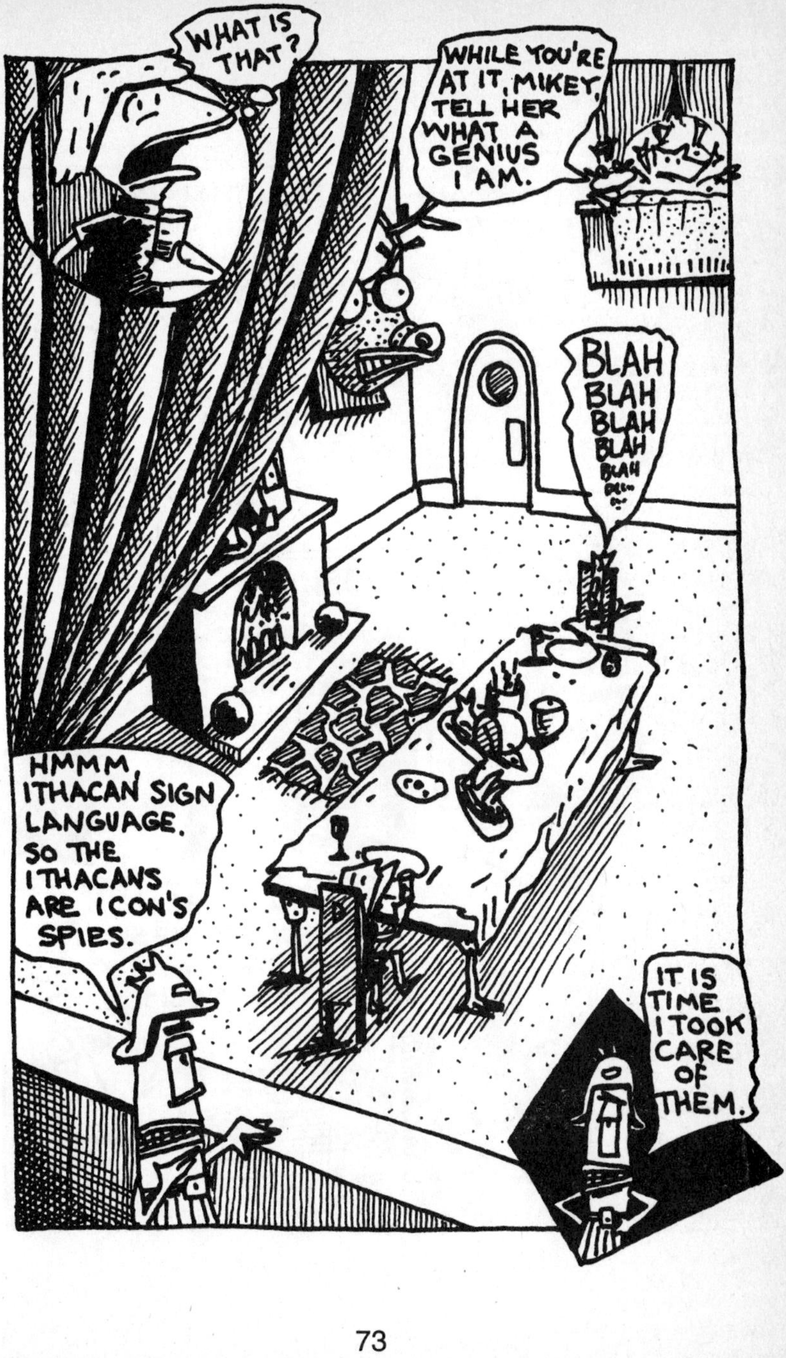
WHAT IS THAT?
WHILE YOU'RE AT IT, MIKEY, TELL HER WHAT A GENIUS I AM.
BLAH BLAH BLAH BLAH BLAH
HMMM, ITHACAN SIGN LANGUAGE. SO THE ITHACANS ARE ICON'S SPIES.
IT IS TIME I TOOK CARE OF THEM.

21

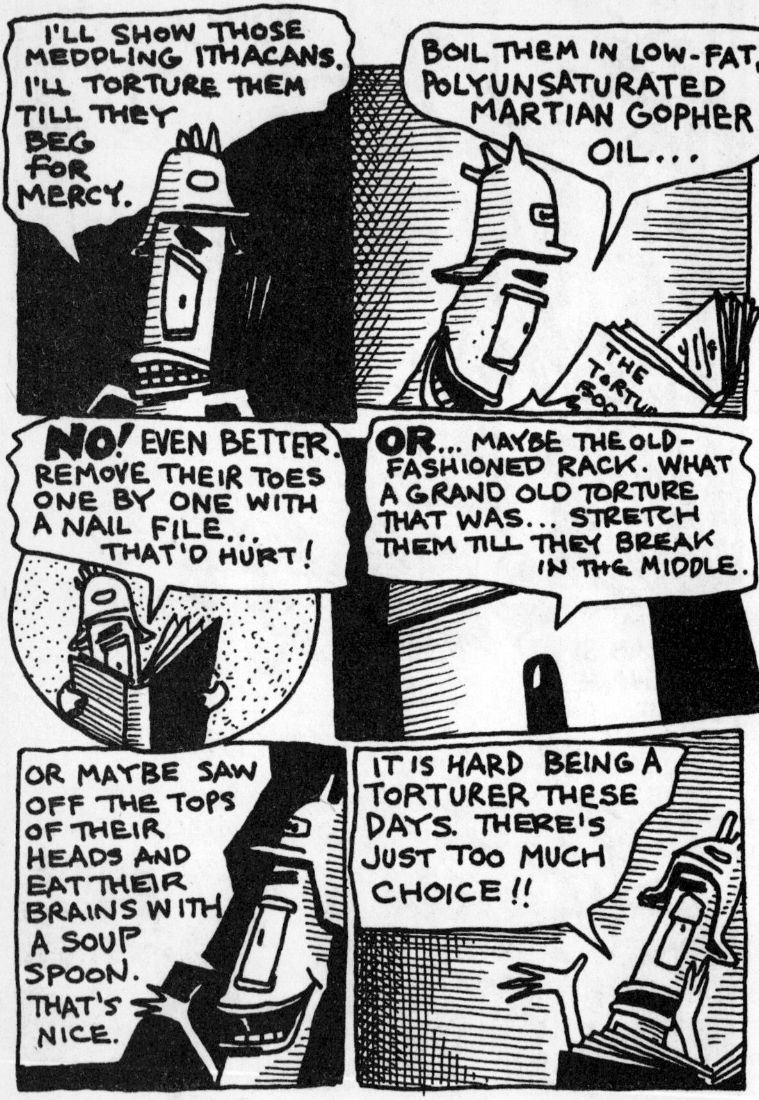
I'LL SHOW THOSE MEDDLING ITHACANS. I'LL TORTURE THEM TILL THEY BEG FOR MERCY.
BOIL THEM IN LOW-FAT, POLYUNSATURATED MARTIAN GOPHER OIL...
THE TORTU
NO! EVEN BETTER. REMOVE THEIR TOES ONE BY ONE WITH A NAIL FILE... THAT'D HURT!
OR... MAYBE THE OLD-FASHIONED RACK. WHAT A GRAND OLD TORTURE THAT WAS... STRETCH THEM TILL THEY BREAK IN THE MIDDLE.
OR MAYBE SAW OFF THE TOPS OF THEIR HEADS AND EAT THEIR BRAINS WITH A SOUP SPOON. THAT'S NICE.
IT IS HARD BEING A TORTURER THESE DAYS. THERE'S JUST TOO MUCH CHOICE!!

22

'What am I doing here? It is all a big mistake.'

Icon is trudging through a dark passageway. He has no idea where he is going. But he knows he can't stop, and he can't go back.

'There is no turning back for Icon, now. But I never wanted to be King. I am not the King type. Not me. It is not fair.'

He turns around. He is sweating. He starts moving more quickly.

'They are coming again,' he says. 'Poor Icon. Lost in the Underworld. Forced to wander the Paths of Doom forever. No one to rescue him. No one for company.'

Now Icon is running – a tired, shuffling run.

'Poor Icon. He must keep ahead of the nasty, bloodthirsty bonecrunchers. They want to be crunching my royal bones. But I do not want royal bones, I just want normal surfer's bones. Salty old sea bones. Catching-huge-curling-wave bones.

'But everyone wants Icon to be King.

Everyone except Icon. They all say Duryllium needs Icon. Why am I so lucky? No! Go away, nasty bonecrunchers.'

He can hear their panting and howling not far behind as he staggers around the winding passages.

'Dead end. Now Icon is bonecruncher meat, for sure.'

The bonecrunchers are very close, now. He feels around in desperation. There is a high, raised ledge. He tries to pull himself up. He can smell the breath of the bonecruchers. They will rip him to shreds. One last effort.

His energy almost gone, Icon manages to clamber up to the ledge. The bonecrunchers are trying to follow. They will get up eventually. But for the moment Icon can rest. Then he must start moving again. He must get as far away from them as he can. Till they pick up his scent and track him down.

23

'Where have you been, Rigo? I have been calling you for ages. Are you turning deaf as well as blind? Clear away the dishes. Then leave us. We want to be alone.'

'As you wish, Your Majesty.'

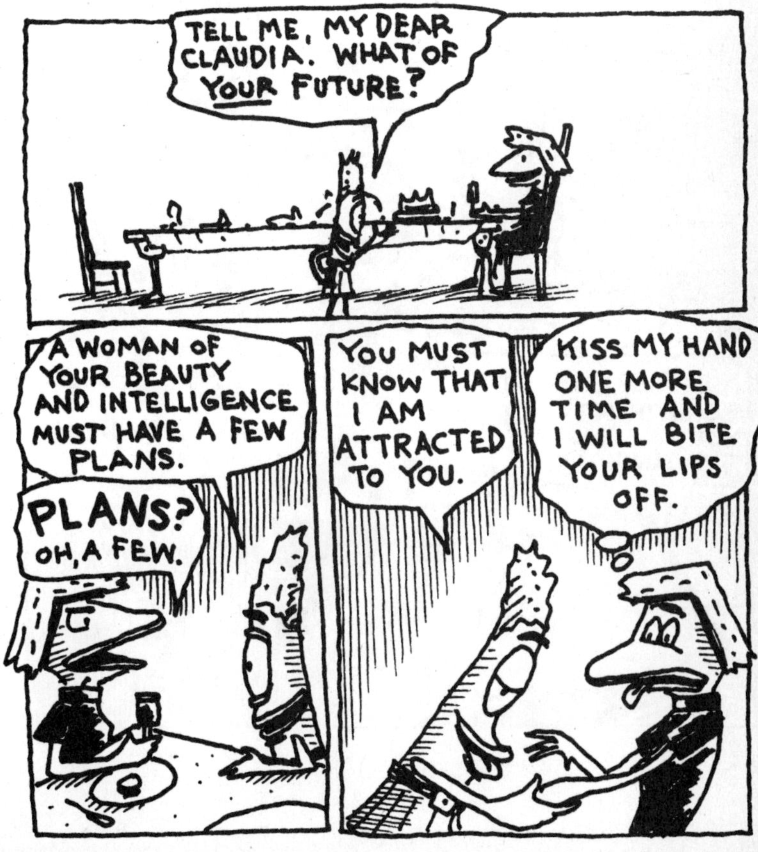
TELL ME, MY DEAR CLAUDIA. WHAT OF YOUR FUTURE?
A WOMAN OF YOUR BEAUTY AND INTELLIGENCE MUST HAVE A FEW PLANS.
PLANS? OH, A FEW.
YOU MUST KNOW THAT I AM ATTRACTED TO YOU.
KISS MY HAND ONE MORE TIME AND I WILL BITE YOUR LIPS OFF.

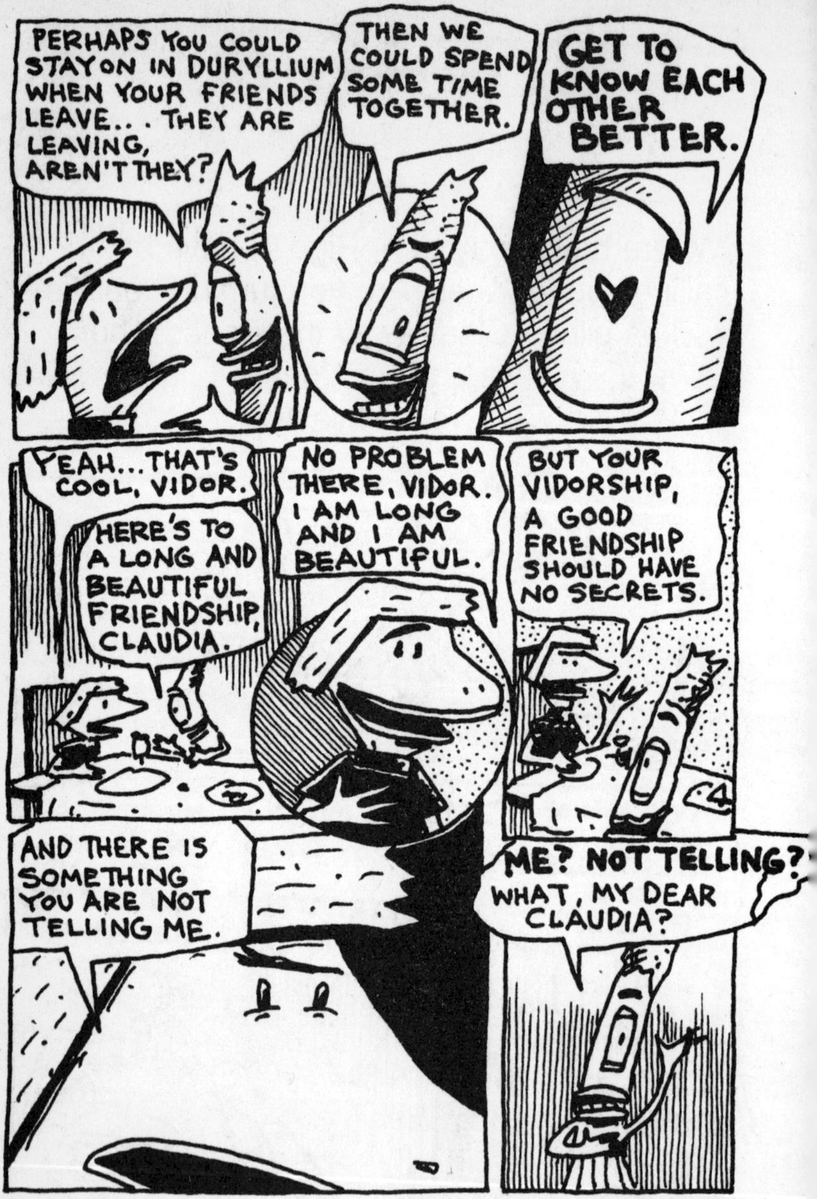
PERHAPS YOU COULD STAY ON IN DURYLLIUM WHEN YOUR FRIENDS LEAVE... THEY ARE LEAVING, AREN'T THEY?
THEN WE COULD SPEND SOME TIME TOGETHER.
GET TO KNOW EACH OTHER BETTER.
YEAH... THAT'S COOL, VIDOR.
HERE'S TO A LONG AND BEAUTIFUL FRIENDSHIP, CLAUDIA.
NO PROBLEM THERE, VIDOR. I AM LONG AND I AM BEAUTIFUL.
BUT YOUR VIDORSHIP, A GOOD FRIENDSHIP SHOULD HAVE NO SECRETS.
AND THERE IS SOMETHING YOU ARE NOT TELLING ME.
ME? NOT TELLING? WHAT, MY DEAR CLAUDIA?

Vidor thinks Claudia can see inside his head. Some clever Ithacan trick. Look inside someone's head and know what they are thinking.

In fact, there was a people on the Other Earth, who could look into each other's heads and thoughts. This proved to be a bit of a nightmare. Imagine if everyone could look inside your head and read what you were thinking. Every time you wanted to kill your parents, they would know. They would just get up and hide all the knives.

This tribe on Other Earth eventually worked out that you could not see through lead. So everyone was fitted out with a lead-head permanently fixed to their skull. It was a great sucess for a while, until the great flood...when it rained for forty days and thirty nights and they all went down head first, never to be seen again.

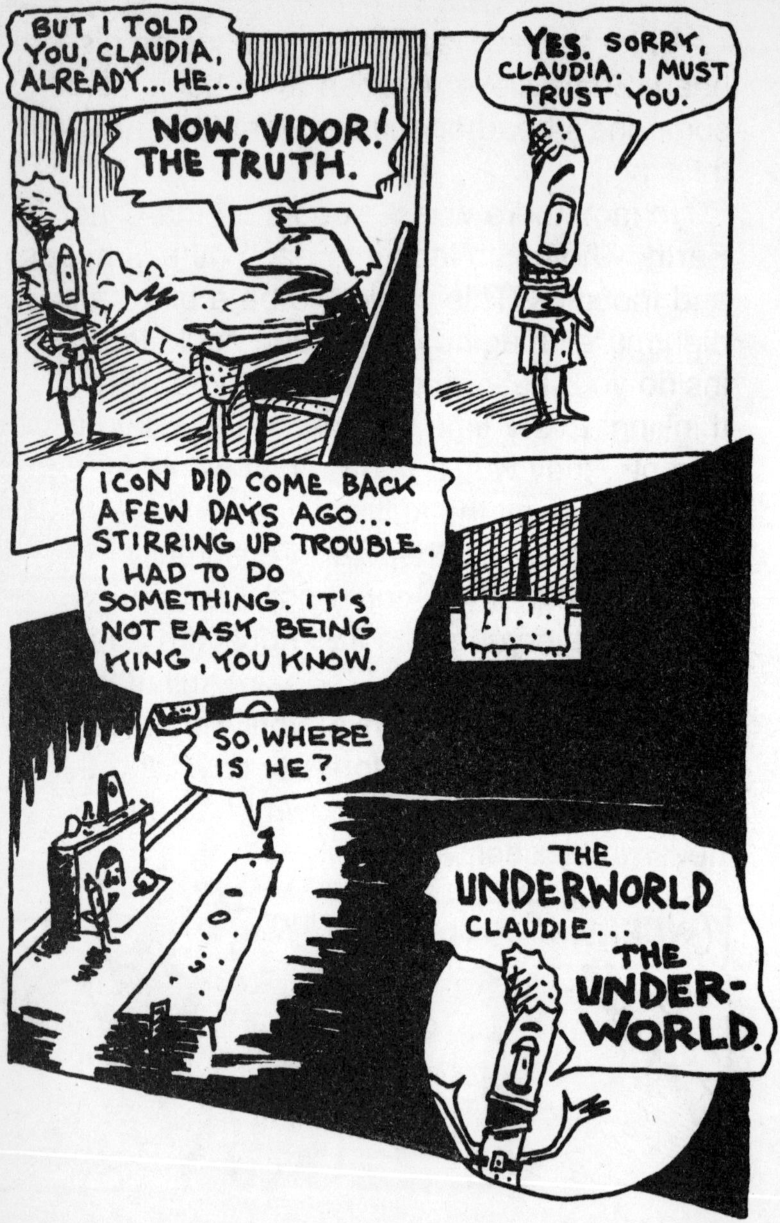
BUT I TOLD YOU, CLAUDIA, ALREADY... HE...
NOW, VIDOR! THE TRUTH.
YES. SORRY, CLAUDIA. I MUST TRUST YOU.
ICON DID COME BACK A FEW DAYS AGO... STIRRING UP TROUBLE. I HAD TO DO SOMETHING. IT'S NOT EASY BEING KING, YOU KNOW.
SO, WHERE IS HE?
THE UNDERWORLD CLAUDIE... THE UNDER-WORLD.

24

Are you familiar with the Underworld? It's not
the sort of place you would go to on holidays.
There was a place in Fifth Millennium Venus,
before it became so icebergingly cold, that
was like the Underworld. We once went there
on a Narrators' convention. It was a disaster,
of course. The cold water was too hot, the hot
water was too cold. The beds were too small.
And the bedbugs too big and vicious. In fact,
two Narrators vanished one night. The
bedbugs ate them. Not that we missed them
that much. No one ever misses a Narrator.
And the food! It was so raw and so feral, you
had to be quick and eat it before it ate you.
We lost another two Narrators one dinnertime.

But that place was heaven compared to
the Underworld. The Underworld is…um…
indescribable. The *NCGUB* says that the
Underworld is the world below our world. It is
a hell. A hell of a rotten place to get sent to.
With hot, sweaty passages, teeming with
slavering monsters whose idea of fun is to rip

your head off and use it for football practice. Fire pours out of holes in the floors and walls. If you sit down in the wrong spot, your buttocks freeze while your head catches fire. And if you ever think you are about to escape, suddenly a trapdoor opens up and you fall back into a pit of acid teeming with nipping, munching piranhas that try to eat you up in teeny-tiny mouthfuls, just so it hurts more. In fact, it's a lot like the secondary school I went to. Except I got out of that.

Eventually.

25

Claudia and Vidor are walking down a corridor in the Royal Palace of Duryllium. Once again Vidor reaches for Claudia's arm. He finds it attached to her shoulder, where it always is. Vidor starts munching away on her hand again. She resists the temptation to resort to violence.

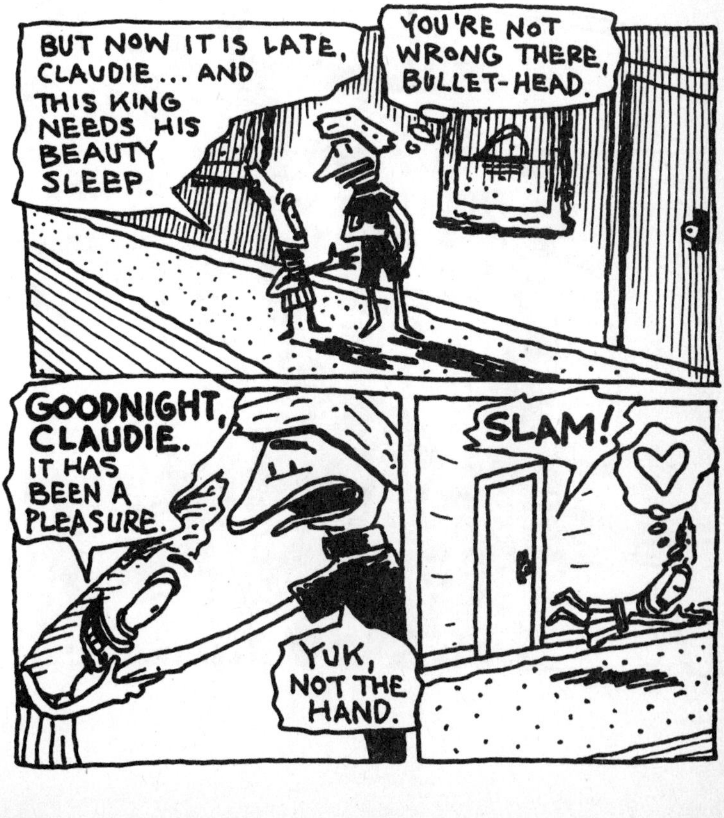

BUT NOW IT IS LATE, CLAUDIE... AND THIS KING NEEDS HIS BEAUTY SLEEP.
YOU'RE NOT WRONG THERE, BULLET-HEAD.
GOODNIGHT, CLAUDIE. IT HAS BEEN A PLEASURE.
YUK, NOT THE HAND.
SLAM!

26

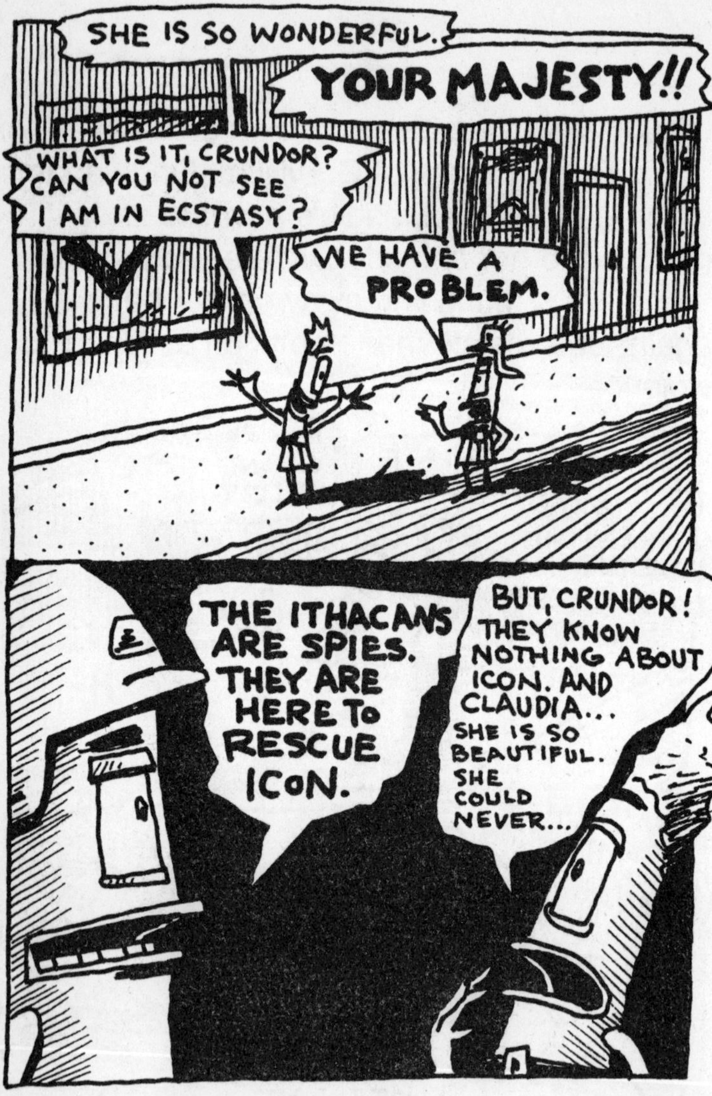
SHE IS SO WONDERFUL.
YOUR MAJESTY!!
WHAT IS IT, CRUNDOR? CAN YOU NOT SEE I AM IN ECSTASY?
WE HAVE A PROBLEM.
THE ITHACANS ARE SPIES. THEY ARE HERE TO RESCUE ICON.
BUT, CRUNDOR! THEY KNOW NOTHING ABOUT ICON. AND CLAUDIA... SHE IS SO BEAUTIFUL. SHE COULD NEVER...

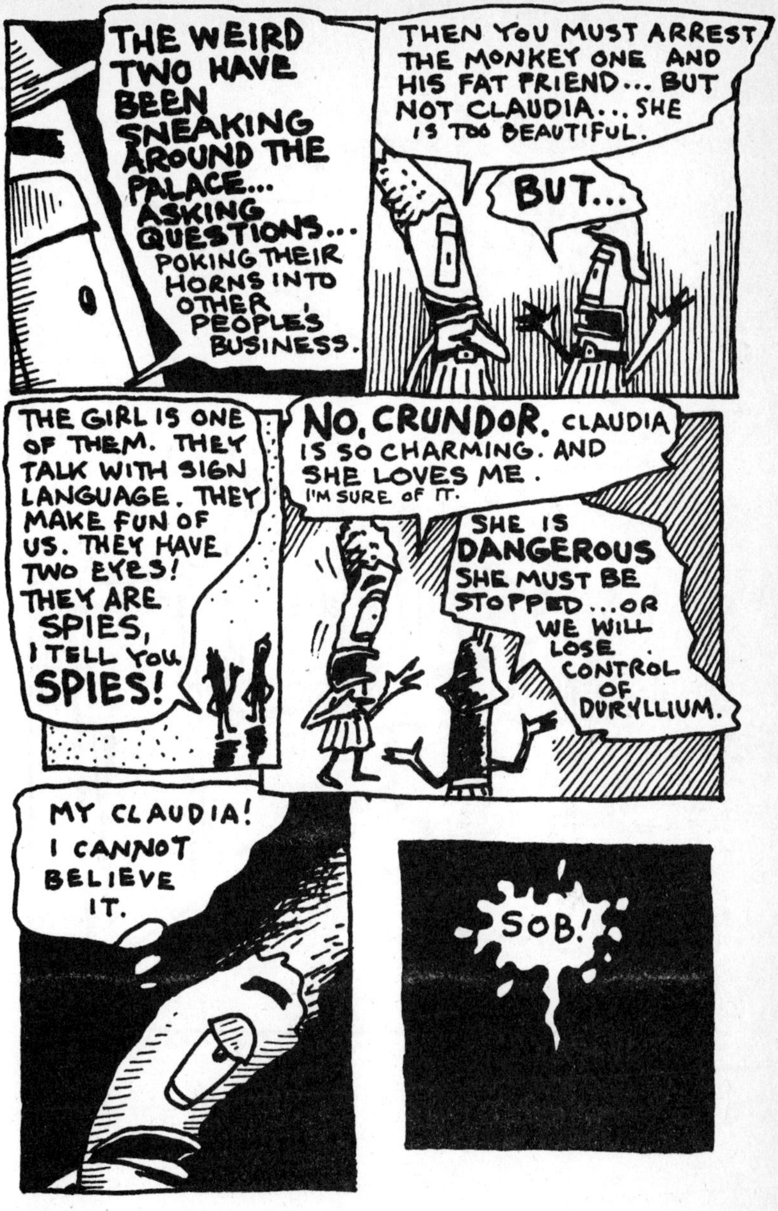
THE WEIRD TWO HAVE BEEN SNEAKING AROUND THE PALACE... ASKING QUESTIONS... POKING THEIR HORNS INTO OTHER PEOPLE'S BUSINESS.
THEN YOU MUST ARREST THE MONKEY ONE AND HIS FAT FRIEND... BUT NOT CLAUDIA... SHE IS TOO BEAUTIFUL.
BUT...
THE GIRL IS ONE OF THEM. THEY TALK WITH SIGN LANGUAGE. THEY MAKE FUN OF US. THEY HAVE TWO EYES! THEY ARE SPIES, I TELL YOU. SPIES!
NO, CRUNDOR. CLAUDIA IS SO CHARMING. AND SHE LOVES ME. I'M SURE OF IT.
SHE IS DANGEROUS SHE MUST BE STOPPED...OR WE WILL LOSE CONTROL OF DURYLLIUM.
MY CLAUDIA! I CANNOT BELIEVE IT.
SOB!

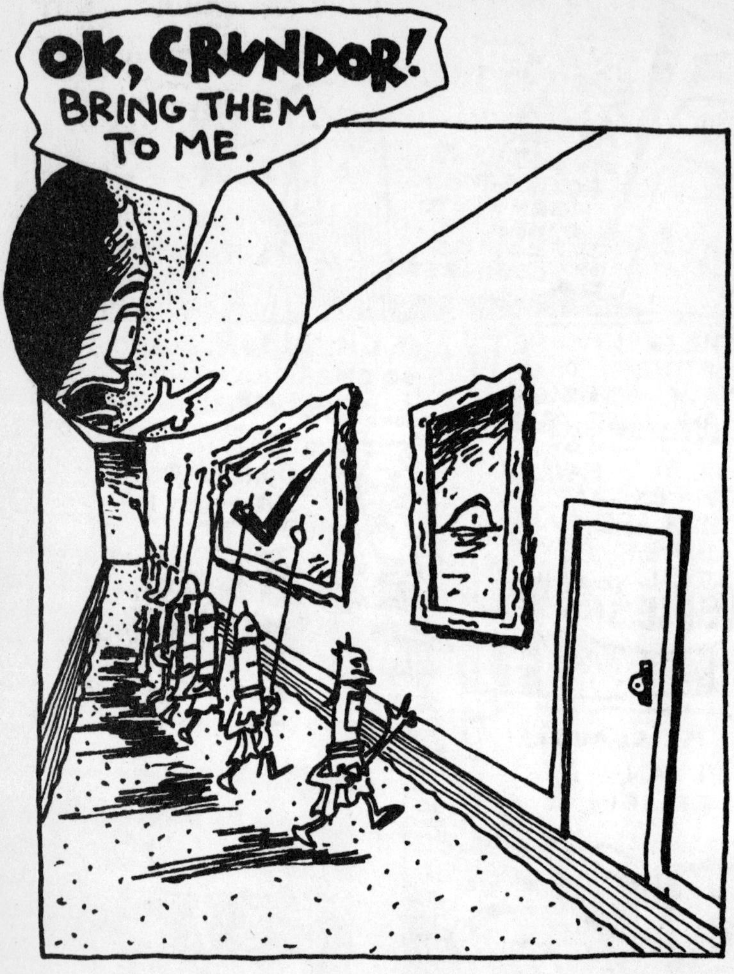
OK, CRUNDOR!
BRING THEM TO ME.

27

In the bedroom, Claudia prepares for sleep.
Vidor has provided for her every whim. There
is a toothbrush, hairbrush – she always
brushes her hair 100 times before bed – and
a clean pair of wetsuit pyjamas. After a long,
hot shower, Claudia slips into bed.

'I wonder where those two idiot mutants
have got to,' says Claudia.

'You called,' says Nico from under the bed-
covers.

'Did you miss us?' It is Mikey up the other
end of the bed.

'Where have you been? What do you
know?' says Claudia.

'We've been everywhere. We know
everything,' says Nico.

'I bet you didn't know that Icon should be
King of Duryllium, but that – '

'Yes, we know!' say Nico and Mikey.

'OK. But I bet you didn't know that Vidor
has sent Icon to the Underworld. And that...'

'YES, WE KNOW!'

'And that Vidor wants to imprison Icon
there forev– '

'YES, WE KNOW!!'

'And that you are both melon-headed know-alls!'

'YES, WE KNO...what??'

Now Claudia is standing up on the bed.

'Well, I'm not letting that little nobody win. We have to rescue Icon,' she bellows.

'Shhh, Claudia. There's a noise outside,' says Nico.

But Claudia is unstoppable when she is in this mood. 'We have the M.I.T. thing. We are going to the Underworld and we are gonna bring him back. Simple as that. And no one had better get in our way.'

'Quiet, Claudia. There's someone at the door,' whispers Nico.

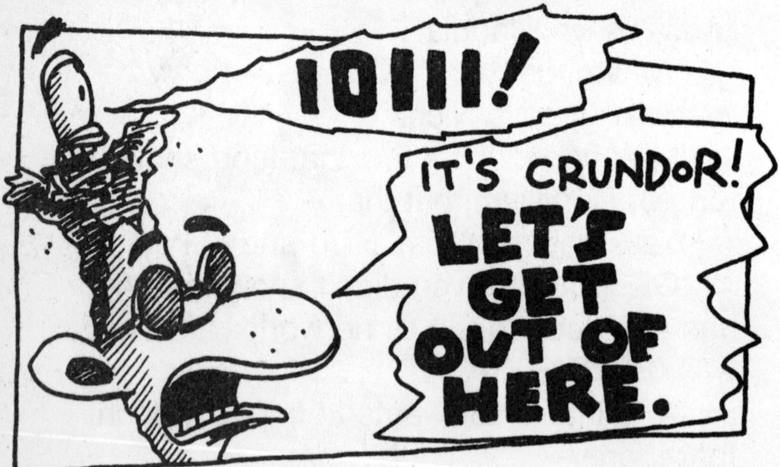
IOIII!
IT'S CRUNDOR!
LET'S GET OUT OF HERE.

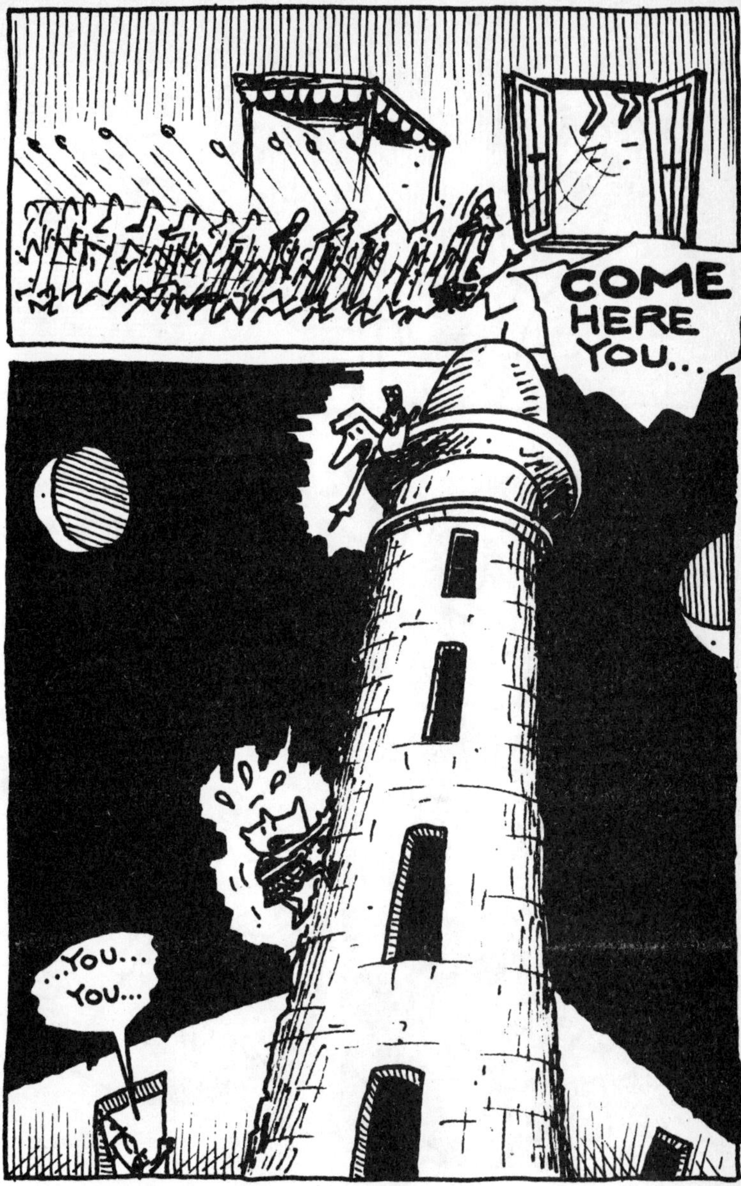
COME HERE YOU...
...YOU... YOU...

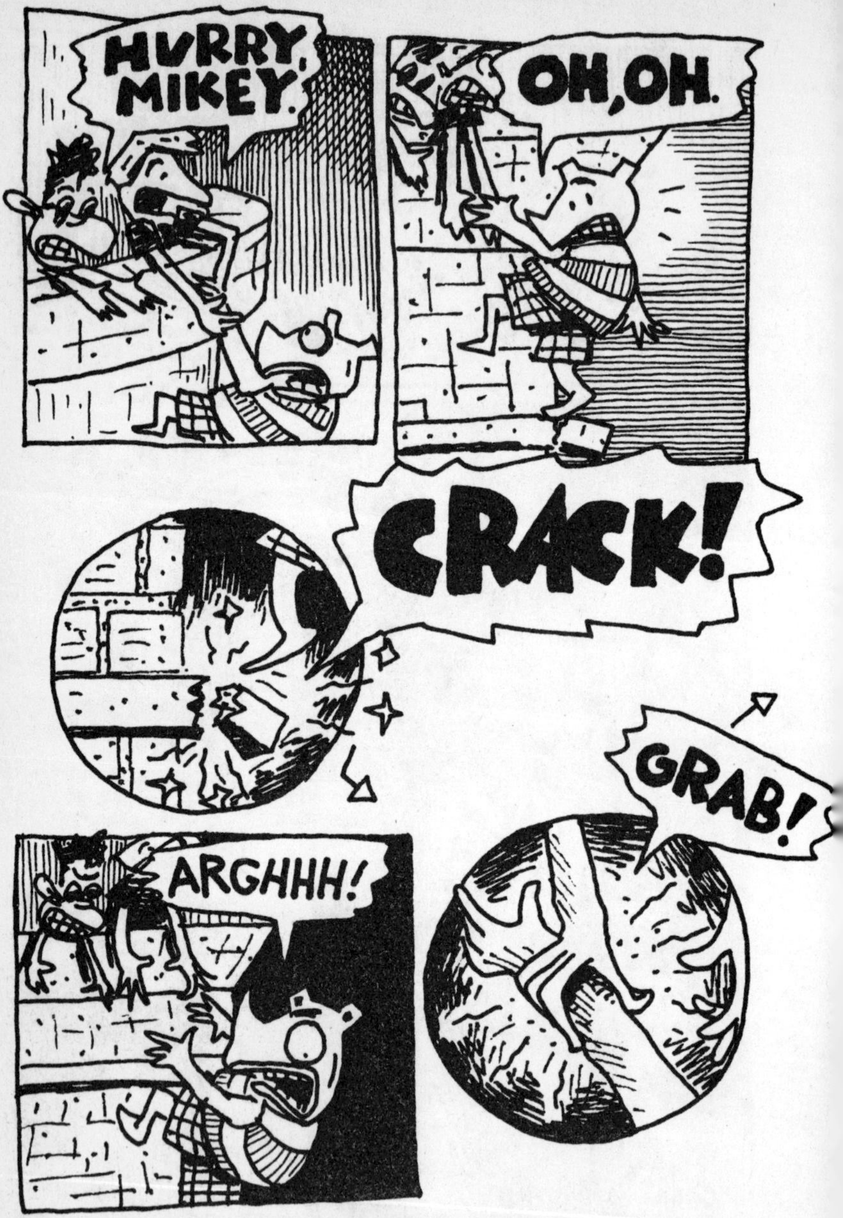
HURRY, MIKEY.
OH, OH.
CRACK!
GRAB!
ARGHHH!

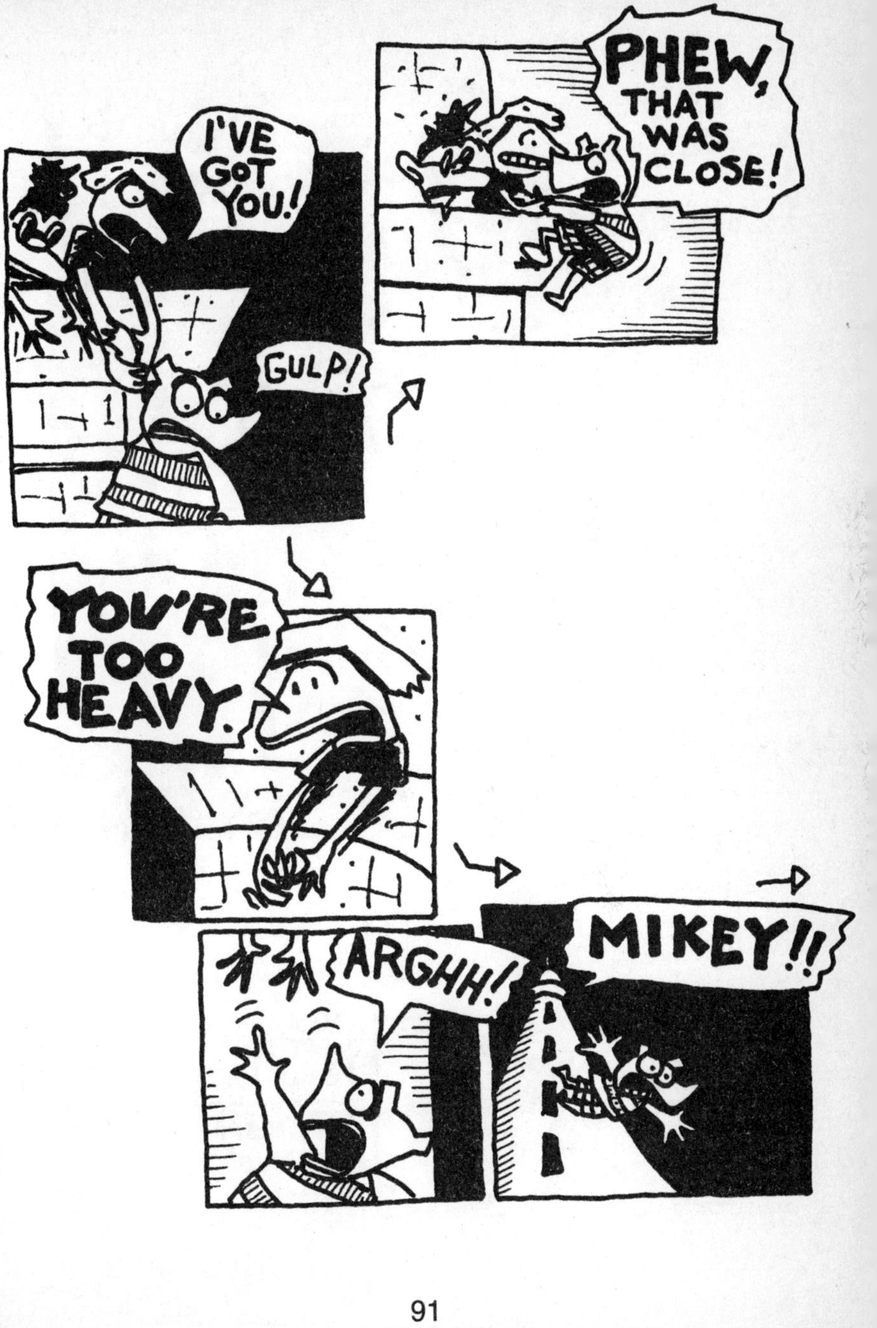
I'VE GOT YOU!
GULP!
PHEW, THAT WAS CLOSE!
YOU'RE TOO HEAVY.
ARGHH!
MIKEY!!

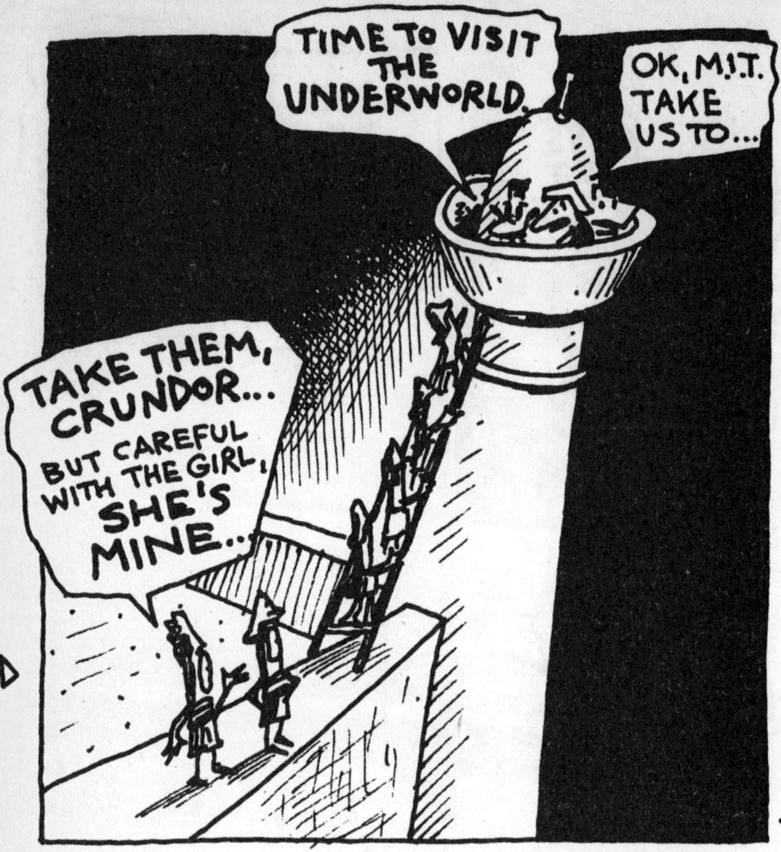
TIME TO VISIT THE UNDERWORLD.
OK, M.I.T. TAKE US TO...
TAKE THEM, CRUNDOR... BUT CAREFUL WITH THE GIRL, SHE'S MINE...

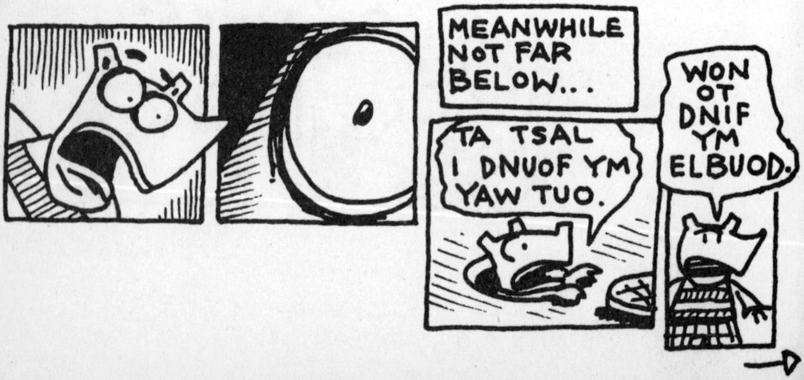
MEANWHILE NOT FAR BELOW...
TA TSAL I DNUOF YM YAW TUO.
WON OT DNIF YM ELBUOD.

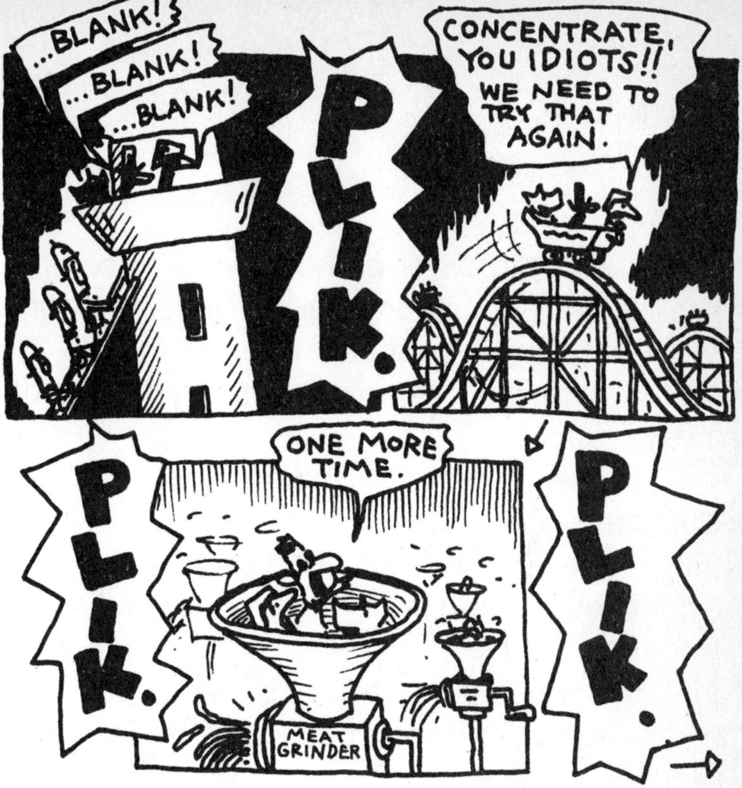
...BLANK!
...BLANK!
...BLANK!
PLIK.
CONCENTRATE, YOU IDIOTS!! WE NEED TO TRY THAT AGAIN.
PLIK.
ONE MORE TIME.
MEAT GRINDER
PLIK.

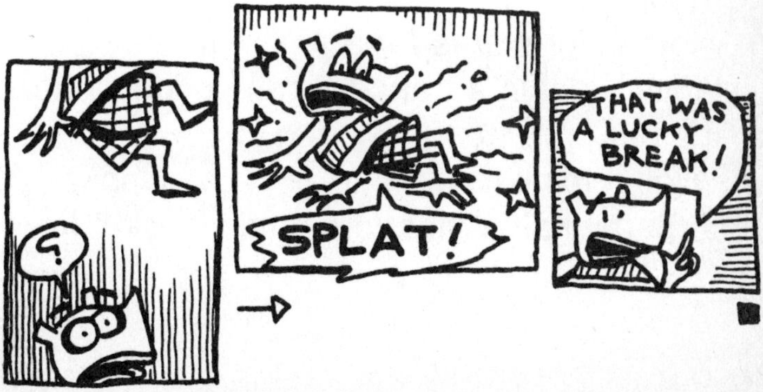
?
SPLAT!
THAT WAS A LUCKY BREAK!

28

High up on the tower of the Royal Palace of Duryllium stands a lone figure. Under the light of three turkey-red moons he gazes out across the plains dreaming of the girl who got away.

'She has fled to the Underworld, poor Claudia. She is trapped there, forever,' says Vidor. 'Even the M.I.T. is useless in the Underworld. There is no escape. She will die with Icon.'

Vidor wipes a tear from his eye.

'Meat for the Bonecrunchers. Oh, my Claudia. My Queen,' he howls. 'What a king must sacrifice for his people.'

Vidor closes his eyes.

'You may never be Queen of my people, oh Claudia, but you will always be Queen of my heart.'

Now Vidor stares for a time into the distance, as if in a trance. Then suddenly he snaps out of it.

'Well, I think it's time to put a new rinse through my hair. What colour this week?'

29

Nico, Claudia and Mikey land somewhere in the Underworld.

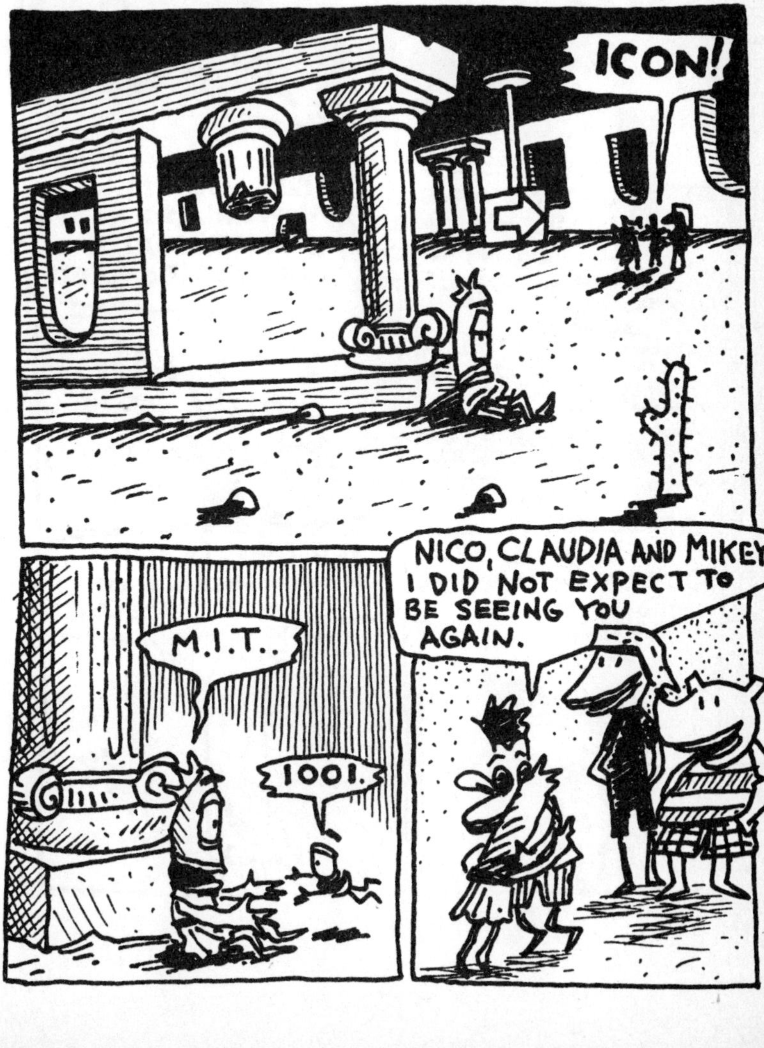
ICON!
M.I.T..
1001.
NICO, CLAUDIA AND MIKEY. I DID NOT EXPECT TO BE SEEING YOU AGAIN.

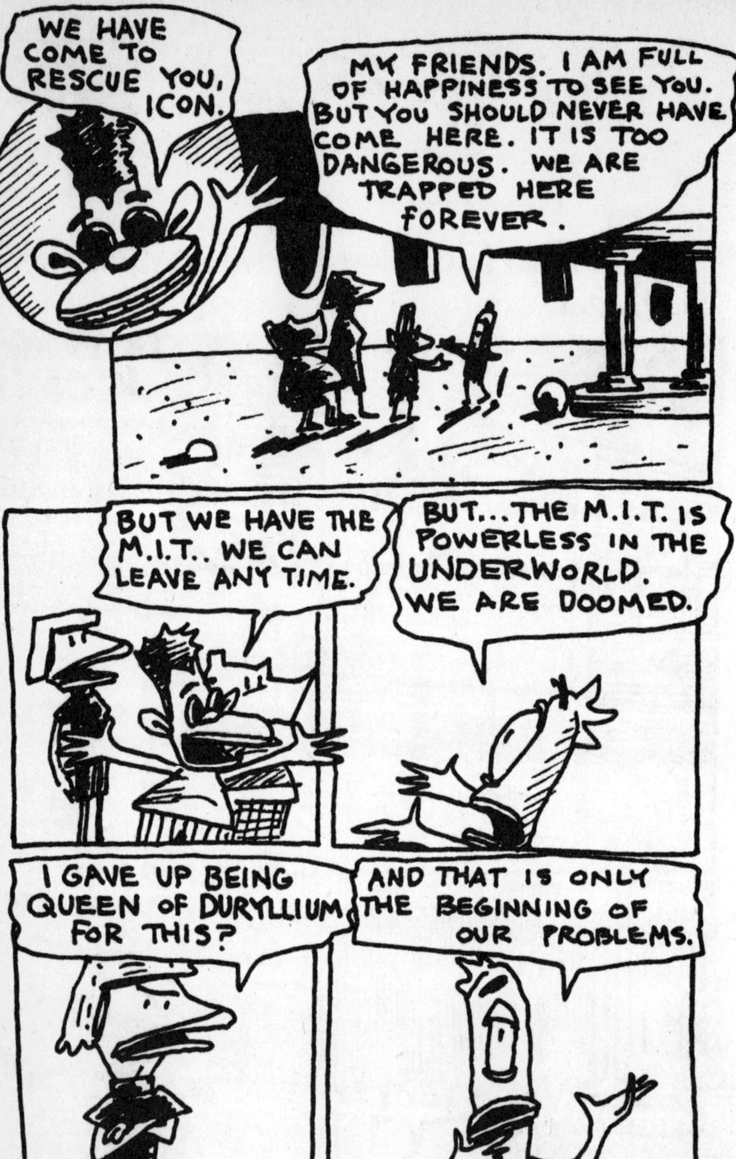
WE HAVE COME TO RESCUE YOU, ICON.
MY FRIENDS. I AM FULL OF HAPPINESS TO SEE YOU. BUT YOU SHOULD NEVER HAVE COME HERE. IT IS TOO DANGEROUS. WE ARE TRAPPED HERE FOREVER.
BUT WE HAVE THE M.I.T.. WE CAN LEAVE ANY TIME.
BUT...THE M.I.T. IS POWERLESS IN THE UNDERWORLD. WE ARE DOOMED.
I GAVE UP BEING QUEEN OF DURYLLIUM FOR THIS?
AND THAT IS ONLY THE BEGINNING OF OUR PROBLEMS.

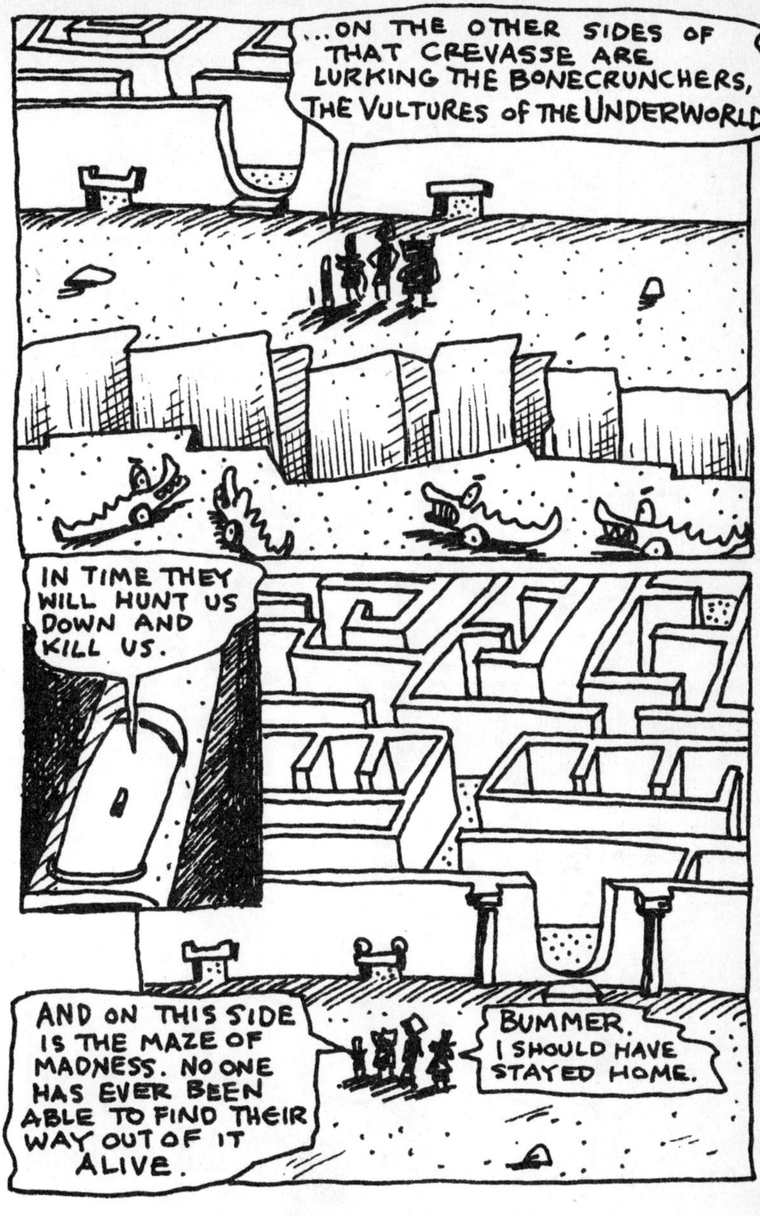
...ON THE OTHER SIDES OF THAT CREVASSE ARE LURKING THE BONECRUNCHERS, THE VULTURES OF THE UNDERWORLD.
IN TIME THEY WILL HUNT US DOWN AND KILL US.
AND ON THIS SIDE IS THE MAZE OF MADNESS. NO ONE HAS EVER BEEN ABLE TO FIND THEIR WAY OUT OF IT ALIVE.
BUMMER. I SHOULD HAVE STAYED HOME.

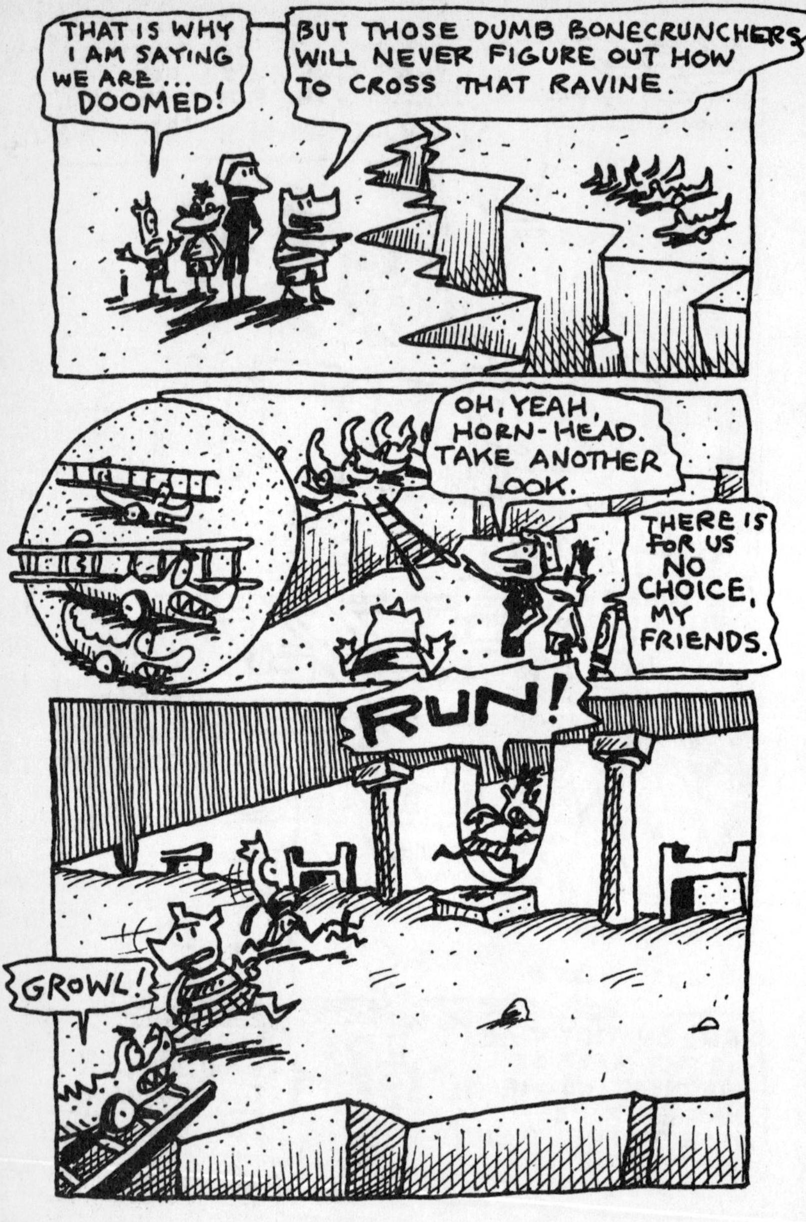
THAT IS WHY I AM SAYING WE ARE... DOOMED!
BUT THOSE DUMB BONECRUNCHERS WILL NEVER FIGURE OUT HOW TO CROSS THAT RAVINE.
OH, YEAH, HORN-HEAD. TAKE ANOTHER LOOK.
THERE IS FOR US NO CHOICE, MY FRIENDS.
RUN!
GROWL!

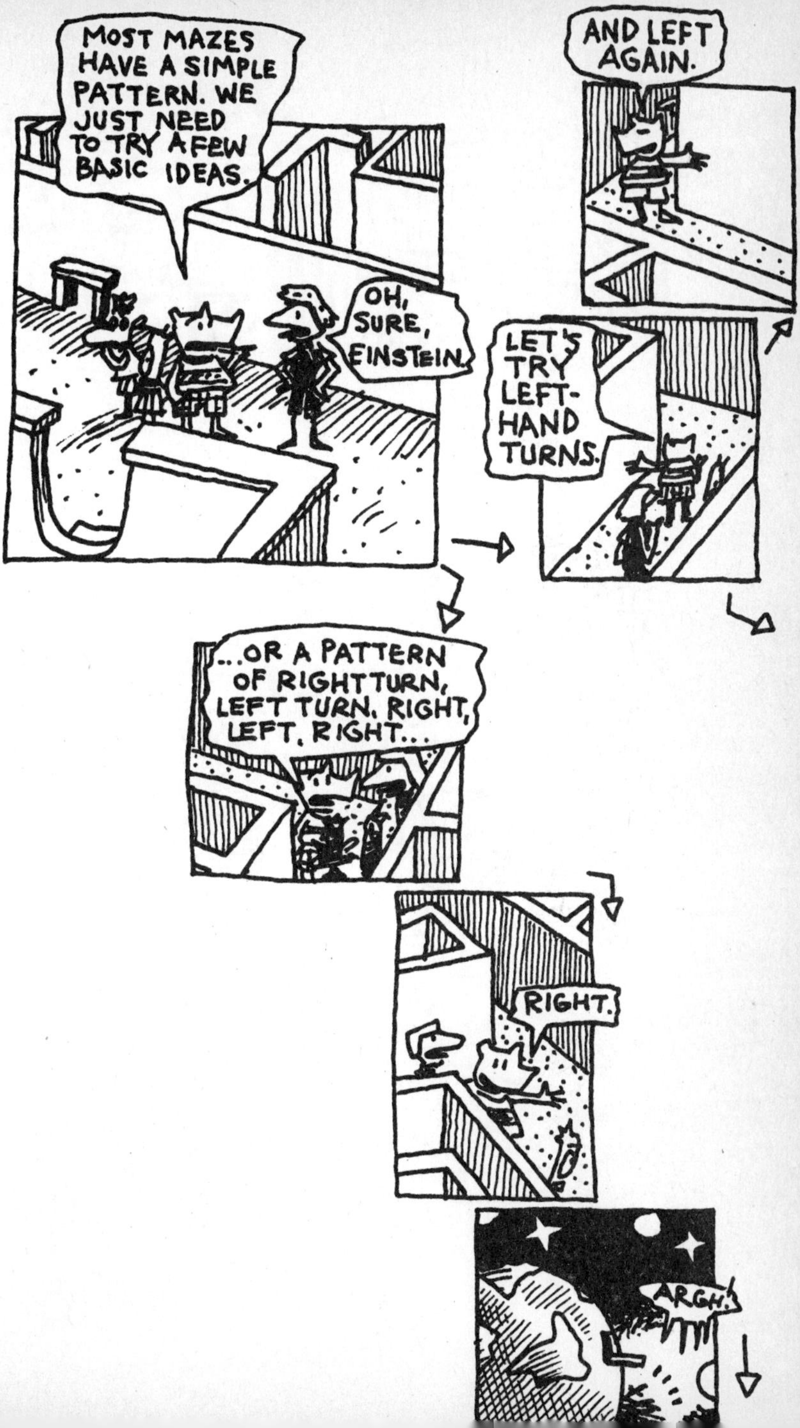
MOST MAZES HAVE A SIMPLE PATTERN. WE JUST NEED TO TRY A FEW BASIC IDEAS.
OH, SURE, EINSTEIN.
LET'S TRY LEFT-HAND TURNS.
AND LEFT AGAIN.
...OR A PATTERN OF RIGHT TURN, LEFT TURN, RIGHT, LEFT, RIGHT...
RIGHT.
ARGH.

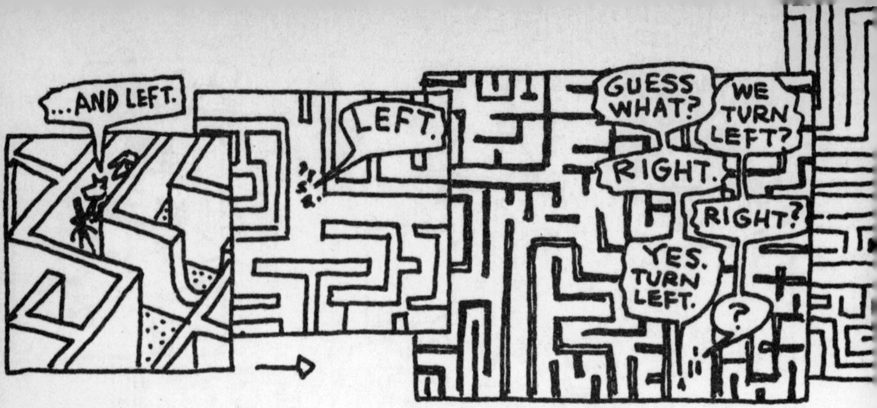
...AND LEFT.
LEFT.
GUESS WHAT?
WE TURN LEFT?
RIGHT.
RIGHT?
YES. TURN LEFT.
?

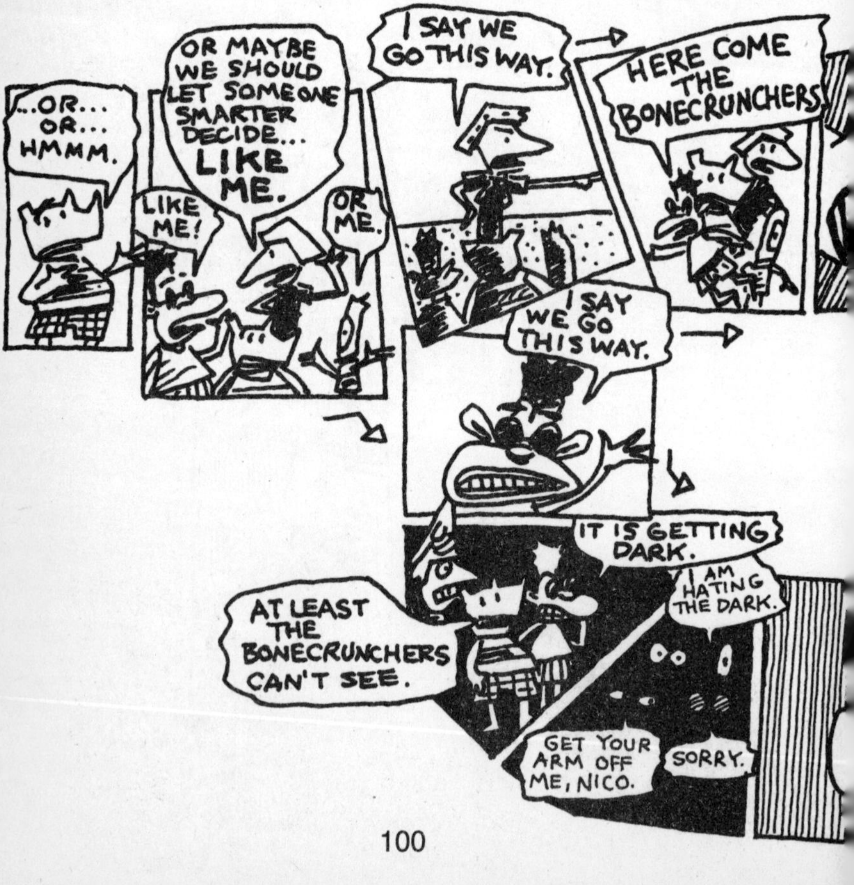
...OR... OR... HMMM.
OR MAYBE WE SHOULD LET SOMEONE SMARTER DECIDE... LIKE ME.
LIKE ME!
OR ME.
I SAY WE GO THIS WAY.
HERE COME THE BONECRUNCHERS
I SAY WE GO THIS WAY.
IT IS GETTING DARK.
I AM HATING THE DARK.
AT LEAST THE BONECRUNCHERS CAN'T SEE.
GET YOUR ARM OFF ME, NICO.
SORRY.

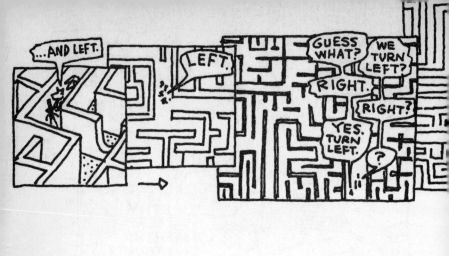

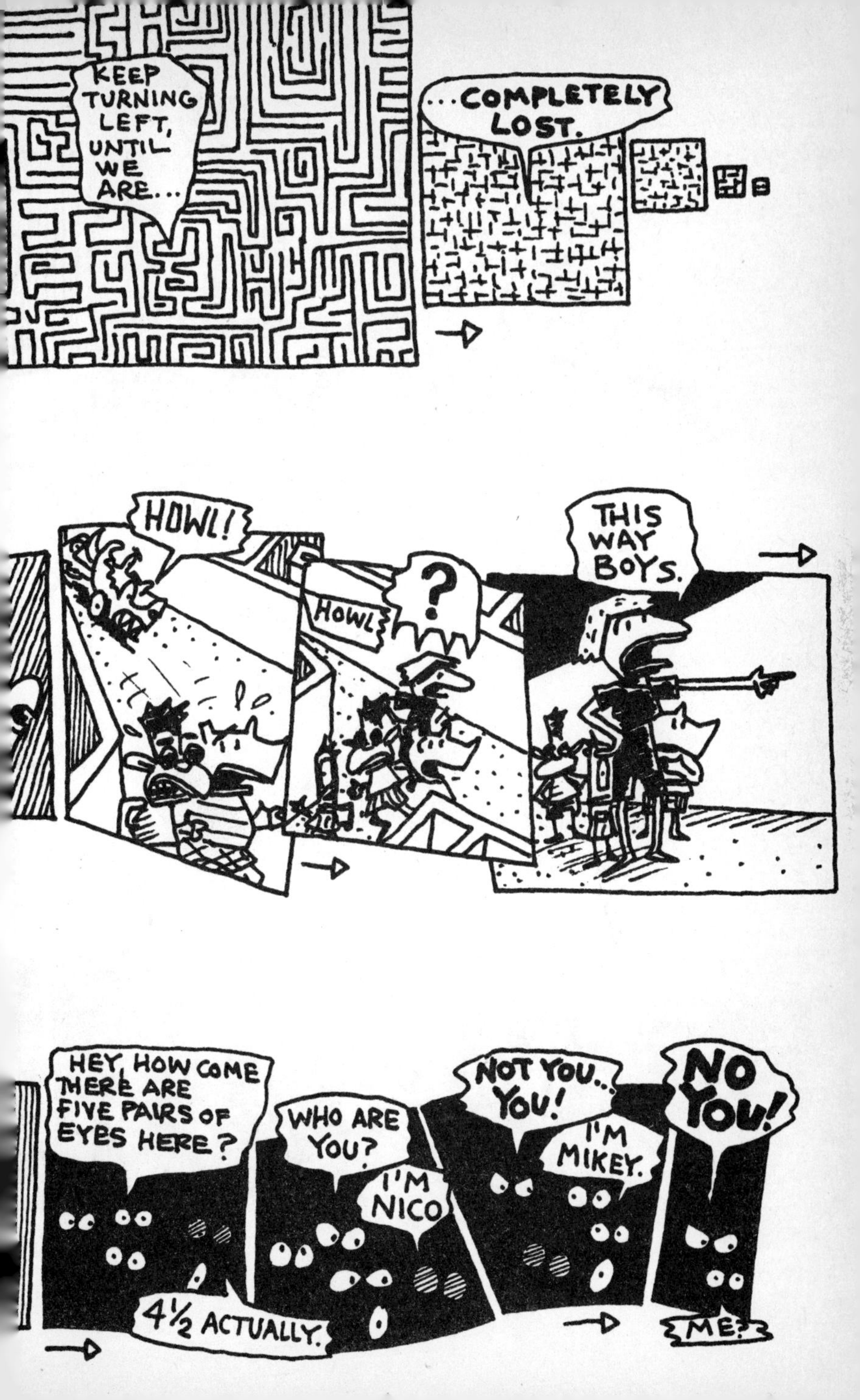
KEEP TURNING LEFT, UNTIL WE ARE...
...COMPLETELY LOST.
HOWL!
HOWL
?
THIS WAY BOYS.
HEY, HOW COME THERE ARE FIVE PAIRS OF EYES HERE?
4½ ACTUALLY.
WHO ARE YOU?
I'M NICO
NOT YOU... YOU!
I'M MIKEY.
NO YOU!
ME?

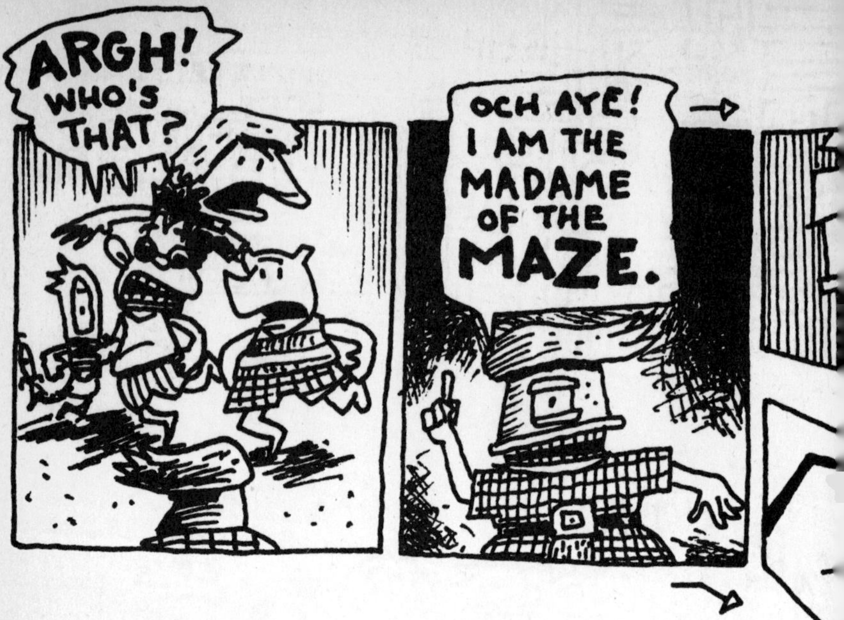
ARGH! WHO'S THAT?
OCH AYE! I AM THE MADAME OF THE MAZE.

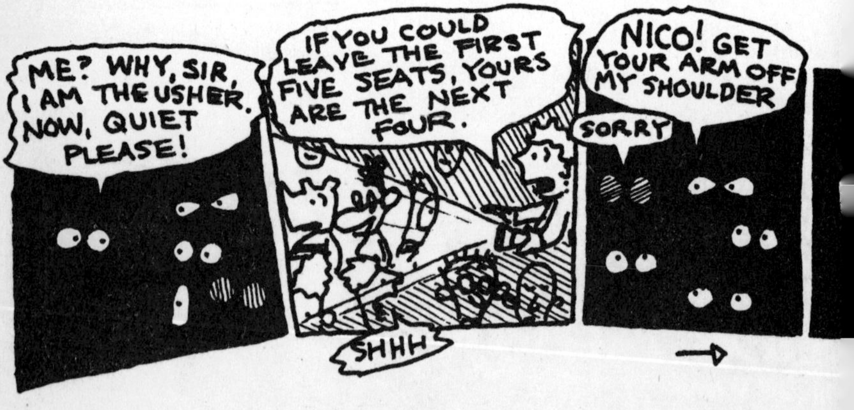
ME? WHY, SIR, I AM THE USHER. NOW, QUIET PLEASE!
IF YOU COULD LEAVE THE FIRST FIVE SEATS, YOURS ARE THE NEXT FOUR.
SHHH
NICO! GET YOUR ARM OFF MY SHOULDER
SORRY

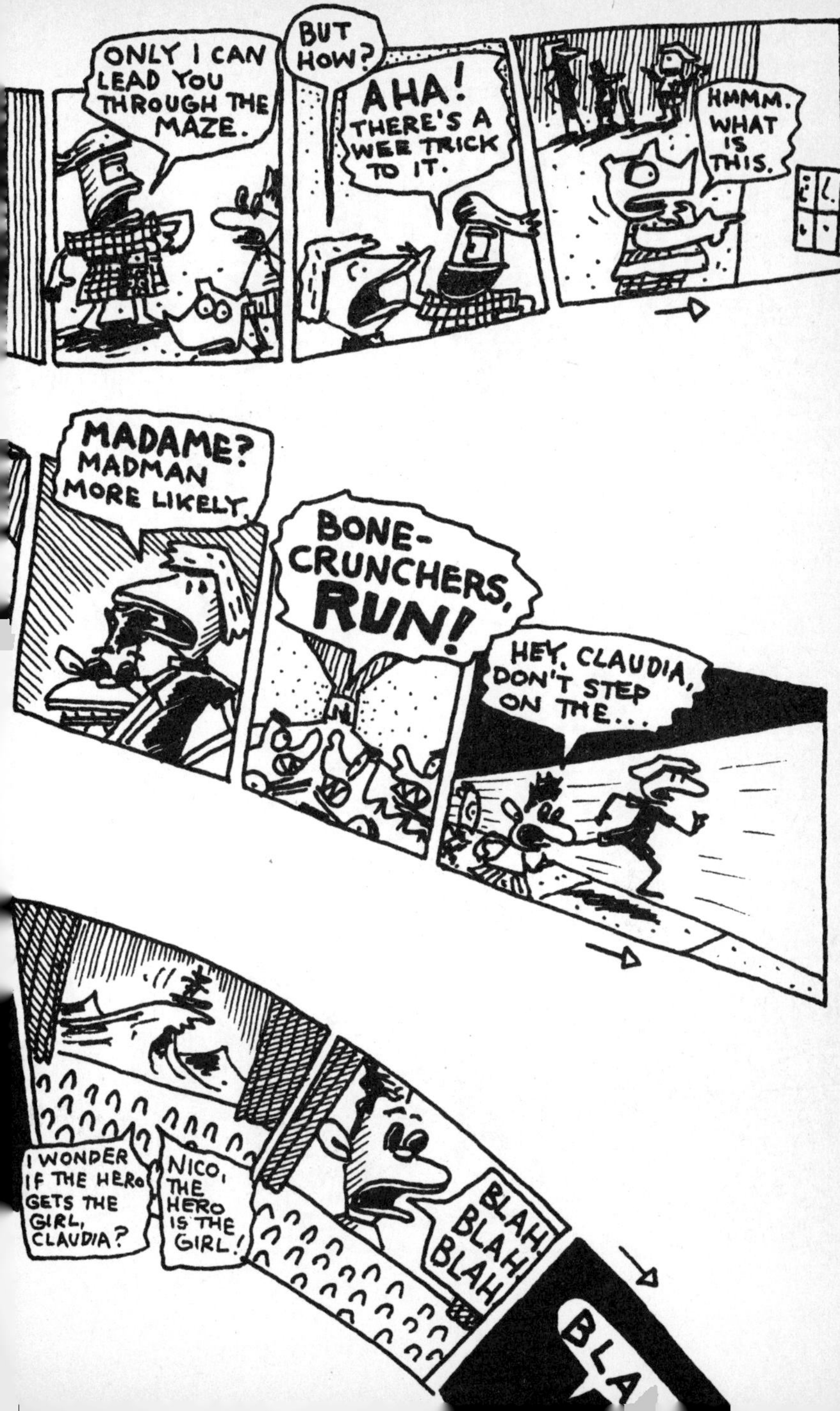
ONLY I CAN LEAD YOU THROUGH THE MAZE.
BUT HOW?
AHA! THERE'S A WEE TRICK TO IT.
HMMM. WHAT IS THIS.
MADAME? MADMAN MORE LIKELY.
BONE-CRUNCHERS, RUN!
HEY, CLAUDIA, DON'T STEP ON THE...
I WONDER IF THE HERO GETS THE GIRL, CLAUDIA?
NICO, THE HERO IS THE GIRL!
BLAH, BLAH, BLAH
BLA

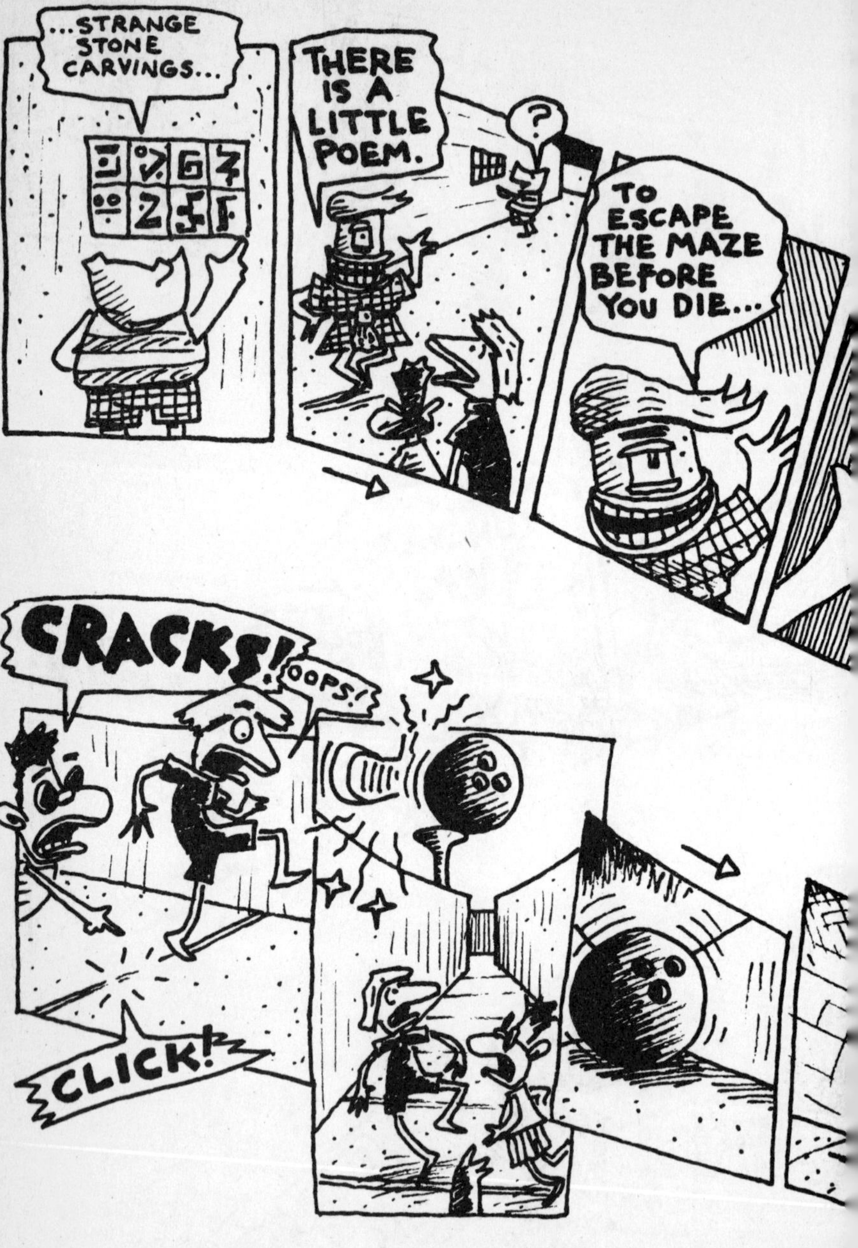
...STRANGE STONE CARVINGS...
THERE IS A LITTLE POEM.
?
TO ESCAPE THE MAZE BEFORE YOU DIE...
CRACKS!
OOPS!
CLICK!

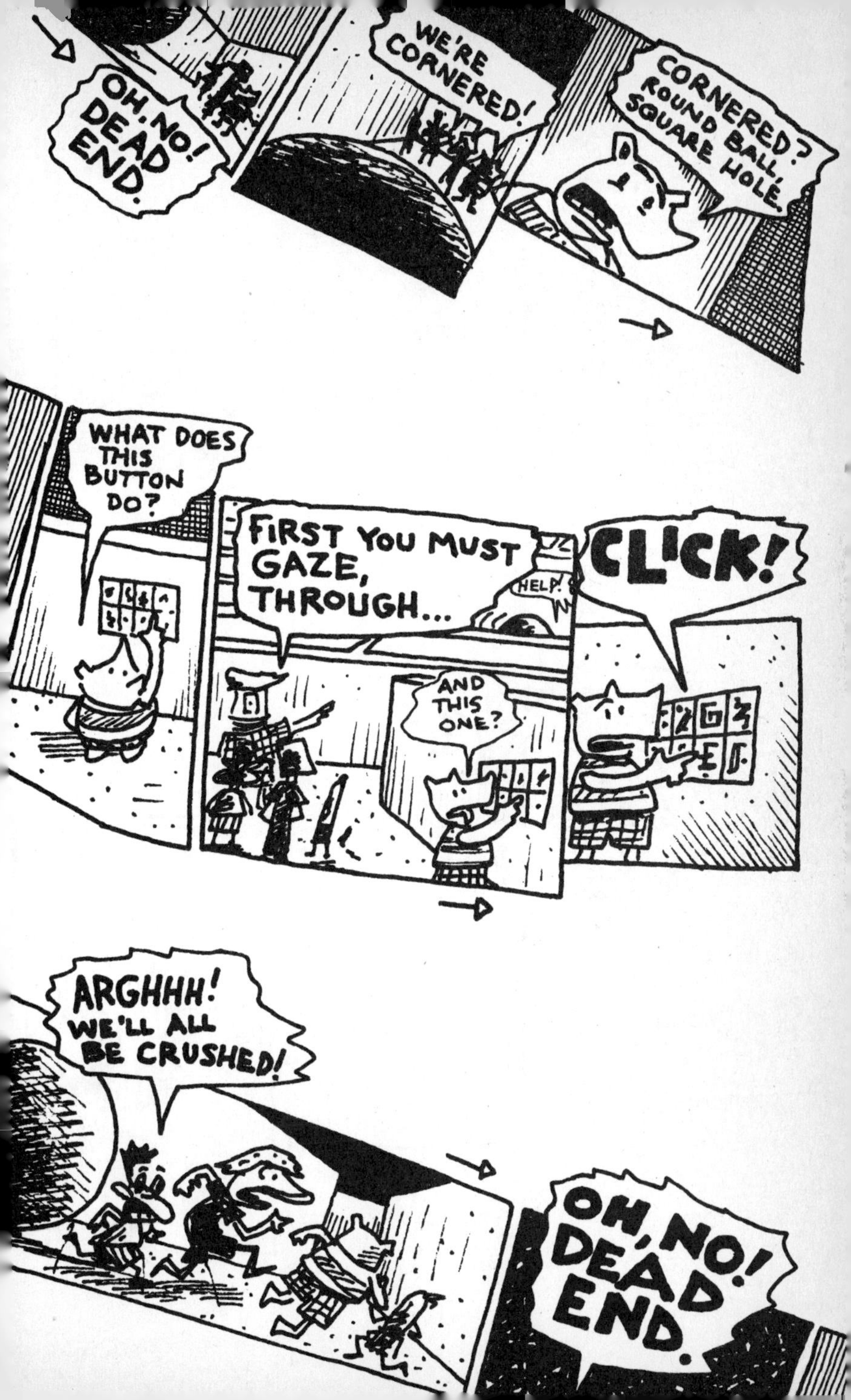
OH, NO! DEAD END.
WE'RE CORNERED!
CORNERED? ROUND BALL, SQUARE HOLE.
WHAT DOES THIS BUTTON DO?
FIRST YOU MUST GAZE, THROUGH...
HELP!
AND THIS ONE?
CLICK!
ARGHHH! WE'LL ALL BE CRUSHED!
OH, NO! DEAD END.

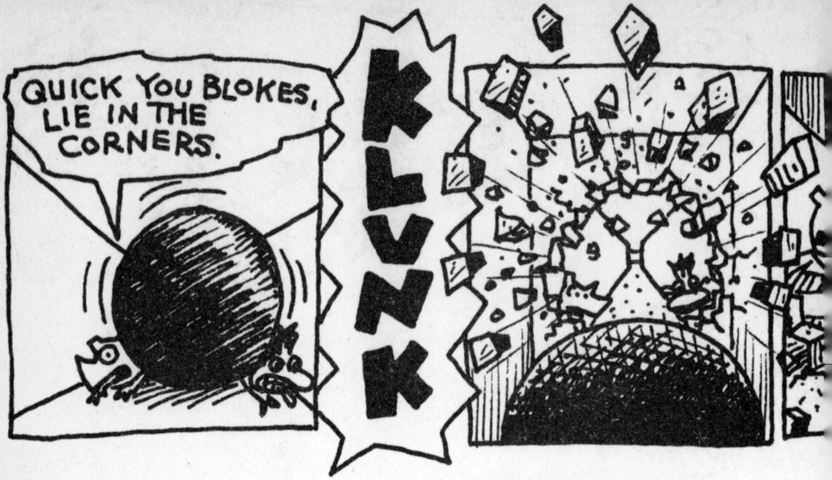
QUICK YOU BLOKES, LIE IN THE CORNERS.
KLUNK

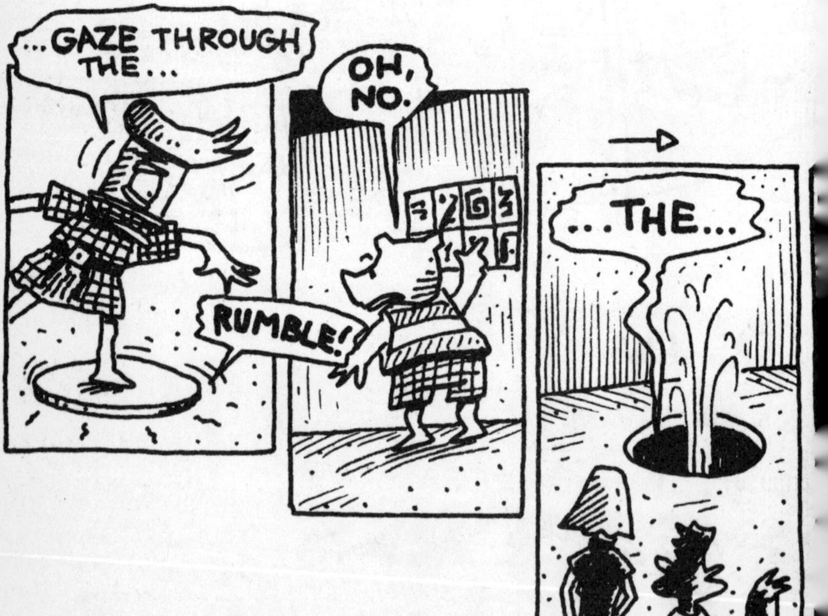
...GAZE THROUGH THE...
RUMBLE!
OH, NO.
...THE...

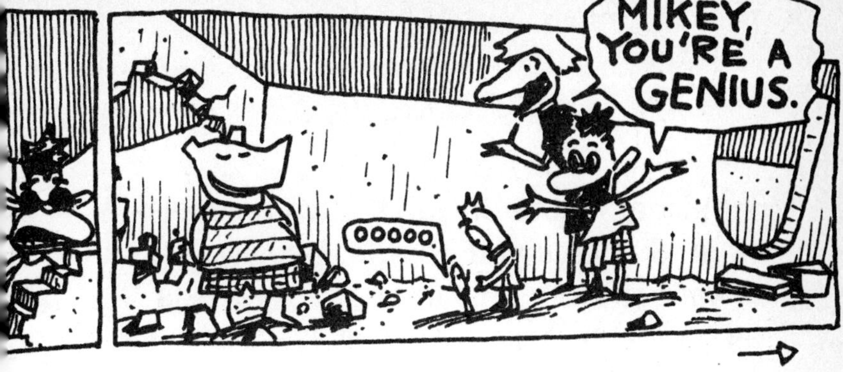
MIKEY, YOU'RE A GENIUS.
OOOOO.

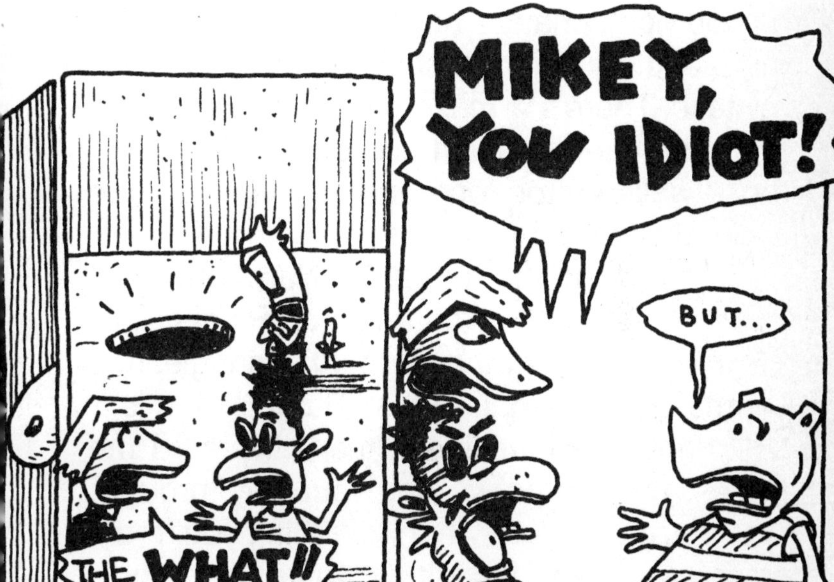
THE WHAT!!
MIKEY, YOU IDIOT!
BUT...

30

Most mazes in the universe have a simple pattern. Simple if you know it. Usually you can just wander around till the pattern reveals itself, or maybe you eventually wander out the other end by luck. It is said that you can get through most mazes if you keep one hand on the wall at all times and just keep walking. Eventually you must find the way out. As long as you don't change hands. Or walls. But on the planet Murillion, that would be a big mistake. There's a maze there that has walls made of razor blades. Keep one hand on those walls for too long and you'll be down to a bloody stump in no time.

There is another maze we Narrators visited once, in the Bahamas, on Planet Earth, not far from the Bermuda Triangle. It seems quite normal, at first. But it isn't. It is built right on a fault line in the Universal Time Plates. You can be walking your way through that maze, and just when you think you're a smartypants and have it all worked out, and you are telling your friends that they have

porridge for brains, the Time Plates shift.
There is a timequake. Next thing you know,
you are in a different maze, on a different day,
in a different millennium, in a different
universe. And you wish you had a change of
undies and a toothbrush, because you may
not get back home for a thousand years. Very
annoying things, mazes.

So our heroes are somewhere in the very
confusing Maze of Madness in the Duryllium
Underworld. Who knows where? Who cares?
It's them, not us. They may well have to spend
the rest of their lives wandering its passages,
chased by bonecrunchers, till they die of old
age, or become dinner.

But, in life, there is a lucky break waiting
for everyone. I have yet to have mine, I should
point out. (Unless you call having to narrate
this book a lucky break. Why didn't I get *Harry
Potter* or *The Hobbit*, instead of *Storymaze*?)
For our heroes, their lucky break is just
around the corner.

They wander into the centre of the maze.
There before them is a huge sculpture.
Michaelangelo's *David*? No. It is a statue of
one of the Great Mythical Creatures of the
Duryllium Dreaming.

31

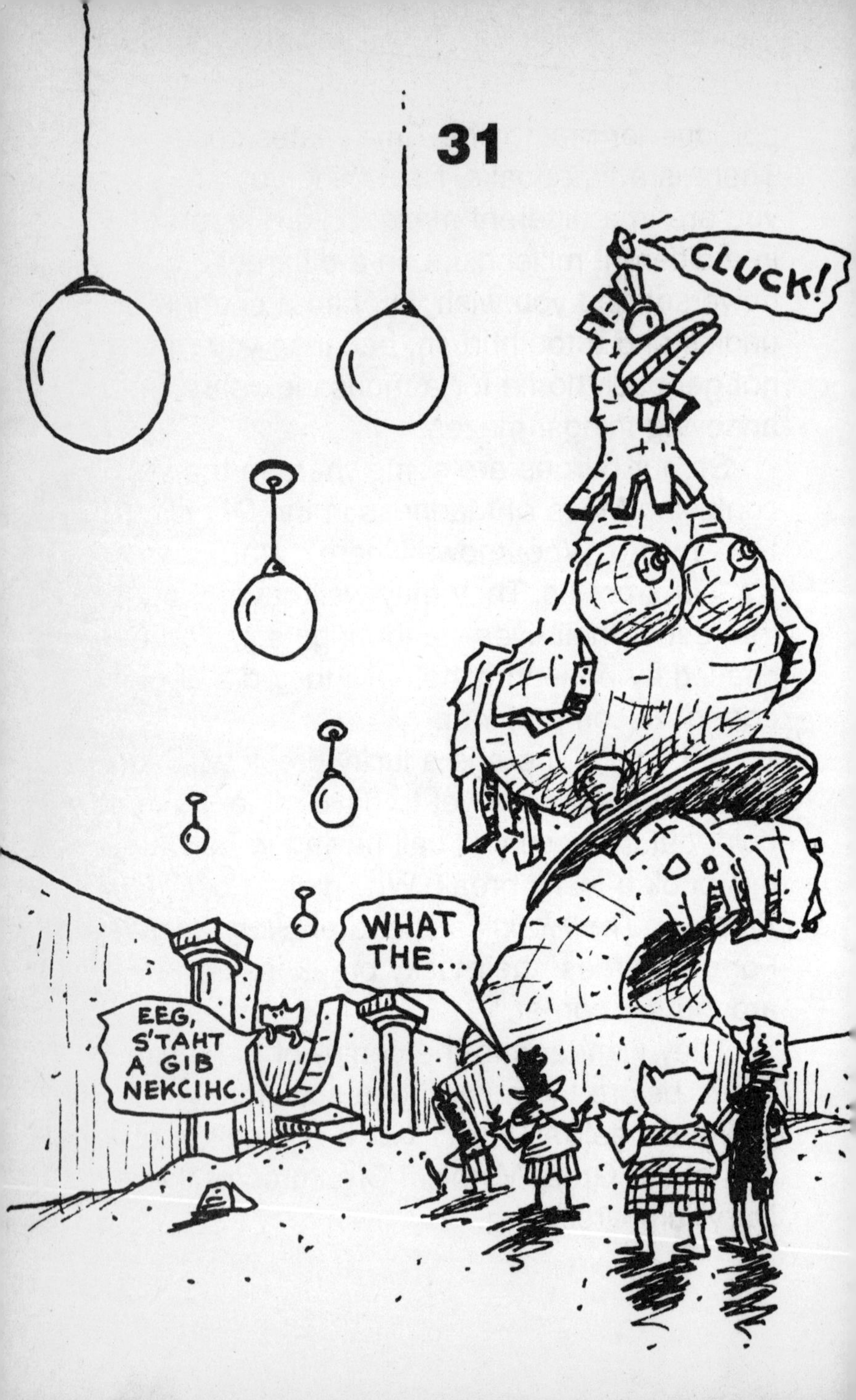
CLUCK!
WHAT THE...
EEG, S'TAHT A GIB NEKCIHC.

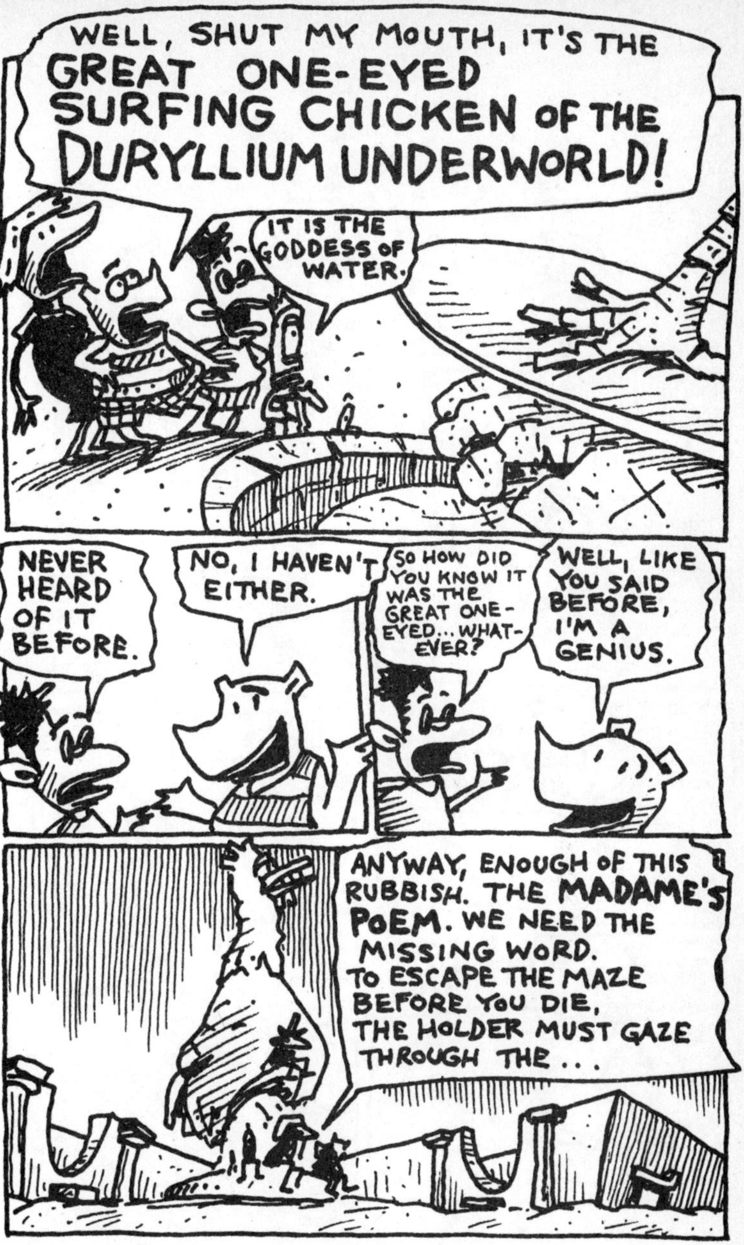
WELL, SHUT MY MOUTH, IT'S THE GREAT ONE-EYED SURFING CHICKEN OF THE DURYLLIUM UNDERWORLD!
IT IS THE GODDESS OF WATER.
NEVER HEARD OF IT BEFORE.
NO, I HAVEN'T EITHER.
SO HOW DID YOU KNOW IT WAS THE GREAT ONE-EYED... WHATEVER?
WELL, LIKE YOU SAID BEFORE, I'M A GENIUS.
ANYWAY, ENOUGH OF THIS RUBBISH. THE MADAME'S POEM. WE NEED THE MISSING WORD.
TO ESCAPE THE MAZE
BEFORE YOU DIE,
THE HOLDER MUST GAZE
THROUGH THE . . .

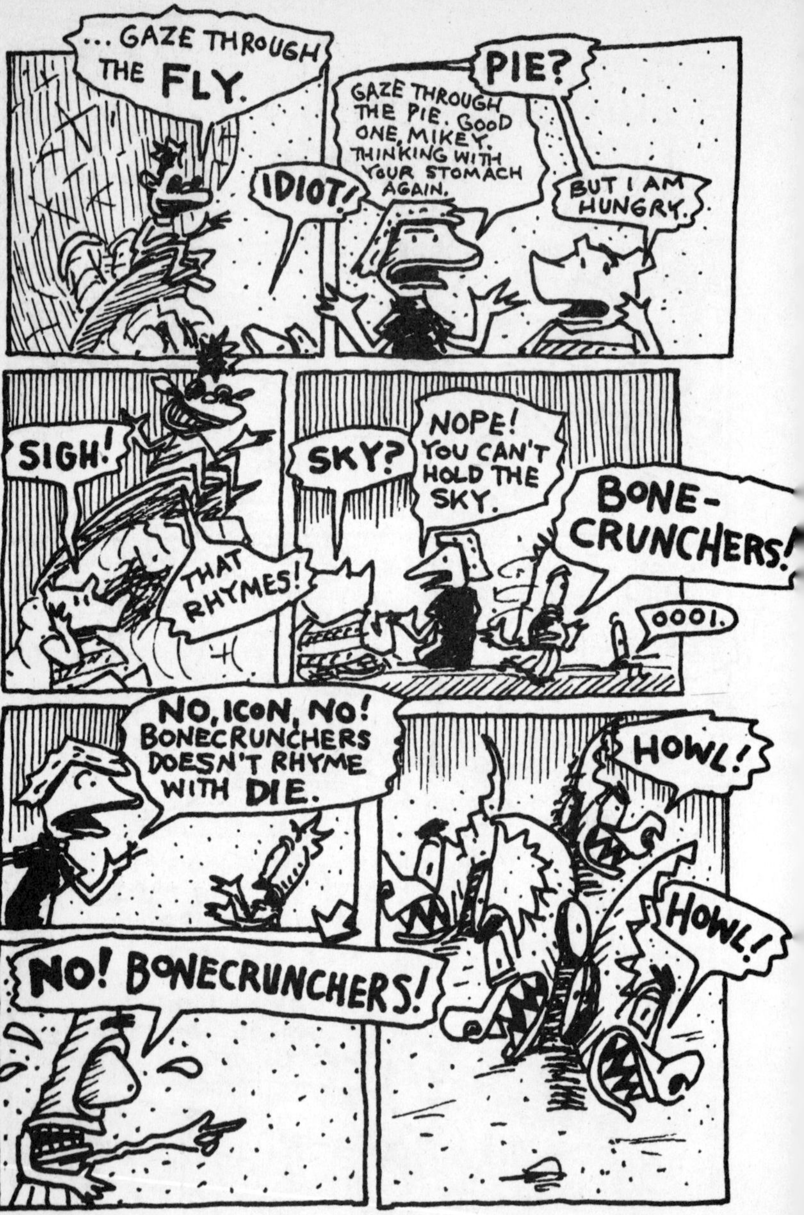
... GAZE THROUGH THE FLY.
PIE?
GAZE THROUGH THE PIE. GOOD ONE, MIKEY. THINKING WITH YOUR STOMACH AGAIN.
IDIOT!
BUT I AM HUNGRY.
SIGH!
THAT RHYMES!
SKY?
NOPE! YOU CAN'T HOLD THE SKY.
BONE-CRUNCHERS!
OOOI.
NO, ICON, NO! BONECRUNCHERS DOESN'T RHYME WITH DIE.
HOWL!
HOWL!
NO! BONECRUNCHERS!

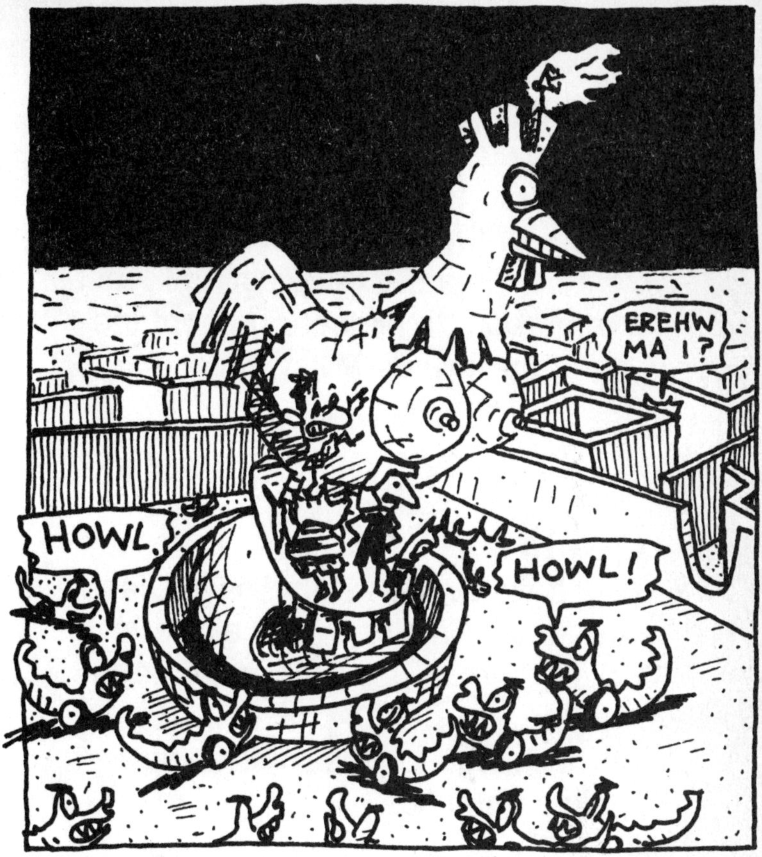
EREHW
MA I?
HOWL.
HOWL!

'Holy Occhilupo!!!' yells Nico, and clambers up the statue of the Great One-eyed Chicken of the Duryllium Underworld.

The others follow. They have no choice. But now they are trapped on the Chicken's back. While the bonecrunchers cannot climb up, our heroes can't get down either.

'Hey, the view's not so bad from up here,' says Nico.

Now they can see the whole maze from above. But they still can't figure how to get out. In fact, in the distance, you can just see the tiny figure of the backwards Mikey lost in the maze. Poor creature. And just as I, your Narrator, am about to blather on about the poor trapped backwards Mikey, Nico interrupts.

'LOOK. THE EYE OF THE CHICKEN. IT'S LOOKING AT ME.'

'You're off your rocker, Nico,' says Claudia.

'I've got to take a closer look at that eye,' says Nico, and he rushes further up the Chicken's neck.

'Come back, you idiot,' says Claudia.

Nico takes no notice.

'THE EYE', he mumbles, standing on the right breast of the Chicken.

'Careful, it could be a booby trap, you fool,' yells Claudia.

But nothing can stop Nico now. He clambers further up the Chichen, till he is perched on the beak, staring into the Chicken's eye, repeating:

'THE EYE. NICO MUST HAVE THE EYE.'

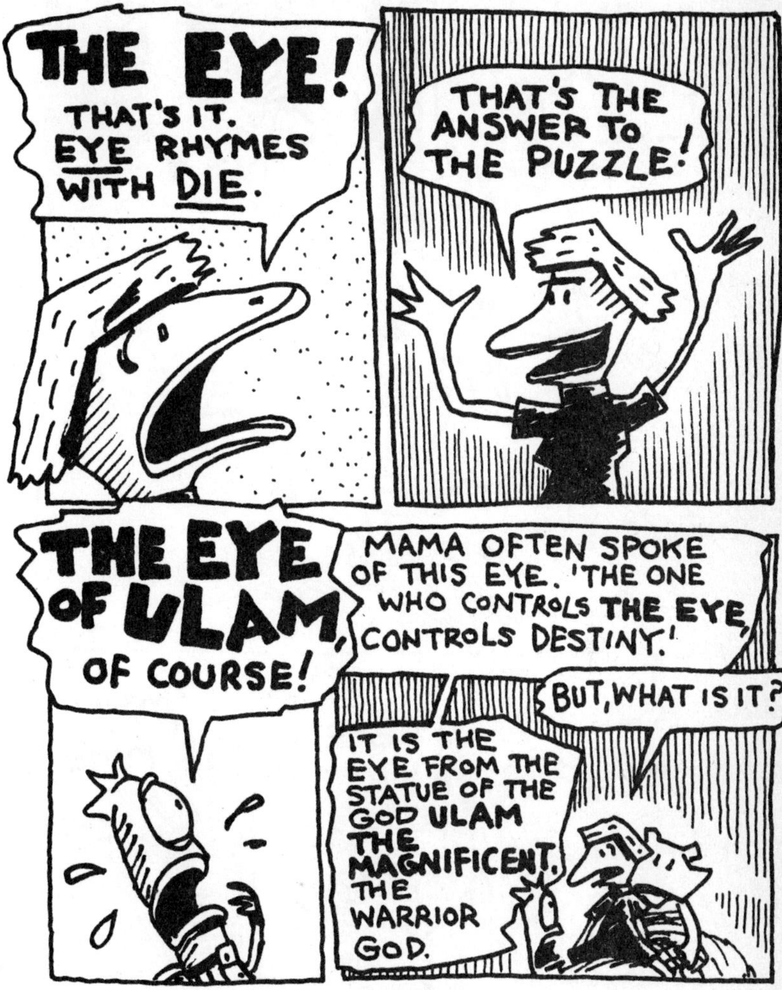
THE EYE! THAT'S IT. EYE RHYMES WITH DIE.
THAT'S THE ANSWER TO THE PUZZLE!
THE EYE OF ULAM, OF COURSE!
MAMA OFTEN SPOKE OF THIS EYE. 'THE ONE WHO CONTROLS THE EYE, CONTROLS DESTINY.'
BUT, WHAT IS IT?
IT IS THE EYE FROM THE STATUE OF THE GOD ULAM THE MAGNIFICENT. THE WARRIOR GOD.

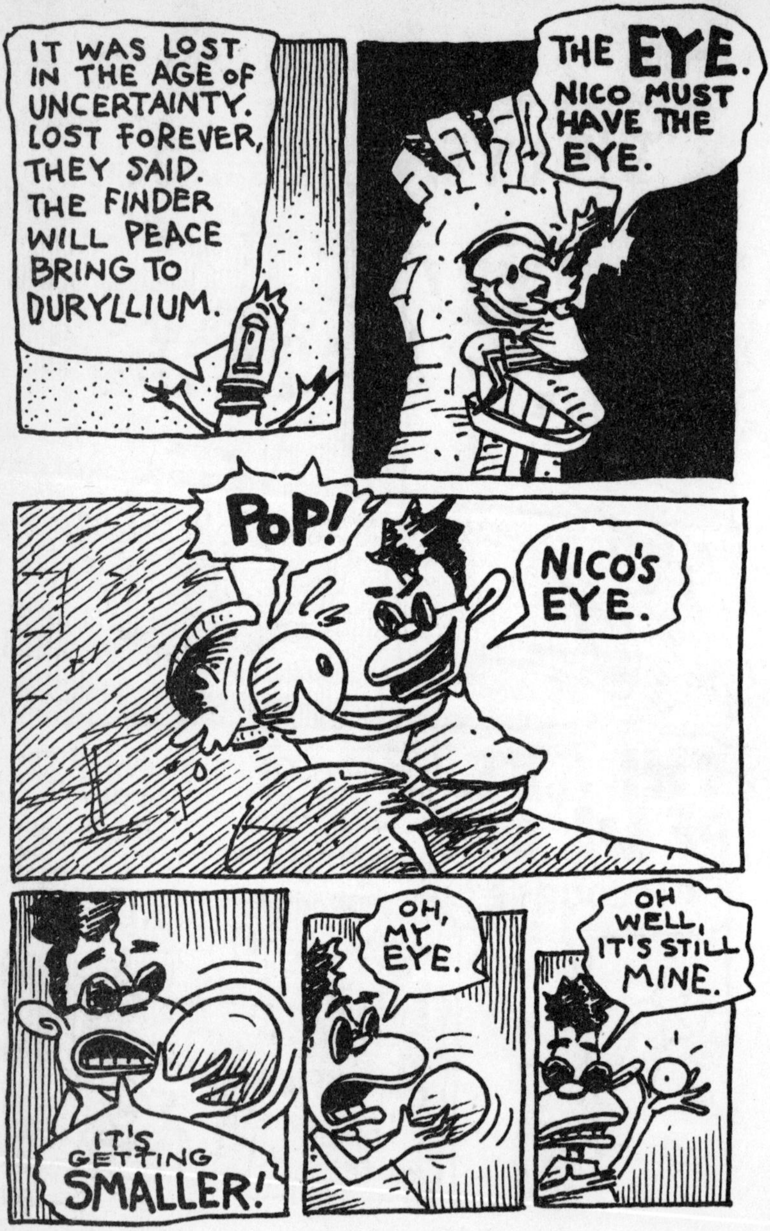
IT WAS LOST IN THE AGE OF UNCERTAINTY. LOST FOREVER, THEY SAID. THE FINDER WILL PEACE BRING TO DURYLLIUM.
THE EYE. NICO MUST HAVE THE EYE.
POP!
NICO'S EYE.
IT'S GETTING SMALLER!
OH, MY EYE.
OH WELL, IT'S STILL MINE.

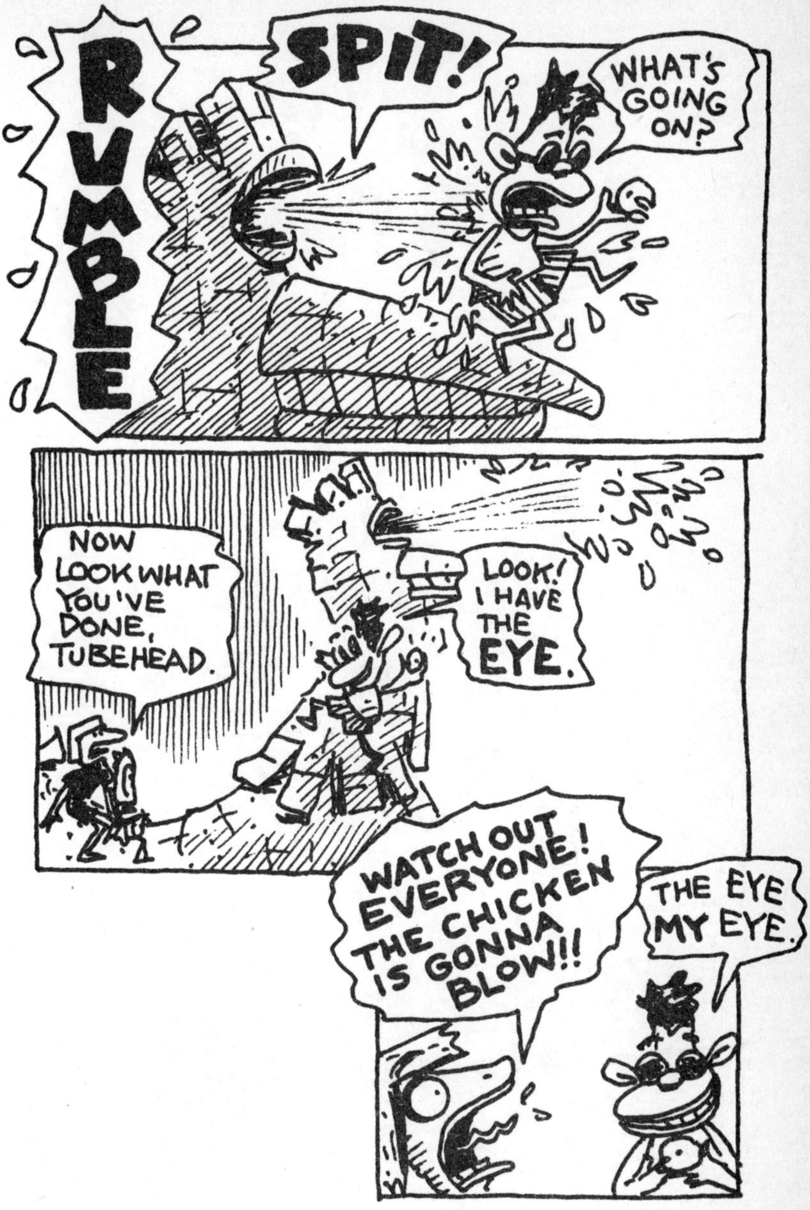
RUMBLE
SPIT!
WHAT'S GOING ON?
NOW LOOK WHAT YOU'VE DONE, TUBEHEAD.
LOOK! I HAVE THE EYE.
WATCH OUT EVERYONE! THE CHICKEN IS GONNA BLOW!!
THE EYE MY EYE.

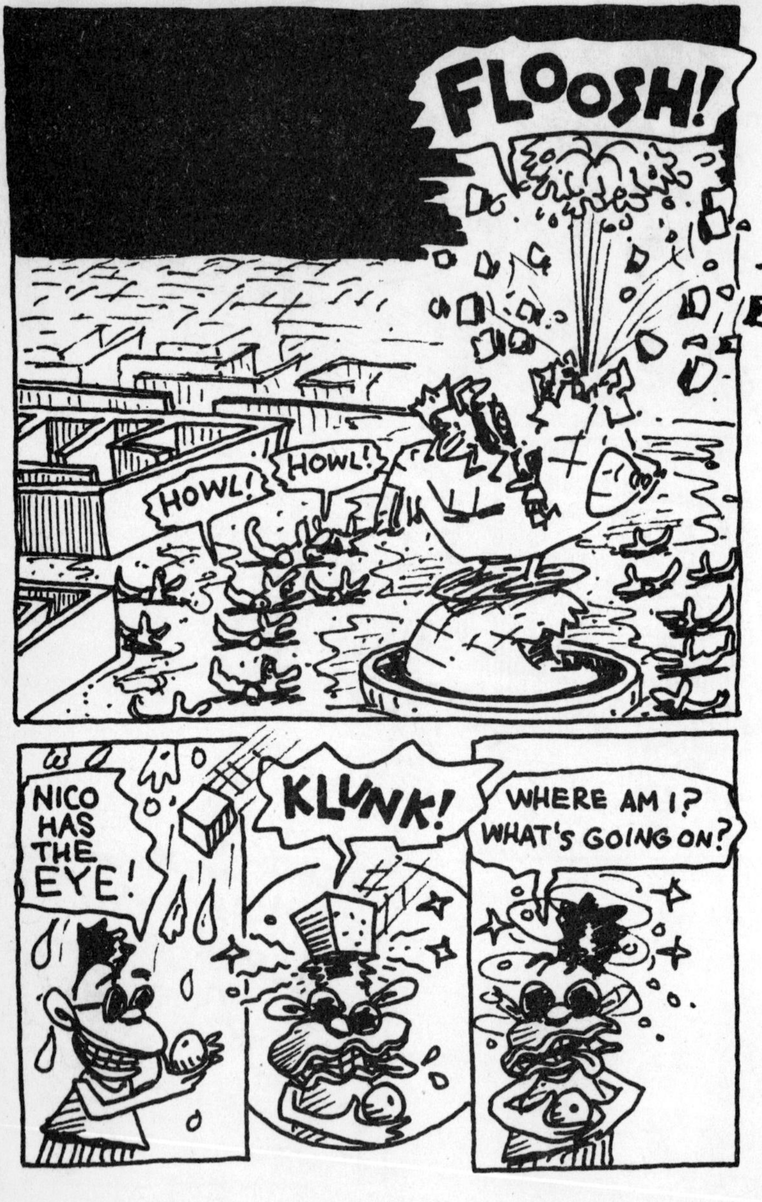
FLOOSH!
HOWL!
HOWL!
NICO HAS THE EYE!
KLUNK!
WHERE AM I? WHAT'S GOING ON?

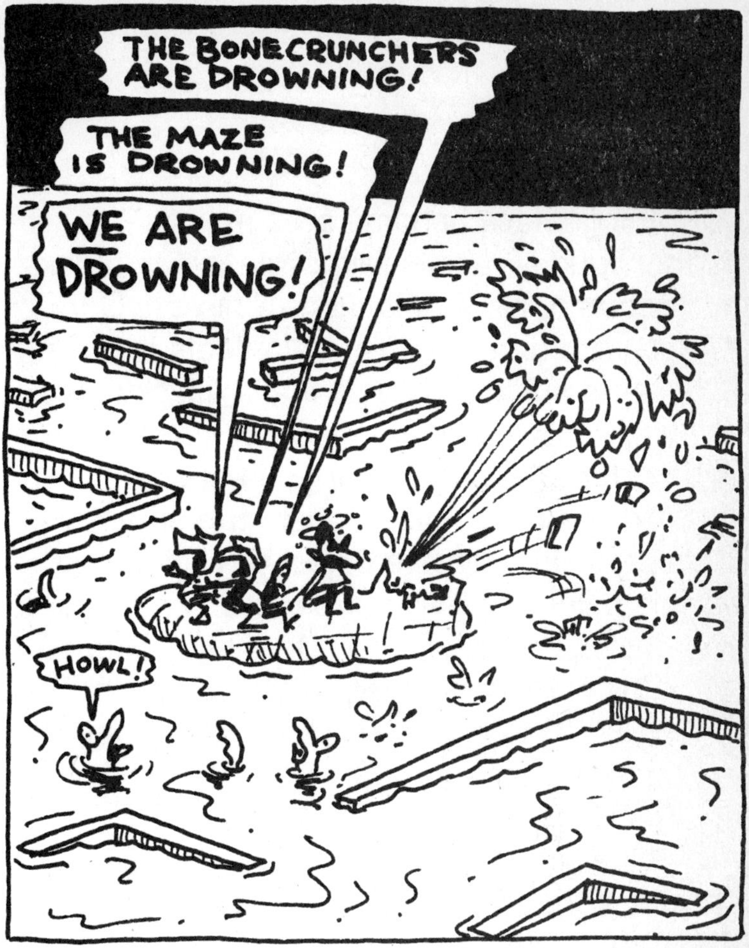
THE BONECRUNCHERS ARE DROWNING!
THE MAZE IS DROWNING!
WE ARE DROWNING!
HOWL!

32

OK, things have become a bit messy. The Underworld is rapidly filling with water, thanks to Nico and that stupid stone Chicken. Our heroes are drowning. Then up floats the Chicken's surfboard. Well, that's a lucky break. Why isn't the surfboard made of stone like the rest of the Chicken, I hear you ask? Well, you ask too many questions. Just read on and accept it. Or insert the object of your choice at this point. Such as the bloated carcass of a long-dead Prime Minister. Or a jet ski loaned to us by our kind sponsor, Petrol Head Inc. It isn't going to matter much because they are going to escape anyway, they just don't know it yet. Ooops, sorry, I gave it away a bit.

Actually they drown. And that's the end. So close the book and go to sleep.

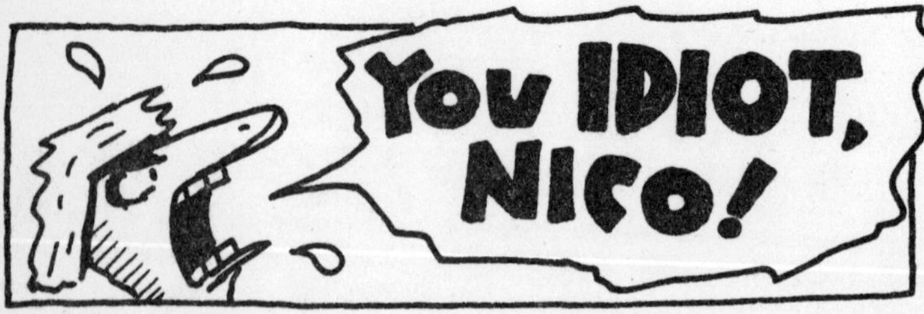
YOU IDIOT, NICO!

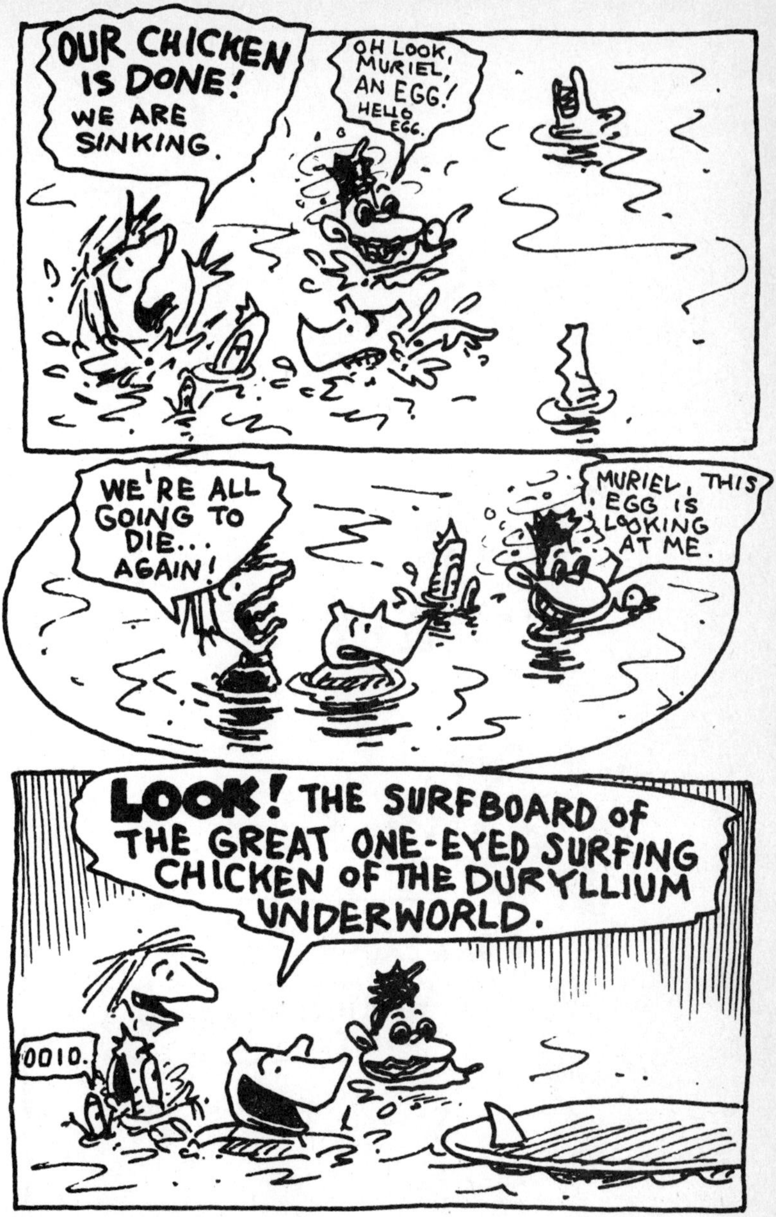
OUR CHICKEN IS DONE! WE ARE SINKING.
OH LOOK, MURIEL, AN EGG! HELLO EGG.
WE'RE ALL GOING TO DIE... AGAIN!
MURIEL, THIS EGG IS LOOKING AT ME.
LOOK! THE SURFBOARD OF THE GREAT ONE-EYED SURFING CHICKEN OF THE DURYLLIUM UNDERWORLD.
OOIO.

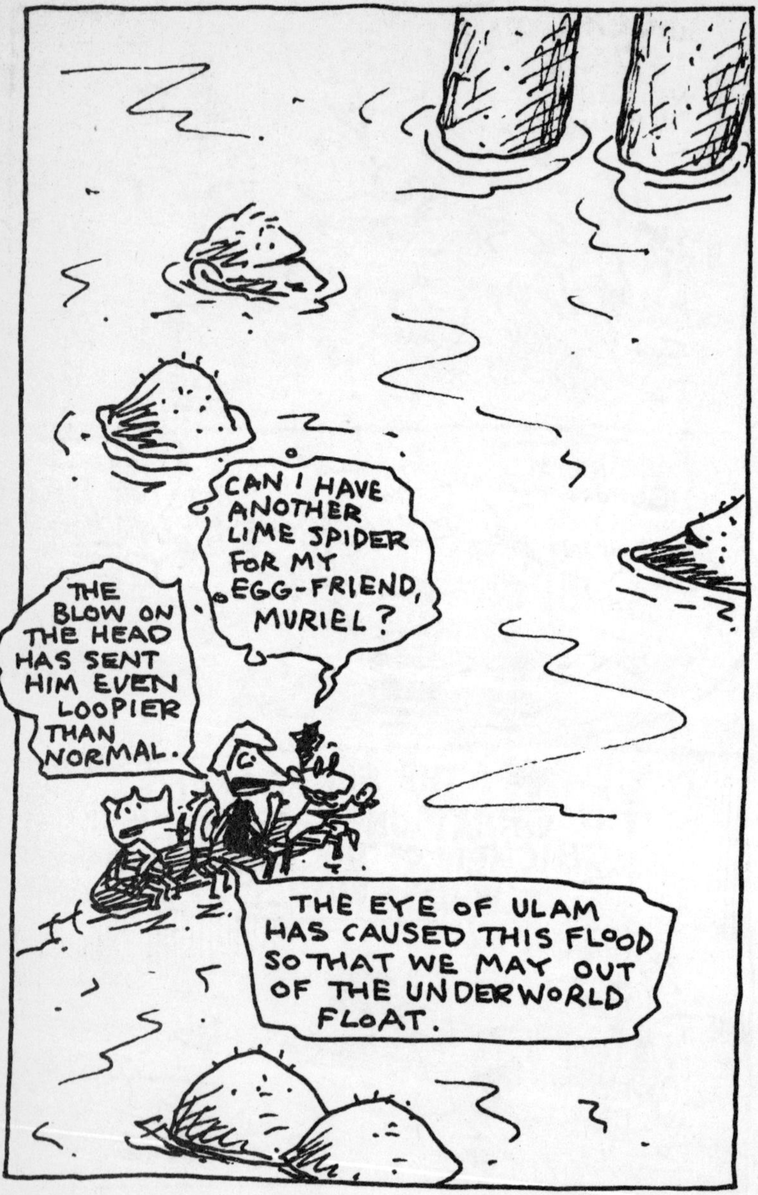
CAN I HAVE ANOTHER LIME SPIDER FOR MY EGG-FRIEND, MURIEL?
THE BLOW ON THE HEAD HAS SENT HIM EVEN LOOPIER THAN NORMAL.
THE EYE OF ULAM HAS CAUSED THIS FLOOD SO THAT WE MAY OUT OF THE UNDERWORLD FLOAT.

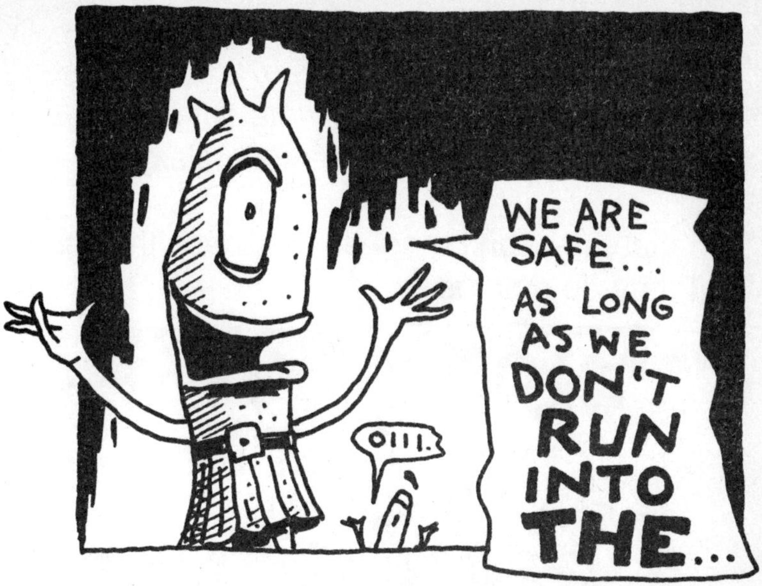
WE ARE SAFE...
AS LONG AS WE DON'T RUN INTO THE...
OIII.

I suppose you are wondering what he is going to say.

'...as long as we don't run into the...'

Now my guess is that he is talking about a Cyclops. I'm saying that because I've read the book. But for those who haven't read the book, you may be thinking: what are they about to meet? If you are trying to leave the Underworld by water, what wouldn't you want to meet?

A giant feral food processor, perhaps? A Very Large Stomping Foot? Or Mmnjhuy76? Which may not make much sense to you, until I tell you that I accidentally leant on my keyboard and it typed out Mmnjhuy76? But it just so happens that Mmnljhuy76 is the name of a huge 1000 metre waterfall on planet Vjsingh, in the Andromeda Galaxy. Spooky eh?

In fact they don't meet any of these things. What they do meet is a...

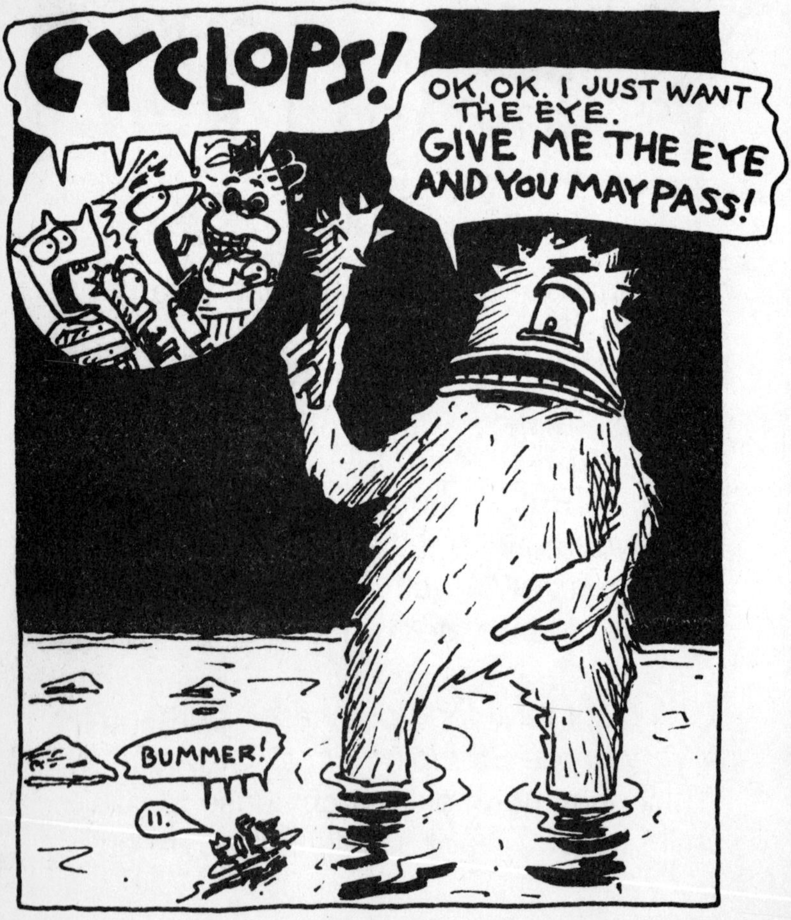
CYCLOPS!
OK, OK. I JUST WANT THE EYE.
GIVE ME THE EYE AND YOU MAY PASS!
BUMMER!
!!.

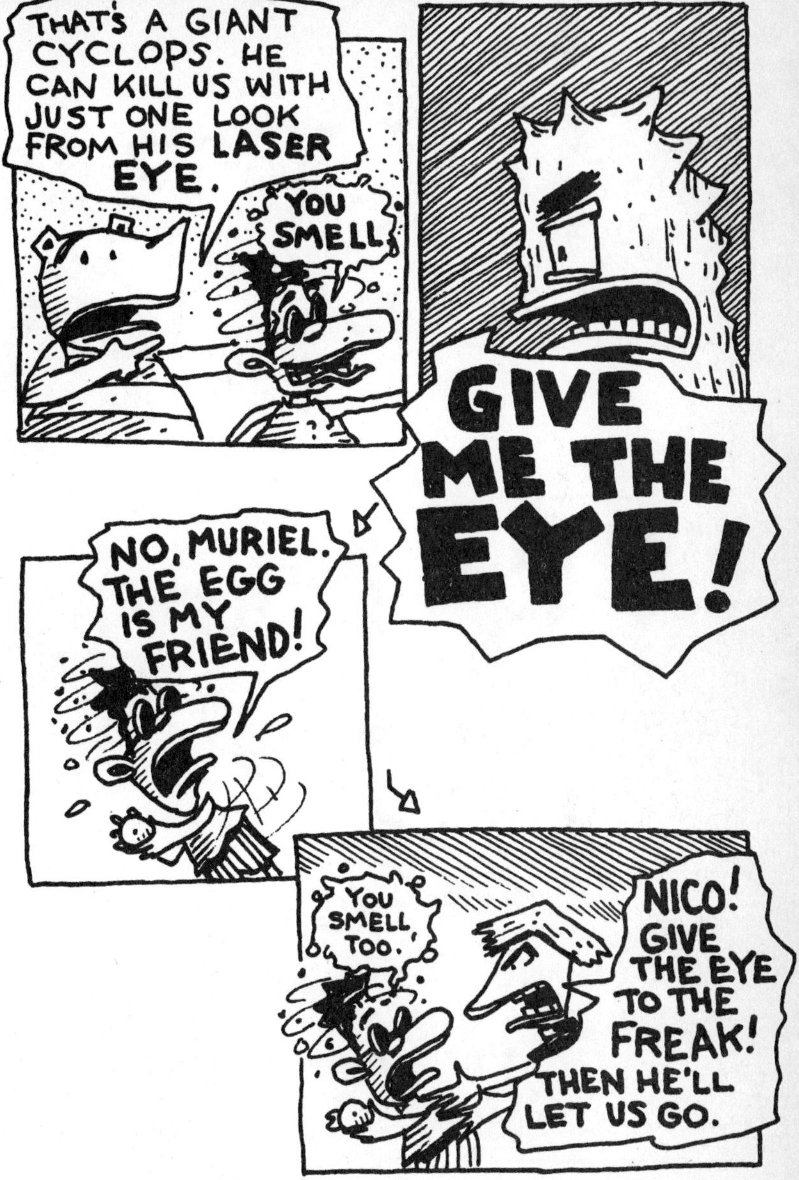
THAT'S A GIANT CYCLOPS. HE CAN KILL US WITH JUST ONE LOOK FROM HIS LASER EYE.
YOU SMELL.
GIVE ME THE EYE!
NO, MURIEL. THE EGG IS MY FRIEND!
YOU SMELL, TOO.
NICO! GIVE THE EYE TO THE FREAK! THEN HE'LL LET US GO.

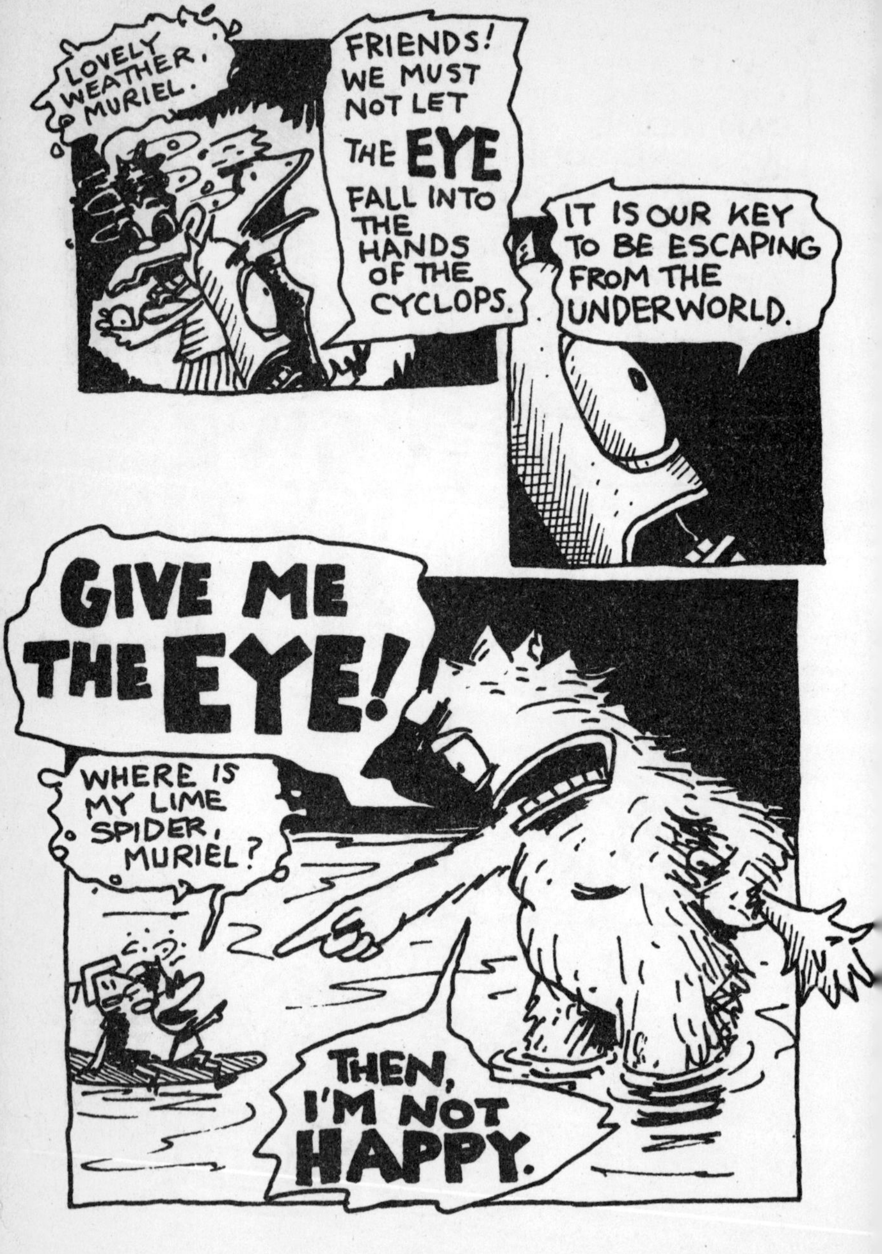
LOVELY WEATHER, MURIEL.
FRIENDS! WE MUST NOT LET THE EYE FALL INTO THE HANDS OF THE CYCLOPS.
IT IS OUR KEY TO BE ESCAPING FROM THE UNDERWORLD.
GIVE ME THE EYE!
WHERE IS MY LIME SPIDER, MURIEL?
THEN, I'M NOT HAPPY.

33

Do you know what a **Giant Cyclops** is? I don't suppose you meet too many of them at your school. Although, in Grade 4 at Narrators Elementary School, I did have this foul-smelling teacher with only one eye. She was very hairy and she did have a laser-like stare which could turn you into a pile of smoking ash. Which, spooky though it may be, is exactly the definition of a Cyclops in the *NCGUB*. So if you're wondering what a Cyclops looks like, look at your Grade 4 teacher.

Back to the action. (Are you still with me?)

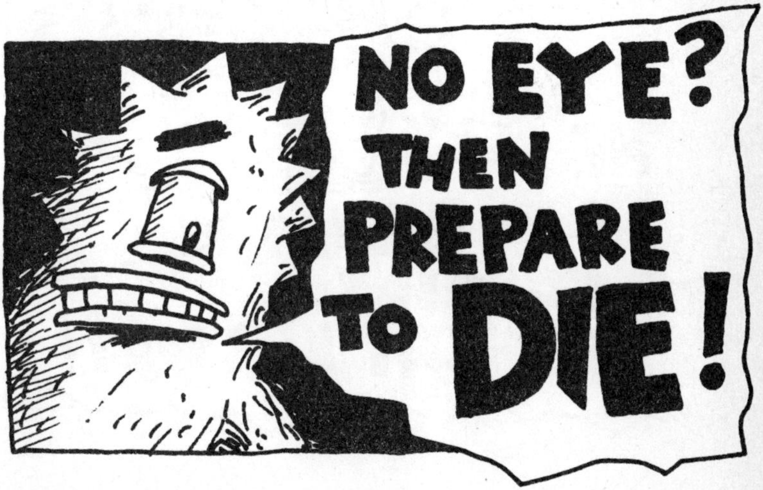
NO EYE? THEN PREPARE TO DIE!

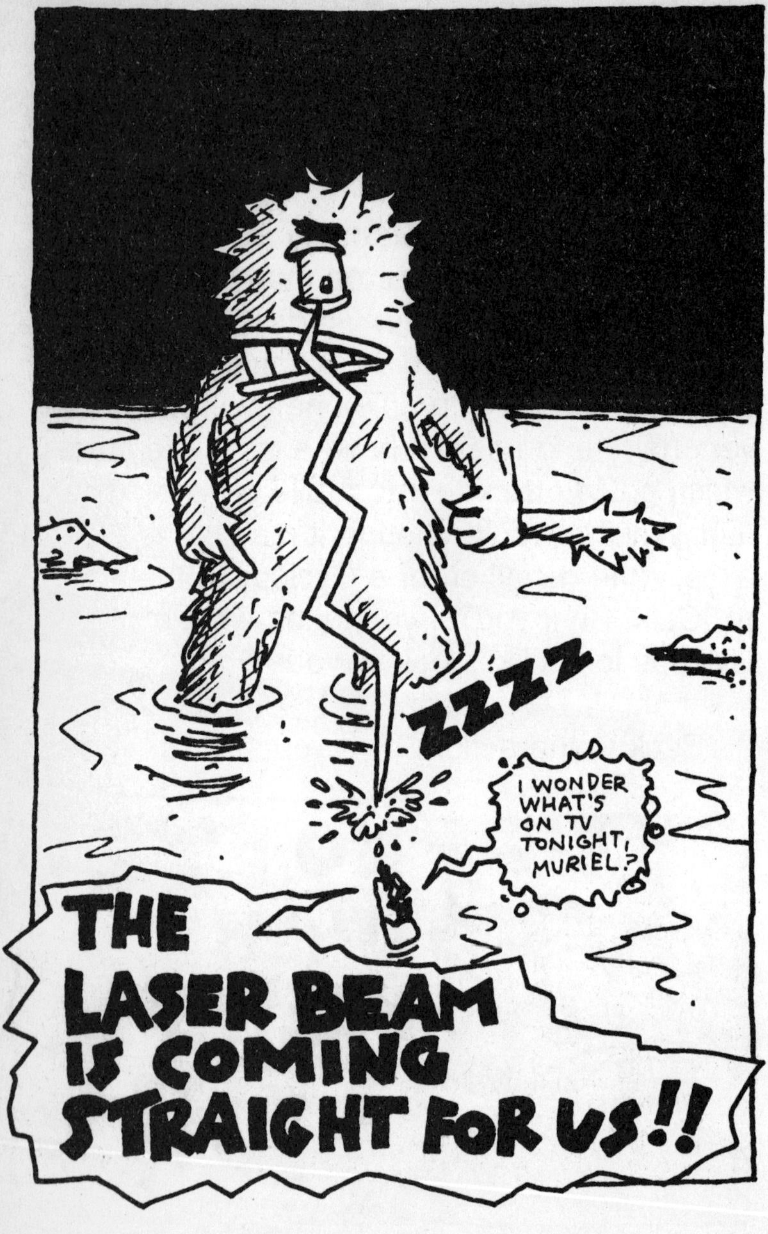
ZZZZ
I WONDER WHAT'S ON TV TONIGHT, MURIEL?
THE LASER BEAM IS COMING STRAIGHT FOR US!!

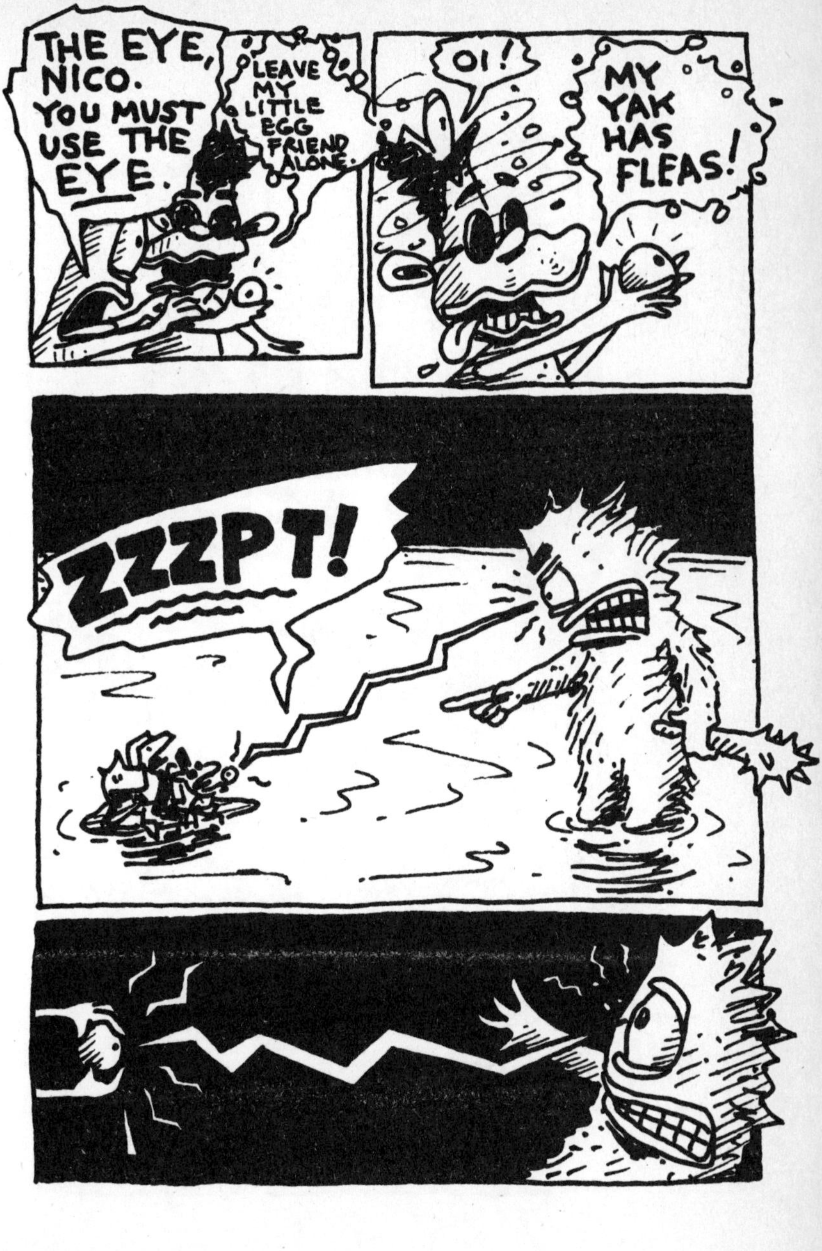
THE EYE, NICO. YOU MUST USE THE EYE.
LEAVE MY LITTLE EGG FRIEND ALONE.
OI!
MY YAK HAS FLEAS!
ZZZPT!

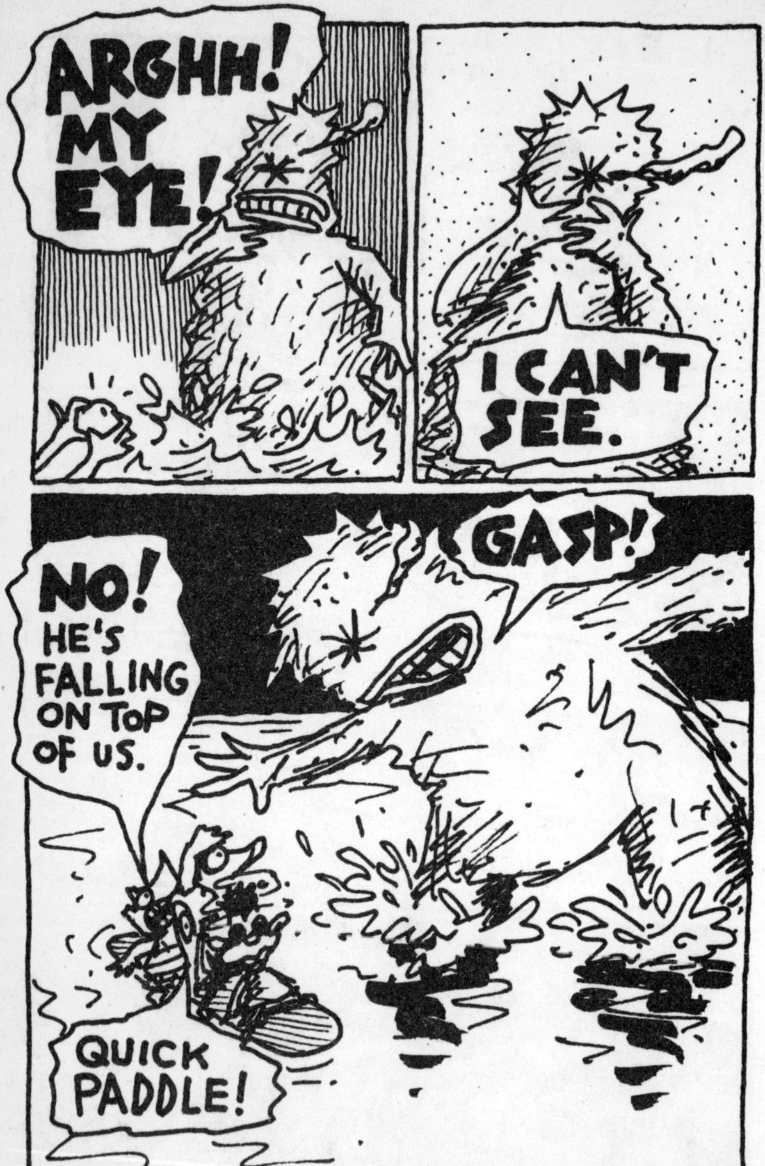
ARGHH! MY EYE!
I CAN'T SEE.
NO! HE'S FALLING ON TOP OF US.
GASP!
QUICK PADDLE!

34

Now, I suppose you're wondering what King Vidor is doing at this very moment. I can tell you one thing, he should not be feeling very kingly. I can see him sitting on the throne. He is thinking he can smell noxious gases wafting up from the Underworld. He is thinking that maybe he hasn't seen the last of Icon. He's got a feeling that stealing power from his brother is not going to be as easy as Crundor had said it would be. Maybe there is a big battle looming. Maybe Icon and Vidor will go head to head in a battle to the death. And then again, maybe not.

Meanwhile, is that a bit of a crowd I hear milling around outside the palace? Chucking things at the windows? Saying they are hungry and they wouldn't mind eating Vidor for their first course and Crundor for afters?

Perhaps I am seeing that. But Vidor isn't. For he is a king. And kings always think everything is going wonderfully, and that everyone loves them, and when they eventually die of old age their coffin will be covered knee-deep in flowers. Fools!

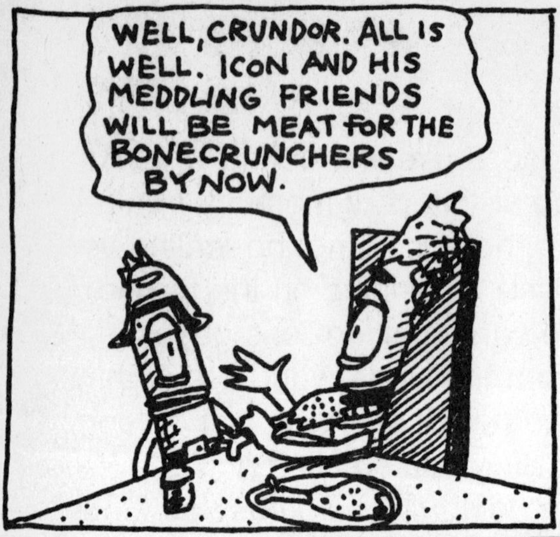
WELL, CRUNDOR. ALL IS WELL. ICON AND HIS MEDDLING FRIENDS WILL BE MEAT FOR THE BONECRUNCHERS BY NOW.

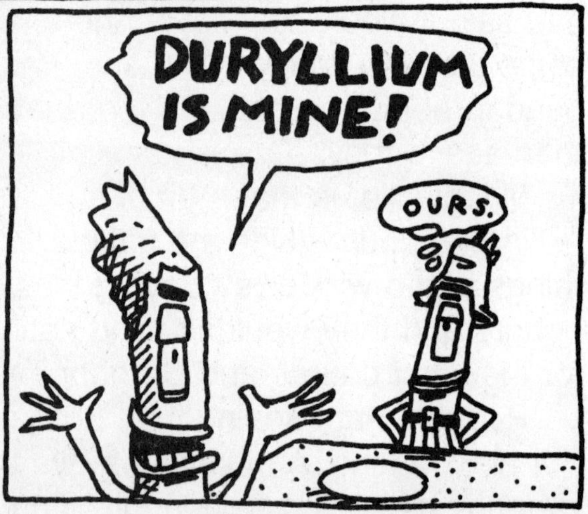
DURYLLIUM IS MINE!
OURS.

Meanwhile, in the Underworld, things are looking up, for everyone except the Cyclops. As he goes down, a giant wave is thrown up.

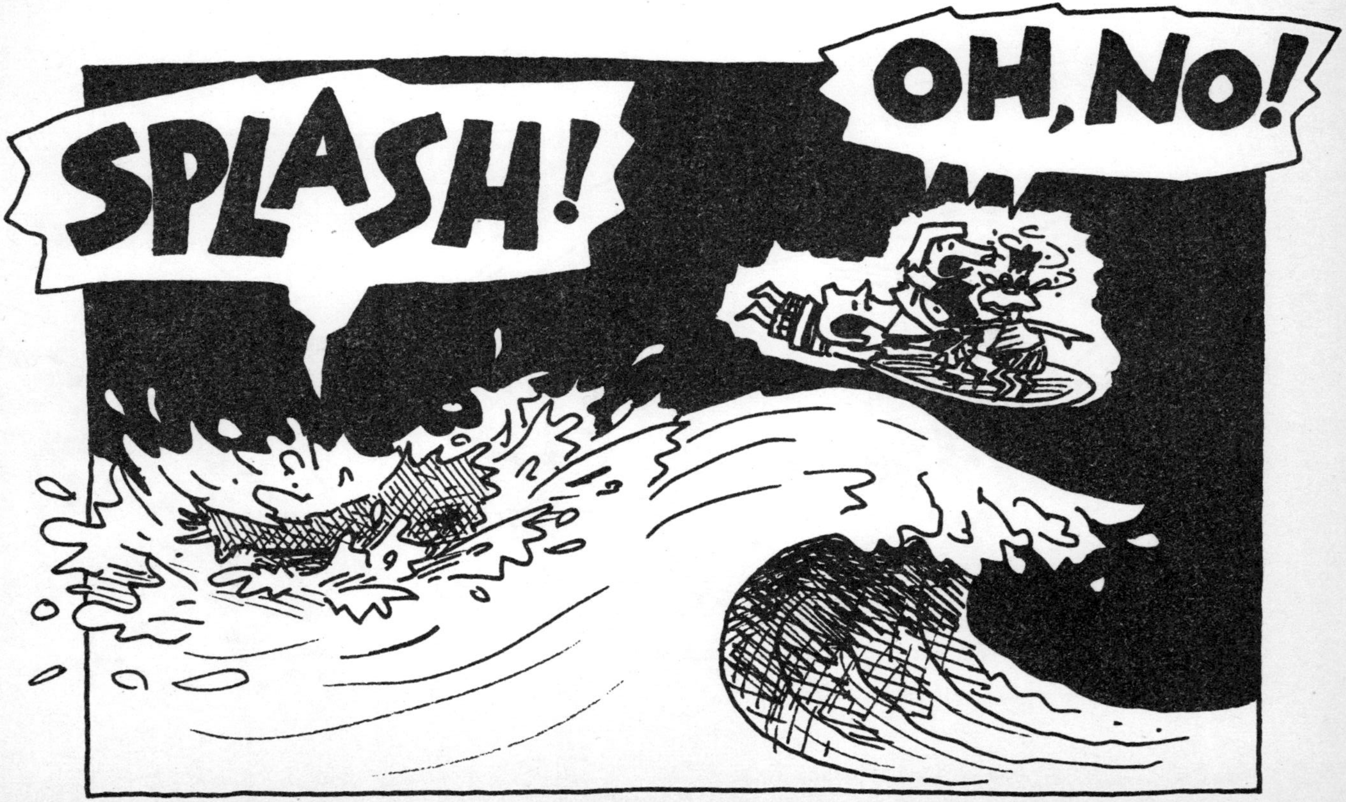
SPLASH!
OH, NO!

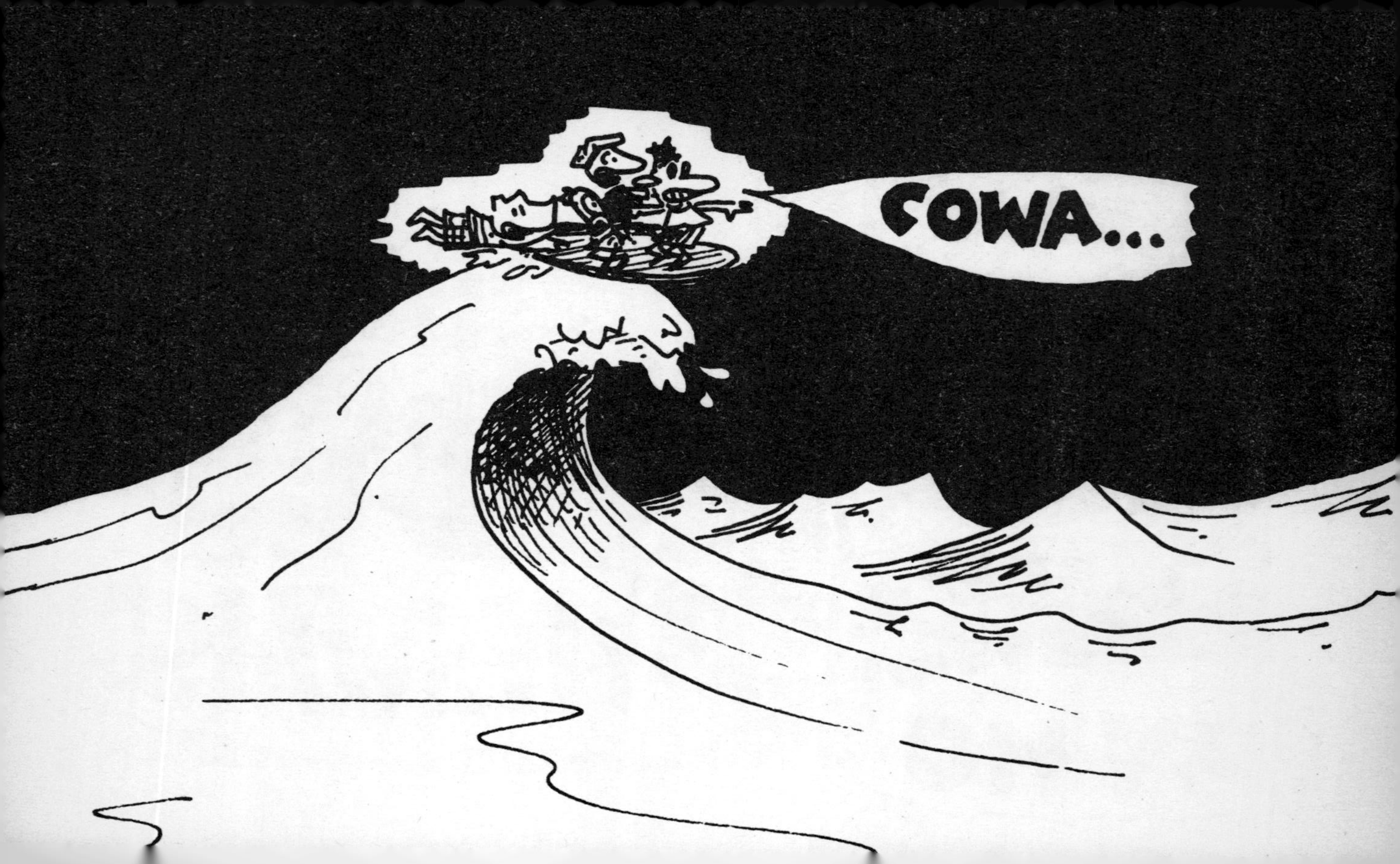
COWA...

35

As luck would have it, our heroes, surfing on
THE ULTIMATE WAVE, fly through space and
time. Where they will end up is a bit of a
lottery. A bit like spinning one of those wheels
at a school fete. The leather strap flicking
across the nails, clacketty, clacketty, clack.
Slowing the wheel down. It could stop on any
number…except mine, of course.

I must be the most unlucky Narrator in the
universe. I never win anything on those stupid
wheels. I remember one school fete.
I desperately wanted to win a battery
operated autocue machine. A very handy
thing for a Narrator. You could take it out in
the countryside, somewhere far, far away,
set it up and start talking about anything you
liked. Maybe pre-program it with a narration
you stole from some TV nature show. What a
buzz. But did I win it? Of course not. I never
win anything.

But enough of my problems.

There's a story to tell. Where were we?
Oh, yes, flying through space and time.

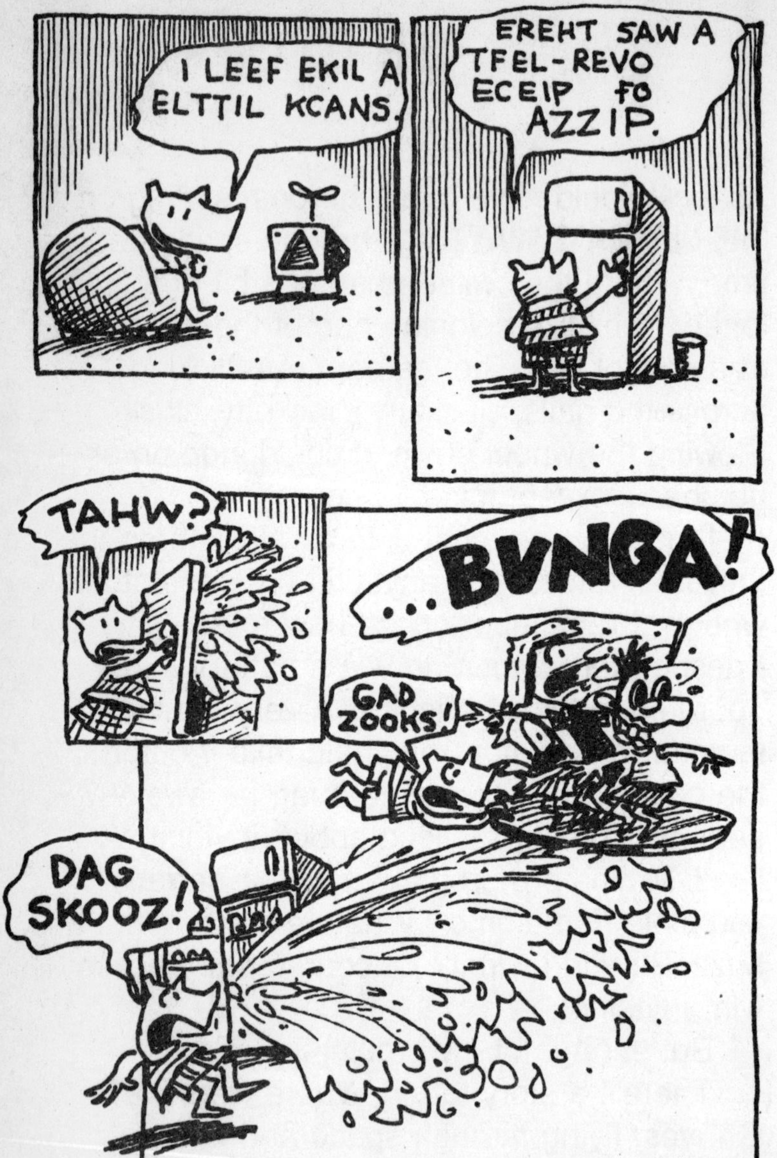
I LEEF EKIL A ELTTIL KCANS.
EREHT SAW A TFEL-REVO ECEIP FO AZZIP.
TAHW?
...BUNGA!
GAD ZOOKS!
DAG SKOOZ!

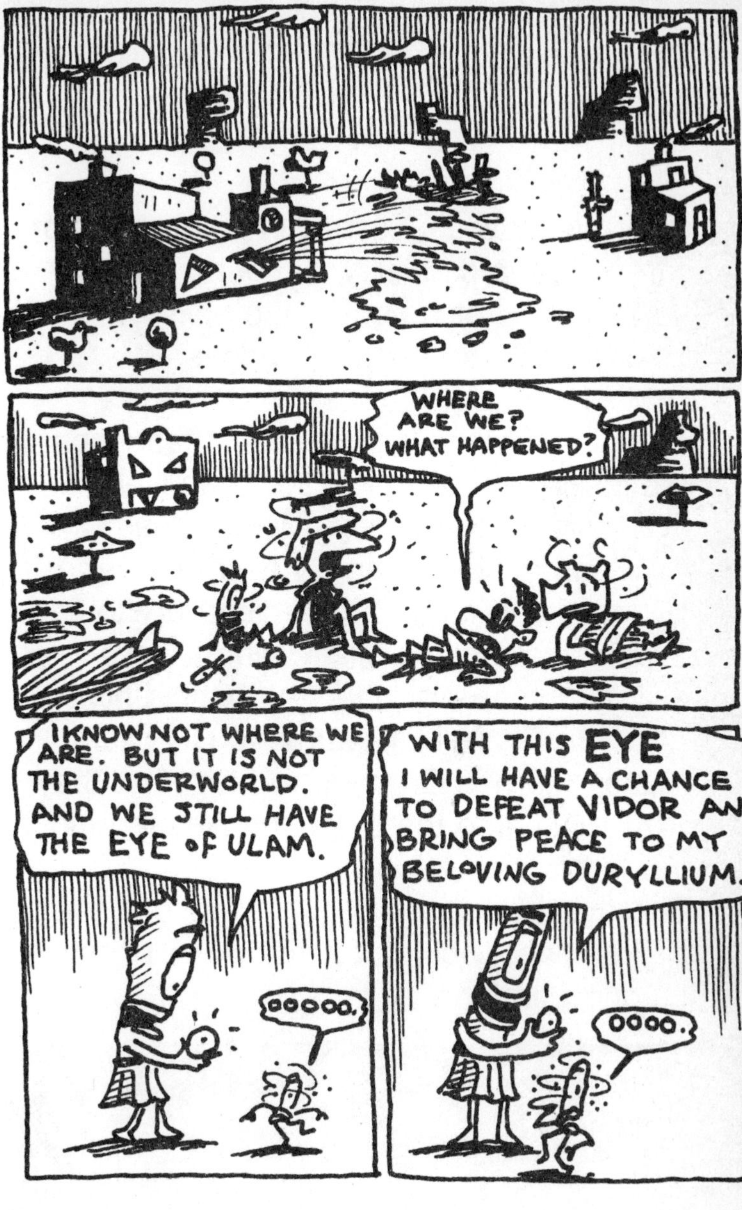
WHERE ARE WE? WHAT HAPPENED?
I KNOW NOT WHERE WE ARE. BUT IT IS NOT THE UNDERWORLD. AND WE STILL HAVE THE EYE OF ULAM.
OOOOO.
WITH THIS EYE I WILL HAVE A CHANCE TO DEFEAT VIDOR AND BRING PEACE TO MY BELOVING DURYLLIUM.
OOOO.

36

Hmmm! Well, I wasn't expecting that. And nor was the backwards Mikey, of course, who would lose a lot of weight in the next few years due to his total fear of fridges.

And what of our heroes?

Well, I can tell you a bit about them. Icon retires to a far-off planet in the Crab Nebula and opens a chicken shop. Nico marries Claudia and they live happily ever after. And Mikey leaves on a journey of discovery to find the elusive backwards Mikey, who always manages to keep just one step behind him. And the M.I.T.? Well, it returns to Duryllium, kills Vidor, marries Crundor and together they turn Duryllium into the biggest turkey farm in the universe.

There is another ending, of course, if you don't like mine. Look at it if you want. I know which one I prefer.

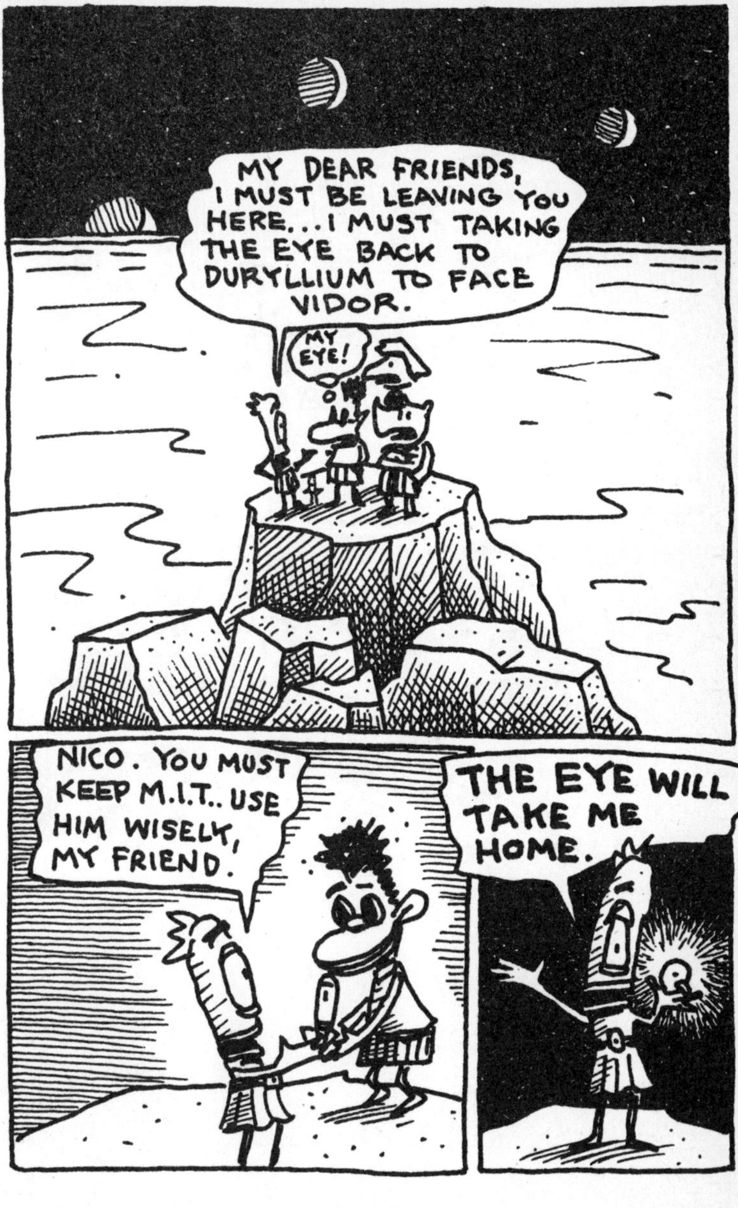
MY DEAR FRIENDS, I MUST BE LEAVING YOU HERE...I MUST TAKING THE EYE BACK TO DURYLLIUM TO FACE VIDOR.
MY EYE!
NICO. YOU MUST KEEP M.I.T.. USE HIM WISELY, MY FRIEND.
THE EYE WILL TAKE ME HOME.

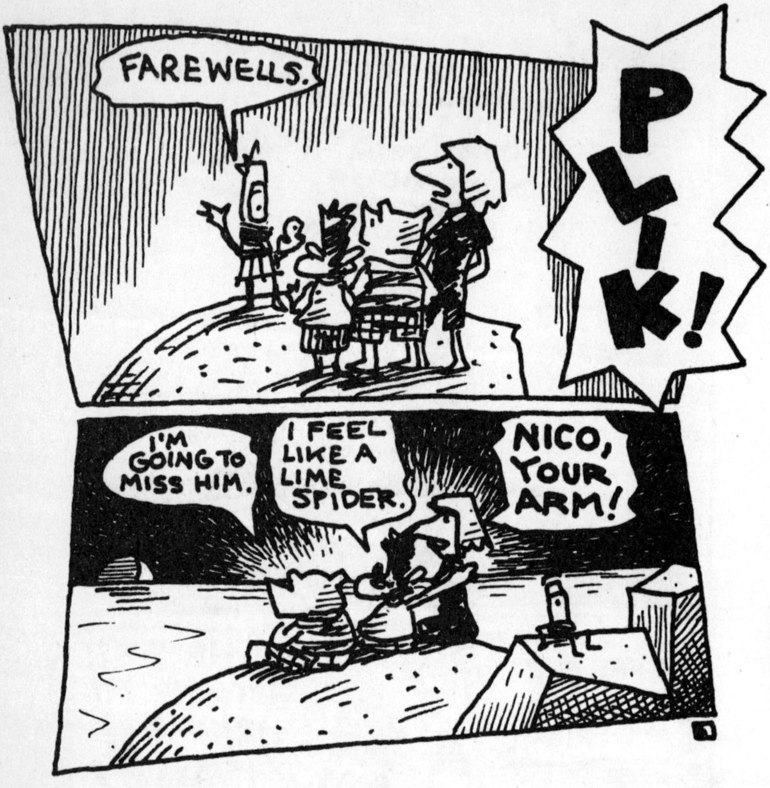
FAREWELLS.
PLIK!
I'M GOING TO MISS HIM.
I FEEL LIKE A LIME SPIDER.
NICO, YOUR ARM!

36a

OK, dear reader, that's it.

Icon returns to Duryllium to challenge his misguided twin brother, Vidor. Nico, Claudia and Mikey use the M.I.T. to leave Planet Acahti and return home to Ithaca.

And you must put this book down and get on with your life. But, congratulations, you have conquered the **STORYMAZE**. Not that it was that hard with such a brilliant Narrator. But, you did find your way through the Maze of Madness without throwing the book against the wall. You have done battle with the Cyclops without turning into a smoking pile of ashes. And most importantly you have learned **THE SECRET OF THE STORYMAZE:**

To reach the end,
is only the beginning.

Or as they say on Ganymede:

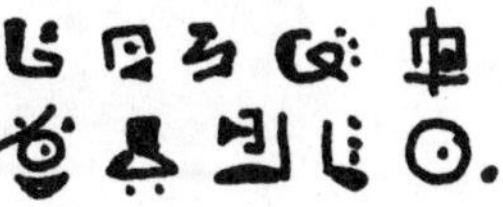

OK. That's it. Close the book.
Thank you, come again.

201

Meanwhile, in a parallel universe on a planet called Acahti, a creature called Yekim has a problem…

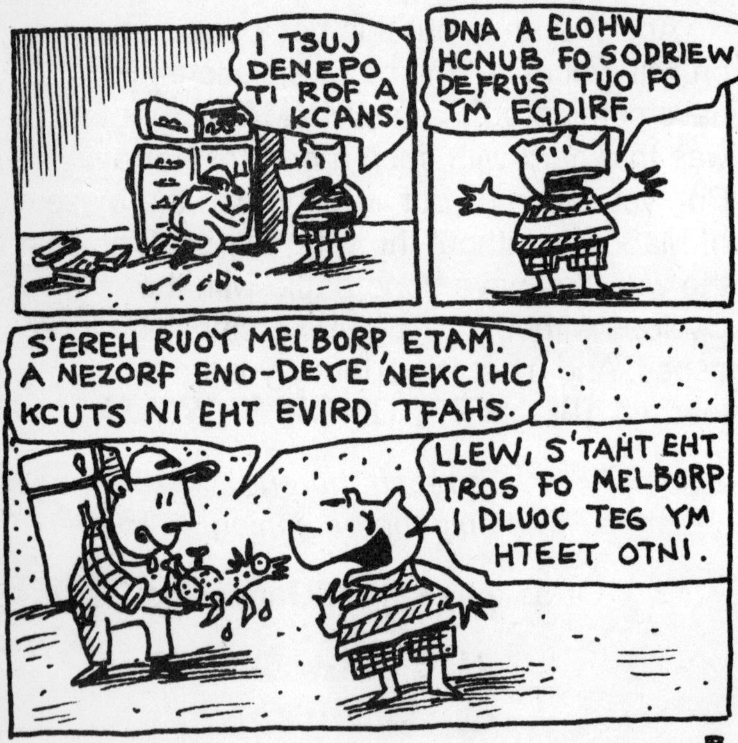
I TSUJ DENEPO TI ROF A KCANS.
DNA A ELOHW HCNUB FO SODRIEW DEFRUS TUO FO YM EGDIRF.
S'EREH RUOY MELBORP, ETAM. A NEZORF ENO-DEYE NEKCIHC KCUTS NI EHT EVIRD TFAHS.
LLEW, S'TAHT EHT TROS FO MELBORP I DLUOC TEG YM HTEET OTNI.

A GUIDE TO M.I.T.'S* LANGUAGE

1	I hate surfing
0	There's lice in here!
01	You idiot!
11	Bummer
010	Hello, master
011	Goodnight
110	Ouch
0000	My yak has fleas!
0010	Oh, joy!
0100	That's handy
0001	HELP!
1001	ICON!
00000	My head hurts
10111	Panic stations!!
100101	Just following orders, fly-breath
100111	Quiet, you stupid animal-head people
101110	What the *&^%$# am I doing here?
111000	As it happens, I play with my feet
111010	I hate water!

*M.I.T. (pronounced *em-eye-tee*) is short for Mental Image Transfer.

LOOK OUT FOR THE NEXT
STORYMAZE ADVENTURE!

THE EYE OF ULAM

*Available at a store
somewhere in the known universe!*